SERAFINA
and the
SPLINTERED HEART

SERAFINA and the SPLINTERED HEART

ROBERT BEATTY

DISNEP·HYPERION

LOS ANGELES NEW YORK

First Edition, July 2017
10 9 8 7 6 5 4 3 2 1
FAC-020093-17139
Printed in the United States of America

This book is set in 12-pt Adobe Garamond Pro, Liam,
Qilin/Fontspring; Minister Std/Monotype
Designed by Maria Elias

Library of Congress Cataloging in Publication Control Number: 2017001301
ISBN 978-1-4847-7504-2

Reinforced binding

Visit www.DisneyBooks.com

Biltmore Estate
Asheville, North Carolina

$\mathcal{S}$erafina opened her eyes and saw nothing but black. It was as if she hadn't opened her eyes at all.

She had been deep in the darkened void of a swirling, half-dreaming world when she awoke to the sound of a muffled voice, but now there was no voice, no sound, no movement of any kind.

With her feline eyes she had always been able to see, even in the dimmest, most shadowed places, but here she was blind. She searched for the faintest glint of light in the gloom, but there was no moonlight coming in through a window, no faint flicker of a distant lantern down a corridor.

Just black.

She closed her eyes and reopened them. But it made no difference. It was still pitch-dark.

Have I actually gone blind? she wondered.

Confused, she tried to listen out into the darkness as she had done when she hunted rats deep in the corridors of Biltmore's sprawling basement. But there was no creak of the house, no servants working in distant rooms, no father snoring in a nearby cot, no machinery whirring, no clocks ticking or footsteps. It was cold, still, and quiet in a way she had never known. She was no longer at Biltmore.

Remembering the voice that had woken her, she listened for it again, but whether it had been real or part of a dream, it was gone now.

Where am I? she thought in bewilderment. *How did I get here?*

Then a sound finally came, as if in answer to her question.

Thump-thump.

For a moment that was all there was.

Thump-thump, thump-thump.

The beat of her heart and the pulse of her blood.

Thump-thump, thump-thump, thump-thump.

As she slowly moved her tongue to moisten her cracked, dry lips, she sensed the faint taste of metal in her mouth.

But it wasn't metal.

It was blood—her own blood flowing through her veins into her tongue and her lips.

She tried to clear her throat, but then all at once she took in a sudden, violent, jerking breath and sucked in a great gasp of

2

air, as if it were the very first breath she had ever taken. As her blood flowed, a tingling feeling flooded into her arms and legs and all through her body.

What is going on? she thought. *What happened to me? Why am I waking up like this?*

Thinking back through her life, she remembered living with her pa in the workshop, and battling the Black Cloak and the Twisted Staff with her best friend, Braeden. She'd finally come out into the grand rooms and daylight world of the fancy folk. But when she tried to remember what happened next, it was like trying to recall the fleeting details of a powerful dream that drifts away the moment you wake. It left her disoriented and confused, as if she were grasping for the tattered remnants of a previous life.

She had not yet moved her body, but she felt herself lying on her back on a long, flat surface. Her legs were straight, her hands neatly lying one over the other on her chest, like someone had laid her there with respect and care.

She slowly separated her hands and moved them down on either side of her body to feel the surface beneath her.

It felt hard, like rough wooden boards, but the boards felt strangely *cold. The boards shouldn't be cold,* she thought. *Not like this. Not cold.*

Her heart began to pound in her chest. A wild panic rose inside her.

She tried to sit up, but immediately slammed her forehead into a hard surface a few inches above her, and she crashed down again, wincing in pain.

She pressed her hands against the boards above her. Her probing fingers were her only eyes. There were no breaks or openings in the boards. Her palms began to sweat. Her breaths got shorter. A desperate surge of fear poured through her as she craned her body and pushed to the side, but there were boards there, too, just inches away. She kicked her feet. She pounded her fists. But the boards surrounded her, closing her in on all sides.

Serafina growled in frustration, fear, and anger. She scratched and she scurried, she twisted and she pried, but she could not escape. She had been enclosed in a long, flat wooden box.

She pressed her face frantically into the corner of the box and sniffed, like a trapped little animal, hoping to catch a scent from the outside world through the thin cracks between the boards. She tried one corner, and then the next, but the smell was the same all around her.

Dirt, she thought. *I'm surrounded by damp, rotting dirt. I've been buried alive!*

Serafina lay in the cold black space of the coffin buried underground. Her mind flooded with terror.

I need to get out of here, she kept thinking. *I need to breathe. I'm not dead!*

But she could not see. She could not move. She could not hear anything other than the sound of her own ragged breathing. How much air would she have down here? She felt a tight constriction in her lungs. Her chest gripped her. She wanted her pa! She wanted her mother to come and dig her out. Someone had to save her! She frantically pressed her hands against the coffin lid above her head and pushed with all her strength, but she couldn't lift it. The sound of her screeching voice hurt her ears in this terrible, closed-in, black place.

Then she thought about what her pa would say if he was here. "Get your wits about ya, girl. Figure out what ya need to do and get on with doin' it."

She sucked in another long breath, and then steadied herself and tried to think it through. She couldn't see with her eyes, but she traced her fingers along the skirt and sleeves of her dress. They were badly torn. It seemed like if she had died and there had been a funeral, then they would have put her in a nice dress. Whoever had buried her had been in a hurry. Had they thought she was dead? Or did they want her to suffer the most horrible of deaths?

At that moment, she heard the faint, muffled sound of movement above her. Her heart filled with hope. *Footsteps!*

"Help!" she screamed as loud as she possibly could. "Help me! Please help me!"

She screamed and screamed. She pounded the wood above her head. She flailed her legs. But the sound of the footsteps drifted away, then disappeared and left a silence so complete that she wasn't sure she'd heard the sound at all.

Had it been the person who buried her? Had he heaved the last shovel of dirt onto her grave and left her here? Or was it a passerby who had no idea she was here? She slammed her fists against the boards and screamed, "Please! I need your help! I'm down here!"

But it was no use.

She was alone.

She felt a dark wave of hopelessness pour through her soul.

She could not escape.

She could not survive this . . .

No, she thought, gritting her teeth. *I'm not gonna let myself die down here. I'm not gonna give up. I'm going to stay bold! I'm going to find a way out . . .*

She slid herself down toward the end of the coffin and kicked. The coffin's rough boards felt thin and crudely made, not like a proper solid casket, but like a ramshackle box nailed together from discarded apple crates. But the earth behind the rickety wood braced the boards so firmly that it was impossible for her to break them.

Then she had an idea.

"Six feet under." That was what her had pa told her years ago when she asked him what they did with dead people. "'Round here they bury folk six feet under," he'd said.

She squirmed inside the dark, cramped space, bending her body up like a little kitten in a lady's shoe box, and positioned herself so that she could put her hands on the top center of the coffin's lid. She figured that six feet of dirt must weigh an awful lot. And her pa had taught her that the center of a board was its weakest point.

Remembering something else he'd taught her, she knocked on the board above her and listened. *Tap-tap-tap.* Then she moved down a few inches and knocked again. *Tap-tap-tap.* She kept knocking until she found a place with a slightly deeper, more hollow sound where the dirt was packed a little less firmly behind it. "That's the spot."

But now what? Even if she managed to crack the board, the dirt above would come crashing down on her. Her mouth and nose would fill with dirt and she'd suffocate. "That's not gonna work . . ."

Suddenly an idea sprang into her mind. She buttoned her dress tight up to her neck and then pulled the lower part of the dress up over her head, inside out, so that the fabric covered her face, especially her mouth and nose. It was cramped in the coffin and difficult to move, but she managed to get the dress bundled around her head and then wriggled her arms out of the sleeves so that her hands were free. If she was lucky, the fabric over her face would give her the seconds she needed.

Knowing that her hands alone weren't strong enough to break the boards, she rolled onto her stomach and positioned her shoulder at the top center of the coffin.

Bracing herself, she pushed upward with her arms and legs and the strength of her whole body. There wasn't enough space inside the coffin to get herself all the way up onto her hands and knees. But she bent herself into a coil and pushed the best she could, slamming her shoulder against the coffin's lid over and over again. She knew that one strong blow wasn't going to do it. And slow pressure wasn't, either. She needed to get a good, hard, forceful rhythm going. *Bang, bang, bang.* She could feel the long boards of the coffin's lid flexing. "That's it, that's what we need," she said. *Bang, bang, bang* she slammed. "Come on!" she growled. Then she heard the center board cracking beneath the weight of the earth above. "Come on!" She kept pushing. *Bang, bang, bang.* The board began to split. Then she felt something cold hit her bare shoulders. She should have been filled with joy that her plan was actually working, but her mind filled with fear. The lid had cracked! The coffin was caving in! Cold, clammy, heavy dirt dumped all over her, pushing her down to the coffin floor. If she hadn't tied her dress over her head, her mouth and nose would have filled with dirt at that very moment and she would have been dead.

Working blind, with nothing but her grasping hands to guide her, she grabbed great handfuls of the incoming dirt and chucked them into the corners of the coffin, packing the dirt away as fast as it poured down through the hole, but it just kept coming, coming, coming. The terrible weight of the dirt surrounded her legs and shoulders and head. It was getting more and more difficult to move. She sucked in breaths through the fabric of her dress as fast and hard as she could. Her chest heaved in panic. She couldn't get enough air!

Finally, when there was no more space in the coffin to push the dirt, she tried to make her escape. She jammed her head straight up through the hole, pushed with her legs, and started digging toward the surface. But the dirt came down so fast, and pushed in so hard, she never had a chance. Even as she dug, the dirt began to suffocate her. Its crushing weight pushed against her chest, driving one last scream from her lungs.

Loose earth poured down around her head and shoulders, collapsing onto her faster than she could dig it away. She felt the pressing weight of it all around her, closing in on her, trapping her legs, but she kept clawing, kicking, squirming her way blindly up through the darkness, desperately trying to pull gasps of air through the fabric covering her face. She felt the material pushing deeper and deeper into her mouth as the dirt pressed in, gagging her, shutting off the flow of air to her aching lungs.

Then she heard a fast scratching sound above her, like the frenzied digging of an animal. She hoped that Gidean, Braeden's dog, was trying to rescue her, but a terrible, low growling sound told her it wasn't her canine friend. Whatever kind of creature it was, the beast's claws tore at the earth, ripping it away with terrific power. Was it a bear digging up its supper? It didn't matter. She had to keep climbing. She had to breathe!

Sharp claws raked across her upstretched hands. Serafina shrieked in pain, but she grabbed hold of the beast's paw. *Gotcha!* She held on for dear life. The force of the paw yanked her body up through the ground.

The snarling beast jerked its paw again, trying to free itself of her, yanking and pulling, but Serafina held on tight.

When her head finally broke the surface of the ground, she sucked in a mighty gasp of air, flooding her lungs with new life. Air! She finally had air!

She lost her grip on the beast's paw and it pulled away, but she clambered out of the dirt until her shoulders and arms were free.

Hope filled her heart. She'd made it! She'd escaped! But as she reached up and pulled the fabric from her head, she heard a loud roaring snarl, and the claws came down at her again, raking across her scalp just as she tried to duck away. Clutching wildly at the earth with her hands, she quickly scrambled out of the grave and got up onto her hands and knees to defend herself.

She had crawled out of the ground into a moonlit graveyard, overgrown by a dense forest of trees and vines. A large stone angel, with her wings raised up around her, stood on a pedestal in the center of the small clearing. Serafina had no idea how she'd gotten here, but she knew this place. It was the angel's glade. But before she could take it all in, she heard something behind her and spun around.

A black panther was coming straight toward her, crouched low for the lunge, its ears pinned back, its face quivering with fierceness as it opened its mouth and hissed with its long fangs bared and gleaming, ready to bite.

Serafina stared into the face of the angry panther. Its bright yellow eyes were as savage as she'd ever seen in a wild animal, filled with a looming and ferocious power. She crouched down low, ready to defend herself. When the panther showed its long white fangs and snarled at her again, Serafina bared her teeth and hissed right back, fierce and fiery, challenging it with everything she had. But to her astonishment, the black panther turned its head away, then slunk into the forest and disappeared.

Overwhelmed with exhaustion, Serafina collapsed to the ground. She sucked in long and heavy breaths, just relieved to be alive. *That big cat had me as good as dead,* she thought. *Why in the world did it slink off like a socked possum?*

As she lay there recovering, she tried to comprehend what had happened. Someone had buried her. But they hadn't just buried her, they had buried her in the old, abandoned grave-yard that had been overgrown by the forest decades before.

And the more she thought about it, the more she couldn't believe what she had just seen. *How could there be a black panther?*

Her mother had been a catamount, a shape-shifter with the ability to turn into a mountain lion at will, but when Serafina finally learned to shift, she was a black panther like her father had been, a rare variant of the race. According to mountain lore, there was only one black panther at a time.

She kept thinking that the panther must have been her father, but her father had died in battle twelve years before, the night she was born. Her pa, the man who had found her in the forest that night and taken care of her ever since, was the only father she had ever known. And the more she thought about it, the more she was convinced that the panther she'd just seen hadn't been a full-grown male, but a young cat, lean and uncer-tain. It might have been her half sister or half brother, but they were just spotted little cubs. When her catamount friend Waysa was in lion form, his fur was dark brown. Maybe the light had been playing tricks on her eyes, but if it had been Waysa, why would he run away from her?

Questions reeled through her mind, but the sensations of her body began to overwhelm her. Her head hurt from the swipe of the panther's claws, which had left a bleeding wound, but it wasn't too bad. After what she'd experienced in the coffin, it felt so good to just have air moving in and out of her lungs. She could feel the warm breeze on her bare skin, and smell the clover and ferns growing nearby, and see the glorious stars above. Her senses seemed more acute than ever before.

As her strength returned to her arms and legs, she brushed the remaining dirt from her body and straightened out the plain beige dress she was wearing. That was when she noticed the large, dark stains around the rips in the material. Frightened, she quickly looked herself over and found dried blood all over her bare torso, shoulders, and arms. But there were no recent wounds. Just scars.

At that moment, memories of her life began to flow slowly through her like a quiet river. She saw herself eating supper with her pa in the workshop, and lying on Biltmore's highest rooftop with Braeden as they counted stars in the midnight sky, and running happily through the forest in panther form with her mother and Waysa. She saw herself sitting in front of the fireplace in Mr. Vanderbilt's library as he told her stories from his books and travels, and sitting quietly at morning tea with Mrs. Vanderbilt, who had recently announced that she was with child.

Then she remembered her friend Essie, one of Biltmore's maids, helping her lace up the beautiful golden-cream gown that Braeden had given her for the Christmas party. She remembered looking at herself in Essie's mirror, seeing a twelve-year-old girl with sharp, feline angles to her cheekbones, amber-yellow eyes, and long, shiny black hair, and thinking, for the first time, she was going to fit in just fine.

The memory of the Christmas party swirled around in her mind. She could so vividly remember the softness of the candlelight, the scent of the wood on the fire, the smile on her pa's face, and the warmth of Braeden's hand on her back as they entered the room together. It was a moment of peace and triumph, not just because she and Braeden had defeated their enemies, but because she felt like she truly belonged.

The last night she remembered at Biltmore, she had been making her rounds through the house on a winter evening. The memory came to her in snatches. She was the Guardian, the protector against intruding spirits and other dangers. Everyone else had gone to bed, and she had the darkened corridors of the house to herself, just like she liked it. She stepped out onto the formal back patio, which the Vanderbilts called the Loggia. The sheer white curtains in the doorway glowed in the moonlight as they fluttered in the cold winter breeze. She looked out across the grounds of the estate toward the forest and the mountains in the distance. The full moon was rising over the peaks.

All was still in the house, but then she felt an unusual movement of air around her and a disturbing chill ran up her spine. The hairs on the back of her neck went up. Suddenly she sensed something behind her. She spun around, ready to fight, but all she could see was a black and roiling darkness where the walls and windows of the house should have been.

Something struck her chest with piercing pain. A storm of wind swept around her. Her mind filled with confusion. She fought with tooth and claw, growling and hissing and biting. Blood was everywhere.

But then it all went black, and the memory faded.

She stood now beside her own grave in the pale light of the moon in the center of the angel's glade and looked around her. She was miles from home. What a strange and haunted place to find herself crawling from the ground! The loose dirt was tracked with human footprints and what looked like shovel marks. There was no gravestone, just a mound of dirt. She reckoned that whoever buried her didn't want her found. Had someone attempted to murder her and then hide the body?

She looked up at the stone angel. "What did you see that night?"

But the angel didn't answer. She stood on her pedestal of stone as mute and immutable as she always did. The angel was old and weathered, mottled with dark moss and green patina. She had long, curling hair and a beautiful face, with tears of dark sap streaming down her cheeks. To Serafina her face seemed to be filled with the silent wisdom of knowingness, as if the angel held inside her the fate and fortune of those she loved, and it was all too much to bear. The angel held her mighty, finely feathered wings above her, and she gripped a long, sharp steel sword in her hand. It was the very sword that Serafina had used to cut and destroy the Black Cloak.

The angel stood in the center of a small clearing of bright green grass. The leaves on the trees and bushes around the angel's glade stayed green all year round, never drying in the summer's sun, or changing color in autumn, or falling to the ground in winter. The angel's glade was a place of eternal spring.

The north side of the glade led deep into the rest of the old graveyard, which had been taken back by the encroaching forest long ago, with vines covering many of the headstones and stringy moss hanging down from the black limbs of crooked trees. The graveyard stretched on for as far as Serafina could see, endless rows of tilting, toppled, half-buried monuments marking the graves of hundreds of dead, rotting bodies and lost souls. A gray whispery mist floated listlessly through the graveyard, as if searching for a place to linger. As Serafina peered across the graveyard looking for signs of movement, she hoped that she was the only body that had crawled forth from the grave tonight.

Finally, she said to her buried companions, "Sorry to be gettin' on my way so soon, but it turns out that I was just a-visiting for a while."

She walked to the other side of the angel's glade, which led into the natural part of the forest that she knew so well. Looking into the trees made her think about her catamount mother. She had learned so much from her mother. They'd run through the forest together and hunted together. She'd learned the sounds of the night birds and the movement of the woodland creatures. She wondered why her mother hadn't sensed her and come to her like she had so many times before.

It began to sink in that her pa hadn't come for her, either, and neither had Braeden.

No one had come.

ROBERT BEATTY

She was alone.

Fear began to well up in her mind. As she thought about what might have happened to the people she loved, her heart felt heavy in her chest. She didn't know what had attacked her or how long she'd been gone. She wondered what the people of Biltmore would think when she walked into the mansion covered in graveyard dirt, but her true fear, deep down, was that they wouldn't be there at all, that she'd find the house empty, full of nothing but shadows.

Anxious to get moving, she headed into the forest, following the path that would take her to Biltmore. She had to get home.

Serafina followed the path through the darkened forest at a quick pace, down into a ravine dense with ancient maple and hemlock trees. Her legs felt strong and steady beneath her as she weaved between the great trunks of the forest's oldest inhabitants.

A chorus of tree frogs, peepers, and insects filled her ears, and the scents of primrose and moonflower wafted past her nose. The evening flowers stayed closed during the day, but opened with their sweet smells at night.

Everything seemed unusually vibrant to her tonight, like her body and her senses were alive with new sensations.

The forest grew thick with rosebay rhododendron bushes glimmering in the silver moonlight. Hummingbird moths hovered over the white and pinkish blooms, dipping into the recesses of the flowers and sipping out the nectar within. It almost felt as if she could hear the beat of the moths' wings against the night air.

Fireflies floated in the darkness above the shiny green leaves of the laurel. Soft flashes of lightning danced on the silver-clouded sky behind them, and a gentle thunder rolled through the darkness, moving on the rising heat of what felt like a summer breeze.

"This is all so strange . . ." she said to herself, looking around her in confusion as she traveled. The last night she remembered, it had been winter, but the air felt strangely warm now. And these plants and insects didn't come out in winter. Had the magic of the angel's glade somehow extended out into the rest of the forest?

When she glanced up at the moon, what she saw stopped her dead in her tracks. The moon was not all the way full, but large and bright, with the light on the right and the shadow on the left.

"That's not right," she said, frowning. That night she was on the Loggia the moon had been full, which meant what she was seeing now was impossible.

She knew that the moon was only full one night a month, then it would wane for fourteen nights, with the light on the left side, getting smaller and smaller until it was dark for a single evening. Then it would wax for fourteen nights, with the light on the right, until it was full once more. Then it would start all over again.

The moon was the great calendar in the sky by which she had marked the nights of her life, wandering through the grounds of Biltmore Estate by herself. The steady phases of her pale companion, the slow sweep of the glistening stars, and the curving transit of the five brightest planets had been her silent but loyal confidants for as long as she could remember. They were her midnight brothers and her dark-morning sisters. She had spoken to them, learned from them, watched them as a girl sees the members of her family moving around her.

But tonight she looked at her sister the moon in confusion, a thumping urgency in her temples as she tried to figure out the meaning of what she was seeing. The moon was lit on the *right* side. That meant it was *waxing*, getting larger each night. But if the moon had been full the last time she saw it, how could it be waxing now?

It was as if she'd fallen backward a night in time. Either that or something equally unimaginable: She'd been underground for more than an entire cycle of the moon.

"That means twenty-eight nights have passed, maybe more . . ." she said to herself in astonishment.

The breeze whispered through the tops of the trees as if the hidden spirits of the forest were nervously discussing that she had discovered the universe's ruse. Time flew forward. Time flew back. Nothing was as it seemed. People were buried underground and people came back. She was in a world of many in-betweens.

Another set of flashes lit up the sky and danced silently

among the clouds, then the thunder rolled on, echoing across the mountainsides.

She had always been able to see things other people could not, especially in the dark of night, but tonight there seemed to be a special magic in the forest. It felt as if she could actually see the evening flowers slowly opening their petals to the moon and the glint of starlight on the iridescent wings of the insects. She felt the caress of the air as it slipped through the branches of the trees, around her body, and against her skin. She sensed the stony firmness of the earth and rock on which she stood. The tiny droplets of dew on the clover leaves around her suddenly glistened, and a moment later, the white light of the distant lightning shone in her eyes. Water and earth and light and sky . . . It was as if she had become intermingled with the faintest elements of the world, as if she were in tune with the slip and sway of the nocturnal realm in a way that she had never been before.

She continued walking, but as she gazed through the trees she spotted what appeared to be a crease of blackness in the distance. She tilted her head in confusion. Was it a shadow? She couldn't make it out. But as she narrowed her eyes to look at it, she realized that whatever it was, it was *moving*, not toward her or away, but hovering in the air, like a rippling black wave.

The skin on her arms rose up with goose bumps. She couldn't help but wonder if what she was seeing was related to the black shape that had attacked her at Biltmore.

She knew she should leave it alone, but she was too curious

to turn away. She slowly moved closer until she was maybe a dozen steps from it, then she stopped and studied the black shape. It appeared to be about five feet long, floating of its own accord a few feet off the ground, like a long banner held in the breeze. And it was utterly black, blacker than anything she had ever seen.

Suddenly, a wind swept through the trees. A gust kicked up from the forest floor, swirling small tornados of leaves around her. The branches hanging above her began to creak and bend, like the swaying limbs of old, twisted men, their long, twiggy hands dangling down onto her head and shoulders. When the cold mist of a coming rain touched her face, she realized that a storm was near. And then she spotted a dark figure making its way toward her through the trees.

Serafina sucked in a breath in surprise and dropped to the ground to hide. She scrambled beneath the base of a half-toppled tree where the spidering roots had pulled up from the earth and created a small cave. Pressing herself in as deep as she could go, she peered out through the small holes between the roots.

The man, or creature, or whatever it was, moved toward her through the forest with a slow and deliberate pace, like a predator hunting for prey. It stalked on two long, gangly legs, its back hunched over and its head hanging down, its shoulders swaying one way and then the other as it gazed from side to side. Even as hunched as it was, the creature was very tall, with long, crooked arms dangling in front of it like a praying mantis, and the elongated fingers of its spindling hands like white, scaly talons, tipped with sharp, curving, clawlike fingernails. It moved with steady purpose, scraping its feet through the leaves of the forest floor, the movement of its bones sounding like cracking branches.

What kind of godforsaken thing is that? she thought, cowering in her hole. *Is it some kind of vile creech that crawled from the grave the same way I did?*

The creature came closer and closer. As it stepped within a few feet of her, Serafina couldn't keep her body from trembling. Her only hope was that the creature wouldn't see her hiding beneath the roots at its feet.

She could hear its breathing now, the slow wheezing, ragged, hissing breath, like a wounded animal, and she could see it more closely than she had before. A white haze lingered about its body like the smoke around a dying campfire, and straggly gray strands hung around its head like the stringy hair of a rotting corpse. When the creature turned and she saw its face, she gasped. The creature's face had been slashed with a savage wound that oozed with the blackish, festering blood of an injury that never healed. She couldn't tell whether the creature was a mortal man or a hellish fiend, or some combination of the two, but its sharp, pointy teeth chattered with anticipation as it scanned the forest, swaying its head back and forth as it crept forward with its dangling claws.

At first it seemed as if the creature was going to pass her by, but then the thing stopped, standing right over her.

Its talon-like hand grasped one of the roots of the toppled tree beneath which she was hiding. Serafina sucked in a startled breath and held it, too frightened to exhale. The creature looked one way into the forest and then the other. It seemed like it knew she was there, that it sensed her presence, maybe smelled her, but it had not yet detected exactly where she was. She held her breath like a trembling rabbit in her little den.

The creature opened its mouth and a low, vibrating, guttural sound emerged. Then Serafina began to actually see the white air rushing from its lungs. It wasn't just an exhalation or a long scream, but a *storm*. The air around her began to twist and turn, the leaves swirling up, the branches on the trees bending and cracking. The air exploded with blowing rain. The terrible noise coming from the creature's mouth was getting louder and louder as the storm rose up all around.

The storm-creech peered down into the mound of roots where she was hiding. Its silver-glowing eyes looked straight at her, shocking her with a blast of fear. The creature's talons closed into a fist, crushing the roots that it had been holding. Then it began tearing the roots away with both hands, its teeth chattering as it ripped its way toward her.

As the creature attacked, Serafina reflexively tried to shift into panther form to defend herself, but it didn't work. For some clumsy reason, she couldn't change. She tried again, concentrating on envisioning herself as a panther, but she couldn't do it. She remained in her human form.

Not knowing what else to do, she cowered down. She tried to stay out of the creature's reach as it ripped the roots away. She thought about leaping up at the thing and fighting it with her bare hands, but it seemed far too powerful. At the last second, just as its claws touched her, she scrambled out of the roots on her belly and darted out the other side.

A storm raged through the forest. The pelting rain roared around her. The wind blew so hard that her hair and clothes pressed against her face and body. It felt like it wasn't going to just blow her away, but tear her into little pieces.

But she couldn't let the storm slow her down. The creature was right behind her. She had to get out of there. She ran headlong into the swirling rain and just kept running.

When she looked over her shoulder, she expected to see the creature charging up behind her, grabbing for her, but it wasn't. It was in the distance, still ripping at the roots where she'd been hiding.

Confused, but relieved that she'd managed to escape the wretched thing, she quickly turned to keep moving, but she nearly ran straight into an eerie black shape similar to what she'd seen before. She stopped abruptly, recoiling from it like it was a venomous snake.

It floated right in front of her now, so sharply black that it seemed like an impossibility. The light of the moon and stars disappeared into it, and she could see nothing on the other side of it. Rain fell in, but did not come out. It was like a tear in the fabric of the world.

The sight of it tightened her chest. Her skin buzzed. She backed away and ducked into a thicket of bushes to hide.

When the black shape drifted in her direction, she caught her breath in surprise. She couldn't tell if it was drifting on the winds of the storm or was actually drawn to her in some way.

The roiling black shape floated slowly closer. She thought that the thick foliage would protect her, but the leaves and branches snapped and hissed as the black shape touched them, bursting them one by one, as it moved toward her.

She frantically squirmed away, but the edge of the black shape touched her shoulder. The searing pain felt like she was being slashed with a burning, white-hot blade. She screamed in agony and wrenched herself away.

Driven by blind fear, she clambered out of the thicket and ran. She spotted a rocky area and sprinted for it. When she saw the drop-off of a steep mountain slope, she jumped.

She hit the ground hard and rolled down the earthen slope, her shoulders and legs thudding against the rocks and trees as she fell, then sprang to her feet and fled.

She tore through the forest, gasping for breath, but pushed herself on, looking over her shoulder for signs of the storm-creech and the black shapes.

As the rain and wind slowly died down, and the storm faded behind her, she kept going at a hurried pace.

Finally, she was relieved to see the glow of the moon peeking through the clouds. Day folk knew that the sun rose in the east and set in the west, but many didn't realize that the moon did as well. Its black shadows among the trees were like arrows pointing the way home. As soon as she got her wits about her, she figured out what direction she needed to go, and went as fast as she could. She had to warn the people of Biltmore about what she had seen.

But just as she began to make progress, she came to the edge of a river blocking her path. She scanned the surrounding area in confusion.

"Don't tell me you've gone and gotten yourself lost," she scolded herself.

She had thought she was close to home. She remembered a creek near here, small and shallow, just a quick leap across. But what blocked her path now was a powerful river, turbulent and strong, ripping through the trees. Its shores weren't the rocky edge of a normal river, but the flooded forest.

It was strange how so much had changed. If the little creek she remembered was now this churning river, then there must have been many other storms like the one she'd just fought her way through. A knot of worry bunched in her stomach. There were few things in the mountains more powerful and damaging than the rushing waters that had formed them.

Knowing she had to get home, she stepped into the dark water of the river to cross it. The current felt like tiny shards tearing at her bare skin. She'd waded across plenty of rivers, but this was a strange and alarming sensation that she'd never felt before. When she took another step, it became very clear that the river was far too deep and turbulent for her to cross. It seemed like it wanted to suck her in and pull her under.

Looking out across the river, she was amazed to see an entire tree—branches, trunk, and roots and all—floating downstream, tumbling through the current, like a great, leafy leviathan. Many of the largest and oldest trees at the edge of the river had toppled into the current, the earth beneath their roots ripped away by the powerful pull of the rushing water.

She stepped back out of the flooded river and away from the edge, convinced that the dark, malevolent water wanted to consume her. She couldn't cross here. But if she was anywhere near where she thought she was, there were no roads or bridges for quite a while.

"We're in a real pickle now, girl," she said, talking to herself the way her pa did. "What we gonna do about it? That's the question."

Then she had an idea.

She made her way upstream along the shore until she found one of the tallest trees hanging over the river, its great, spreading boughs almost reaching across and touching the trees on the other side. She knew the relentless current tearing at its roots would soon bring the tree crashing down into the river, but for now it was her path.

She climbed up the trunk and then outward on the limbs, high up over the river's tumbling flow, moving from branch to branch, her goal to cross over the river the way she'd seen squirrels do it, using the canopy of the trees as her bridge.

But as she crawled farther out, the tree's branches became slender green saplings bending and whipping in the wind. It felt like the wind was going to sweep her away. Every muscle in her body clenched as she bobbed and swayed in the upper branches. She could see the closest tree on the other side, a great pine with sturdy branches thick with needles, but she couldn't leap across such a great distance. It was just too far.

Looking down, all she could see a hundred feet below her was the swirling black water of the river. If she lost her grip here, or tried to jump to the tree on the other side, then she'd go plummeting down. She'd either die when she hit the water or get swept away in the current and drown. One way or another the river would have her, just like it wanted.

As she was trying to figure out what to do, she heard a stick break on the forest floor down below her, back in the direction from which she had come. She swiveled, scanning the forest for danger. Had the storm-creech followed her scent and tracked her here? But then she spotted a robed figure moving slowly through the trees.

What kind of devil-spawn is comin' now? she thought in exasperation. *I just want to get on home!*

She squinted her eyes and peered down through the branches of the trees, trying to make out who or what was down there.

It was a man wearing long robes, and a hood of some sort covered his head, like one of the old Celtic druids from ancient Britain that she'd seen depicted in Mr. Vanderbilt's books.

As he made his way through the forest, the robed man opened a pale and delicate hand in front of him. Suddenly, a glowing, hissing torch of blue light, like a tiny ball of lightning, rose up from his palm and hovered over his shoulder, lighting his way through the darkness.

Some kind of sorcerer, Serafina thought as she crouched lower. Her heart began to pound in her chest. *The storm-creech, the floating black shapes, the storms . . . They were all his doing.* Everything she had seen must have been the sorcerer's conjurations. Had it been the sorcerer who attacked her on the Loggia? Had he already taken over Biltmore? She had to get home.

But how? She was stuck up in a tree a hundred feet above a raging river.

When the dark-robed sorcerer stopped walking, the hair on the back of Serafina's neck stood on end. Her whole body began to shake. Every sense inside her was telling her to fight or flee. *Flee*, her mind kept telling her. *Flee before it's too late!*

The sorcerer slowly lifted his head and looked up into the trees in her direction.

Serafina scurried for cover, pushing herself farther out onto the thinner branches of the tree even as they bent and twisted in the wind, lifting her and dropping her in sudden movements that made her stomach feel like it was floating.

She scanned the branches on the opposite side of the river. A moment before, it had been too far to jump, but her muscles were bursting now, her whole body filled with panic.

She focused her eyes on the branch she had to jump to, tilted her head to study the angle, then leapt for it with a mighty grunt.

As she flew through the air she envisioned herself as the black panther deep inside her soul and tried to shift her shape.

She could see her panther form clearly in her mind. This was the moment. She was in midair. She *had* to do it now!

But the shift didn't come.

She reached out desperately with her thin, human arms as she sailed through the air, trying to grab hold of the branches of the pine tree on the other side. When she felt her hands touch the branches, she grabbed hold. She had made the distance! But her body swung too hard, and she immediately lost her grip and continued to fall.

Her arms flailed, reaching out in all directions as she tried to catch hold of something, *anything*, on the way down.

She slammed into a thick branch. It knocked the wind out of her with a painful crack. She twisted around and frantically tried to hold on to the branch, but couldn't.

She fell again, hit the branch below her, reached out, fell, grabbed, fell, slipped again, reached out, slipped, then grabbed hold with an infuriated snarl and finally held fast.

She found herself clinging to the bough of a pine tree some fifty feet lower than where she'd started. Her arms and legs were scratched and bleeding. The long, curving spine of her back, usually so supple and strong, hurt something fierce. Grabbing at the hard branches on the way down had jammed her measly human fingernails painfully into her fingers.

Frightened to make any more racket than she already had, and still wincing from the pain of the crashing fall, she gritted her teeth and quickly crawled into the cover of the pine tree's inner branches and hid.

She peered out from her hiding spot, sure that the sorcerer must have heard her. She expected to see him staring up at her, or casting a spell, or summoning one of the black shapes to finish her off.

Instead, the smoking, hissing blue ball of burning light came toward her, floating up into the trees, illuminating everything around it in a bright halo as the sorcerer looked on from below. Serafina cowered into her hiding spot in the thick cluster of pine needles as the eerie blue light came closer.

The buzzing, burning light smelled like a lightning storm, and made her hair float up around her head. But she stayed hidden where she was, her skin tingling.

Finally, the light floated on, and the sorcerer continued his journey through the forest.

Serafina let out a deep sigh of relief and started breathing again.

She watched as the sorcerer made his way through the ferns that grew along the edge of the river. He leaned down and pulled some sort of plant from the ground, then moved on.

Suddenly, Serafina noticed something out of the corner of her eye, something moving much closer to her. Snapping her head toward it, she saw a large, silvery spiderweb glistening in the starlight, its eight-legged spinner lurking on the outer edge with its many eyes watching her. As the spider moved, tiny droplets of dew on the web shimmered in the light, some jostling loose and falling to the forest floor below, others moving like quicksilver along the strands. Serafina knew it was impossible, but she swore she could not just see, but *hear* the droplets sliding along the strands of the web. She could actually *feel* them skittering along, like a shudder down her spine.

Startled, she climbed away from the spider's web and looked back down into the forest. The druid-sorcerer, or whatever he was, had gone down onto his knees now. The burning blue orb hovered over him like a lantern, giving him light to work. He dug through the boggy area at the edge of the river, gathering the tall, pitcher-shaped carnivorous plants that grew there.

Just as she was about to creep away, the sorcerer spoke. He did not stop his work or look around him. He didn't speak in a deep and frightening man's voice like she expected, but a surprisingly soft, calm, steady tone. It was as if Serafina wasn't hidden in a tree a hundred feet away but concealed in the bushes beside the hooded figure.

"I can't see you, but I know you're there," the voice said.

Serafina burst out of her hiding spot and fled. She leapt from branch to branch down through the tree. As soon as she hit the ground, she ran, her bare feet thrashing quickly across the forest floor. When she looked over her shoulder, she didn't see any sign of the sorcerer, but she kept running.

Putting the dark river behind her, she fled way up into the rocks and trees of a high ridge, then through a wide, forested valley. When she finally slowed down, she could tell by the type and age of the trees that she was getting closer. She could see a soft glow of light in the distance, and it drew her home like a beacon.

As she made her way along the edge of Biltmore's bass pond, she noticed that the little stream that normally trickled into it was swollen with rain, filling the pond with more water than usual. *The storms are coming,* Serafina thought.

The calm, flat water of the pond reflected the light of the stars and the moon, but she didn't linger to admire it. She was anxious to get home, to make sure Braeden and her pa were all right, and to warn them about what she'd seen in the forest.

She followed the garden path up through the pink and orange azaleas, which were blooming as bright as the moon itself. When she saw a faint green glow up the hill toward the rest of the gardens, she paused, uncertain. She knew Biltmore's gardens well, but had never seen a greenish light like this before.

Her first thought was that the sorcerer was already here, had already taken over and made Biltmore his domain. Then she heard the murmur of many voices.

As she approached more closely, she saw that the green glow wasn't a sorcerer's spell, but the Conservatory all lit up for an evening party, the light shining through the leaves of thousands of orchids, bromeliads, and palms, and out through the greenhouse's many panes of glass.

She crept along the edge of the building and looked into the Walled Garden, where she saw hundreds of ladies in formal summer dresses and gentlemen in black tailcoats gathered for the party. The windows of Biltmore House blazed above, the south walls and towers of the mansion rising like an enchanted castle into the night.

The Walled Garden had been strung with the kind of softly glowing Edison bulbs that her pa used. And smaller lights hung along the wooden arbor that covered the central path of the garden, the lights tucked among the leafy vines and flowering blooms like little faeries taking refuge among the leaves. She had never seen so many beautiful lights in her life.

Hiding in the bushes near the rose keeper's stone shed, she scanned the crowd for Braeden, but she didn't see him. He was a reserved boy, not always the center of attention, but his aunt and uncle usually encouraged him to attend the estate's social events. She and Braeden had shared so many adventures. And they had been through so much together. He was her closest and most trusted friend. She couldn't wait to see him.

The fancy folk were mingling about on the perfectly manicured paths of the garden, holding champagne flutes in their elegant, flawless hands, chatting and sipping lightly as they promenaded among the roses, dahlias, and zinnias. Bathed in the Conservatory's glow, a string quartet played a beautiful song. Footmen in their formal black-and-white livery strolled among the crowd serving custard tarts, cheeses, and freshly baked cream puffs from their trays. Serafina suddenly felt pangs of hunger.

But everything about this party flummoxed her. It must have taken weeks of planning to arrange all this, and yet she hadn't heard anything about it. And why wasn't Braeden here? There were so many strangers. Where were Mr. and Mrs. Vanderbilt?

A few of the more adventurous adult guests and a coterie of their fancifully attired children huddled together and lit candles inside small paper lanterns, then held them aloft. As if by magic, the rising heat of the candles lifted the lanterns upward out of their hands into the nighttime sky. Serafina watched with the other children as the lanterns floated slowly up into the heavens. She couldn't help but smile at the sight of it, but then a sadness swept through her. She knew it was foolish after everything she'd been through, but she felt so sad that she hadn't been invited to this wonderful party. It was an *evening* party. And she was a creature of the night! If anyone should have been part of it, she should have been! It felt like so much had changed, like the whole world had been slipping by without her.

After destroying the Black Cloak and freeing the estate's lost children from its dark imprisonment, she had entered the daylight world upstairs. The Vanderbilts had welcomed her into their home. She had become part of Biltmore now. Hadn't she? So why wasn't she at this party? It made her qualmish in her stomach thinking about it. What had happened? What had she missed? Hadn't anyone noticed that she wasn't there?

It was hard to understand how all these fancy-dressed people could gather for this lovely party, when just a few miles away a storm had raged through the forest. A short distance down the hill the inlet stream was quietly flooding the pond. A dark force was coming, but they seemed to have no idea.

When she heard Mrs. Vanderbilt's gentle laugh in the distance, Serafina turned hopefully toward the sound. She saw right away that Braeden wasn't there, but Mr. Vanderbilt and Mrs. Vanderbilt were standing together with several of their guests near one of the rose trellises.

Mr. Vanderbilt was easily recognizable with his black hair

and mustache, and his lean, shrewd face with dark, inquisitive eyes. He was dressed in a handsome black tux with tails and white tie. Many of the men she'd spied on over the years were loud of voice and boisterous of manner, but Mr. Vanderbilt was a quieter, more refined, thinking kind of gentleman. Usually, if he wasn't reading in his library, he was watching and learning from those around him. He was always kind and welcoming in spirit when he spoke to people, whether they were guests or servants or workers on the estate, but he also seemed to enjoy watching people from a distance at parties, taking everything in.

Mrs. Vanderbilt was more outgoing, more talkative and social with the guests. She had dark hair like her husband, and a similar spark of intelligence, but she had an easy charm and a gracious smile. She wore a lovely, loosely flowing mauve dress, but what truly stunned Serafina was that Mrs. Vanderbilt's belly was large with her baby. The last time Serafina had seen her, she couldn't even tell that she was with child.

It hasn't just been twenty-eight days, Serafina thought. She felt as if she were being lowered into a deep, dark well. *I've been gone for months . . . They've all forgotten about me . . .*

"And where is that dear nephew of yours tonight?" one of the lady guests asked Mrs. Vanderbilt.

"Yes, indeed," said the lady's husband. "Where is Young Master Braeden?"

"Oh, he's around," Mrs. Vanderbilt said lightly, but Serafina noticed that the mistress of the house didn't actually look around her when she said these words. It was as if she already knew her nephew wasn't nearby. She was acting cheerful in front of her guests, but Serafina could hear the twinge of concern in her voice.

As Mrs. Vanderbilt and her friends continued their conversation, Mr. Vanderbilt stepped back from them and looked up toward the Library Terrace. Serafina could see the wrinkles of worry around his eyes and mouth.

"So, how has Braeden been doing?" one of the guests asked Mrs. Vanderbilt.

"Oh, he's fine," Mrs. Vanderbilt said. "He's fine. He's doing well."

One *he's fine* was enough, Serafina thought, but two was too many. There was definitely something wrong.

"If you'll excuse me for a moment," Mr. Vanderbilt said. He touched his wife's arm, and then left them.

As Mr. Vanderbilt walked quickly through the crowd, several people tried to talk to him, for he was host of the grand party, but he kindly gave his regrets and kept moving.

Ducking through the hedges, Serafina followed him. After being away for months, the sight of her was no doubt going to startle him, but as soon as he was alone, she was going to tell him about the dangers she'd seen in the forest. She could show him the rising water of the pond as evidence of it all. But she sensed the urgency in his movement.

Mr. Vanderbilt ascended the steps through the Walled Garden's arched stone entrance and up the next set of steps to the path through the shrub garden. Serafina darted through the roses and then weaved behind the fruit trees to follow him, careful to avoid the detection of the guests. She had lost her ability to shift shape, but she certainly hadn't lost her knack for sneaking unseen or unheard. She was as fast and light on her feet as she had always been.

She followed Mr. Vanderbilt up past the purple-leafed beech and then the elm tree with its low, splaying branches, until he went up the steps and reached the Pergola.

"Wine, sir?" a footman said as he hurried down from the house toward the party with his tray restocked.

"No, thank you, John," Mr. Vanderbilt said. "Do you happen to have a sweet tea on your tray?"

"Oh, yes, sir, I do," the footman said in surprise, for iced tea was not his master's normal drink. *Braeden,* Serafina thought.

"Thank you very much, John," Mr. Vanderbilt said as he took the tea and kept moving. "Take good care of everyone."

"I will, sir," John said, a worried twinge in his voice as he watched his master rush up the steps toward the terrace.

Finally the footman turned and continued on his way toward the party.

As Serafina slipped behind a tree trunk to avoid the passing footman's notice, she couldn't help but wonder about how little people noticed the things around them. She knew that theoretically she could walk openly among the guests of the house, and she had felt left out about not being there, but the truth was, she still felt far more comfortable spying on a party than attending it. And the soaking wet, grave-dirtied, dress-torn, bloodstained look of her would have shocked them all.

Right now, she had her eyes fixed on one person, and that was Mr. Vanderbilt.

Serafina went right after him. She ran across the gravel path, making barely a rustling step of noise, then bounded up the stone steps at the southeast corner of the house to reach the Library Terrace. It was a flat area just outside the glass doors of the Library with a view to the forest and the Blue Ridge Mountains. The terrace was covered by an arbor heavily laden with long, hanging purple wisteria. The vines grew thick and twisty around the arbor's stout posts and up into its latticework above. The warm amber light of the Library fell through the open doors onto the terrace.

A boy was sitting on a bench, facing out toward the forest. When she first saw him, she didn't recognize him. But as she crept closer and saw his face, she knew.

It was Braeden.

But what she saw—the way he was sitting and the look of his face—struck her such a blow that she couldn't help but suck in a gasp of air. She was too startled to move immediately toward him like she normally would have. She watched from the shadows and tried to understand what she was seeing.

The first thing she noticed was that Gidean, Braeden's once-beloved black Doberman, wasn't lying at his young master's feet like he normally did. The poor dog was lying twenty feet away, his head down, his ears drooped, a sad, dejected expression on his face, as if Braeden had sent him away, scorned and unwanted.

Braeden sat on the bench alone. There was a plaid blanket around his legs despite the fact that it wasn't cold outside. He was twelve years old, but he looked smaller, frailer than she had ever seen him before. His brown hair was longer, his skin different, paler, like he hadn't been outside as much as he usually was. But what caught her most of all was that there were long, jagged scars on the side of his face, and his right leg had been strapped into some sort of leather-and-metal brace, with hinges at the knee.

Her heart swelled with grief. She wanted to reach out to him. What had happened to Braeden? Had the dark forces she'd seen in the forest already attacked him?

"It's just me," Mr. Vanderbilt said softly as he approached his nephew. "Are you all right?"

"Yes," Braeden said, his voice somber, "I'm all right," but his words were laced with tones that tugged at her heart.

Braeden seemed so sad. His mouth hung grim. His eyes were dull of spirit. And as she crept closer to him, an even darker, more despairing expression clouded his face, as if something was suddenly causing him even more anguish than moments before.

But she could see him trying to steady himself the best he could, at least for his uncle's sake. "Did you come all the way up here for me?" he asked.

"There wasn't anything to do down there," Mr. Vanderbilt said, smiling a little, and Braeden gave him a wan, knowing smile in return.

Mr. Vanderbilt offered him the glass of sweet tea. It had

always been Braeden's favorite. But as he reached out with his left hand to take the glass from him, his hand was shaking so badly that it was clear that he wouldn't be able to hold the tea without spilling it.

"I don't want that!" Braeden snapped at his uncle, knocking the tea away.

Mr. Vanderbilt stepped back and took a long breath. The master of Biltmore wasn't at all used to someone treating him like that, but after a moment, he stepped closer once more.

"Try it again," he said gently, handing the glass to Braeden. "Your right hand works better, I think."

Braeden looked at him sharply, but slowly reached over with his right hand and took the glass. His right hand was trembling, too, but not nearly as badly as the left.

Steadying the glass of tea in two hands now, Braeden took a long drink in silence. When he was done, he nodded. It was as if he had forgotten how much he liked the drink. "Thank you," he said to his uncle, almost sounding like his old cheerful self again for a moment, but then he pressed his lips together and shook his head, barely holding back tears.

Mr. Vanderbilt sat on the bench beside him. "Is it bad tonight?"

Braeden nodded. "For the last few weeks it finally felt like I was getting a little better, but all of a sudden, I feel so awful."

"Is it the party?" Mr. Vanderbilt asked regretfully.

"I don't think so," Braeden said shaking his head, "I don't know . . . maybe . . . maybe it's the beautiful night, the moonlight, the stars. She loved nights like this."

"I'm sorry," Mr. Vanderbilt said.

"Sometimes, I almost feel like I'm going to get back to normal again, but other times I feel a terrible aching inside, like she's standing right beside me."

I am, Braeden, Serafina thought. *I'm here!* But she was so transfixed by what she was seeing and hearing that she couldn't speak or move. It was like she was locked in a dream that she could only watch.

"Sometimes," Mr. Vanderbilt said gently, "you have to push on through your life even when you don't feel too well. She might have left Biltmore for any number of reasons. But if the worst has happened, then we need to keep her in our hearts. She'll live on in your memories of her. And she'll live in my heart as well. She was a good, brave girl, and I know she was a very special friend to you."

Braeden nodded, agreeing with everything his uncle was saying, but Serafina noticed a peculiar expression on Braeden's face, a hesitation in his movement. Serafina knew him well enough to know that there was something he wasn't telling his uncle.

Mr. Vanderbilt put his arm gently around his nephew. "No matter what's happened, we'll get through this."

It was strangely fascinating to watch and listen, to imagine a world where she had disappeared, but Serafina couldn't stand it anymore. She had to tell them that she was alive and well, that she was finally home. And more than anything, she had to warn them. The talon-clawed creature, the black shapes, the storms, the dark river, the sorcerer . . . they were coming.

Taking in a deep breath, she stepped out from behind the column and showed herself to both of them.

"Braeden, it's me. I'm back."

Braeden and Mr. Vanderbilt didn't turn toward Serafina or react to her in any way. They seemed not to hear her or see her even though she was right in front of them.

"Braeden, it's me!" Serafina said again more loudly as she stepped even closer to them. "Mr. Vanderbilt, it's Serafina! Can you hear me?"

But neither of them responded. She couldn't believe it. This was impossible.

"Braeden!" she shouted frantically. She was standing right in front of them and they couldn't see her! What in the world was going on? Her body began to tremble with fear.

Preparing to return to his guests, Mr. Vanderbilt patted

Braeden's shoulder. "Stay here as long as you like," he said gently. "But when you're feeling up to it, think about coming back down to the party."

"I will," Braeden said. "It *is* beautiful. I can see the lights from here."

"I think maybe Serafina's pa was trying to light Biltmore up so brightly that she could find her way home," Mr. Vanderbilt said, his voice filled with a warm and gentle melancholy.

Gidean, still lying twenty feet away, watched Mr. Vanderbilt walk back down toward the party, then looked glumly back at Braeden.

"Gidean, can you hear me, boy?" Serafina said to her old friend, but he didn't look in her direction, and his long, pointed ears didn't perk up. He just gazed at Braeden with sadness in his eyes.

How was all this possible? She was right in front of them, as plain as night.

Serafina studied Braeden, and then looked at herself. The rays of moonlight coming down through the vine-covered lattice above her shone onto her body, casting her in an eerie, dappled-white light.

Am I truly here? she wondered.

Or am I still buried underground in the coffin and just imagining that I crawled out?

Have I been cursed by a spell?

Or am I some sort of whispery ghost or haint or spirit?

She thought about how quickly she'd been able to dart away

51

from the talon-clawed creature in the forest, how skillfully she'd escaped the sorcerer, how quietly she had slipped past all the guests at the party.

She brushed back tears as the emotion welled up inside her. What had happened to her?

Determined to make it stop, she stepped closer to Braeden.

"It's me, Braeden. I'm back. It's me," she said again, her voice cracking.

But Braeden did not respond. He looked out across the moonlit forest and fields. His heart seemed forlorn, his mood dark. There was a tension in his face that she'd never seen before.

She lifted her hand and looked at it. She slowly turned it one way and then the other in the moonlight. It seemed normal in every way to her, and yet he could not see her. She had felt hungry earlier, but maybe it was because she had seen the food at the party. She had felt pain when she fell from the tree, but maybe that was what she *thought* she should be feeling. Was she just *remembering* how things felt?

Braeden breathed a long, heavy sigh, then began to move. He gripped the side of the bench, and with much effort, his arms shaking, he managed to get himself up onto his crooked legs. He stood lopsided, tilted over like his body had been broken. Clearly exhausted by the exertion of getting onto his feet, he rested there, leaning his shoulder against the column for a moment.

When he tried to take a few steps forward, it seemed at first as if he was going to be all right, but then he winced and his leg buckled beneath him. The metal brace tripped him up and he lurched off-balance. Serafina reflexively darted forward to catch him so that he didn't fall, but he hit the ground anyway, grunting in pain as he crashed into the gravel.

Serafina stepped back in confusion. She was certain she had reached him in time, but she hadn't been able to hold him up.

As Braeden struggled to get to his feet, she stepped forward again and grabbed his arm to lift him. At first she thought she was touching him. She *had* to be touching him, because she could see her hands were on him. But then she slowly realized that she could not actually feel him the way she should, the true warmth of his living body. She knew she *should* feel it. She could *imagine* feeling it. But this was more like a *memory* of feeling.

Her spirit was remembering the physical world the way an amputee lying in a hospital bed remembers his missing leg, feels the movement of it, suffers the pain of it, even though it's gone.

She slowly reached out and tried to touch his shoulder, and then his bare hand. There was something there, something like a physical object, but she couldn't feel the living warmth of it, and it was clear that he couldn't feel her at all.

Up to this moment, she'd been interacting with the world based on her memory of her past life. But now she was like the amputee who sees with his own eyes that his leg is actually gone. It was becoming clear to her that she could no longer affect the physical world around her. It was as if the more she realized what was happening to her, the more she faded away.

Gritting her teeth, she tried to hold herself together, but it was no use. She pressed her hands to her face and squeezed her eyes shut, trying just to breathe. She began to cry in confusion and fear. A dizzying nausea swept through her stomach. It felt like she was going to pass out, but she had to hold on.

Braeden slowly dragged himself and his bad leg over to the terrace's stone railing. He clung to the top of the railing for support as he looked out into the night. He seemed lost in thought, like he was remembering something. At first she thought he was gazing out at the trees and the bank of clouds rolling in across the night sky, but then she realized that he was looking in the direction from which she had come. He was looking specifically toward the graveyard and the angel's glade.

"No, she's not *missing*," Braeden said as if his uncle was still there. "She's dead and buried."

Serafina stepped back in horror. *She's dead and buried,* Braeden said.

Was Braeden the one who buried me?

Is it possible that I'm actually dead?

She knew she'd been buried, there was no denying that, but *dead?*

She didn't *feel* dead.

And even in Braeden's discouraged hopelessness she sensed something else, some other uncertainty in his eyes and tone of voice. He seemed to be waiting, frustrated, biding his time. Despite everything, despite the anguish and pain, there seemed to be a faint trace of *hope* in him.

After Mr. Vanderbilt went back down to the gardens to

rejoin his wife and the guests at the evening party, Serafina wanted to stay with Braeden, just to keep him company if nothing else, but the longer she stayed there, the more upset he seemed to become. She could see it in the shaking restlessness of his hands and legs, in the pained expression of his face, and even the unsettled way he was breathing. The mere closeness of her presence seemed to sadden and disquiet him.

After Braeden went to bed and the partygoers went up to their rooms in the mansion, Serafina went down into the basement to see her pa. She passed maids and manservants she knew by name. She saw footmen and assistants. But none of them saw her.

When she finally came to the workshop, she found it empty. There was no sign of her pa. She waited a few moments, thinking he would soon return, but he did not.

Her heart began to fill with a terrible dread. Had this, too, changed?

She searched the basement room by room, the kitchens and pantries, the workrooms and the storerooms. Biltmore was just too large! She finally found her pa repairing the small, wheeled electric motor that powered the house's dumbwaiter. She sighed with relief.

Her pa was on his knees, pulling a wrench. The muscles on his bare, sweating forearm bulged. He was a large, gruff man with a barrel chest and thick limbs. He wore simple work clothes, a leather apron, and a heavy leather belt laden with tools. She had seen him working a thousand times, had handed him screwdrivers and hammers when he needed them, had run to retrieve parts and materials for him. But she'd never seen him like this. There was no joy in his work tonight, no sense of purpose. He moved slowly, doggedly, his eyes mournful. He was going through the motions of his life, but his spirit was gone.

"Pa . . ." she said, standing before him. "Can you see me?"

To her surprise, her pa stopped his work. He slowly turned as if gazing at the empty air around him. It was clear that he couldn't see her, but he stared at the emptiness for a long time as if he was sure something was there.

After a few moments, he pulled out a rag and wiped his brow. Then he lowered his head and wiped his eyes, a wave of emotion racking through his shoulders. She could see the flicker of memories in his face, the sadness in his eyes. She didn't know what Braeden knew of her demise, but one thing was certain: her pa thought she was dead.

She could see it in his face and in the way he moved. His dream of having a daughter had been the joy of his life for these twelve years. But now she was gone. He was alone, true and certain.

Seeing him there by himself, her heart broke.

Finally, he gave up on fixing the machine and sighed as if it was all pointless anyway. She'd never seen him break from a job before the job was done. The idea of leaving a machine unmended was inconceivable.

As he hoisted his leather tool satchel over his shoulder and trudged back toward the workshop, Serafina followed him. He walked slowly, without spirit or purpose, like a wanderer who has nothing to go home to.

She stayed close to him as he moved back and forth in the shop, putting his tools away and preparing his late-night meal.

As he cooked his supper of chicken and grits over his little cook stove and then ate alone, she sat across from him in her old chair. It was here that she used to listen to his stories and share her own, telling him about the rats she had caught or the falling stars she'd seen streaking through the sky. But now her plate and her spoon sat on the bench, unused for months.

"I'll eat my grits, Pa, I swear I will," she said out loud as tears welled in her eyes.

A little while later, when he lay in his bed and fell asleep, she crawled onto her own empty cot behind the boiler and lay down. She didn't know what else to do.

When you're dreaming, what happens if you fall asleep in your dream? Do you dream? And is your dream real life?

If she was dead and buried, how could she be tired?

She didn't know, but maybe sleep wasn't about the body, but about rest for the mind and the spirit.

All she knew was that she was exhausted. Trembling and forlorn, she curled up in a ball.

As she fell asleep, she slipped into a dream where she was biting and clawing, fighting in a black, swirling world, and then it all fell away and all she could feel was the earth and the river and the wind, a vast world without form, and she felt herself being swept through it like she was nothing but a particle of dust, and then a tiny droplet of water, and then a wisp of air, until she finally dissolved into nothingness.

She started awake with a violent jerk.

When she looked around the workshop she didn't know whether she was awake or asleep. Did she just dream of her death? Or was her death the reality and what she was experiencing now the dream?

She remembered the frightening sensation of her feet being torn into little pieces by the current of the river, and the feeling of the wind high in the trees almost sweeping her away. *I only have so much more time left here,* she thought, *and then I'm going to fade away completely.*

She looked at her surroundings, trying to understand. It was dark, the witching hour between 3:00 and 4:00 a.m.

Still shaking from the dream, she rose from her bed and stood in the workshop, not sure what to do. She just stood there and breathed and tried to figure out whether she was truly breathing or dreaming of breathing or remembering breathing.

Finally, she went over to her pa sleeping on his cot.

She tried to touch his side to make sure he was truly there. She felt a vague shape, but no warmth, no response to her touch. It was just as it had been with Braeden.

Even though she couldn't feel her father's warmth, and he couldn't feel hers, she curled up beside her pa like a little kitten so small and light that it wasn't even felt against its master's chest. And she tried not to sleep.

In the morning, when her pa woke and began his day, she tried to touch him, tried to speak with him, tried to tell him what was happening to her, tried to warn him about what she'd seen in the forest, tried to tell him to check the stream flowing into the pond, but the more she tried, the more sadness it seemed to cause him. Her presence wasn't a comfort to him, but a sorrow. She was *haunting* him.

Finally, when he gathered his tool bag and went off to work, she let him go, not because she wanted to let him go, but for mercy's sake.

11

Serafina sat alone at the bottom of the basement steps, her head on her hands. She had to figure out a way to get back into the world and warn everyone that they were in danger. She'd been attacked, and clearly Braeden had been attacked, and she was sure that there were more attacks to come.

"But what can I do?" she asked herself. How could she talk to the people she loved? How could she warn them?

She had found Mr. and Mrs. Vanderbilt, Braeden, Gidean, and her pa, but there was one more person at Biltmore who might be able to help her. She went up the back stairway to the fourth floor and down the corridor into the maids' quarters.

When she came to the particular maid's room she was looking for, the door was ajar.

As Serafina paused, a bad feeling crept into her.

"Essie?" she asked quietly. "Essie, are you there?"

Finally, Serafina slipped slowly into the room.

Her friend Essie's room was empty and lifeless. Essie's books and newspapers weren't on the nightstand by the bed. Essie's drawings of flowers and plants weren't on the wall. Essie's clothes weren't strewn across the floor and chair. The bed had no sheets or pillows.

Serafina's heart sank.

No one was living in this room anymore.

Essie was gone.

Remembering her friend's old mountain stories of haints and nightspirits and other strange occurrences, Serafina had hoped that maybe Essie could help her, that maybe she could even talk with her in some way, but it was all for naught.

It just seemed so unfair, so wrong. She was home, but she felt homesick. Why couldn't everything just stay the way it had been? She'd made friends and found new family. She'd worn beautiful dresses and had English tea with lots and lots of cream! She'd met her mother and run at her side. She'd nuzzled her head and felt her purr. But what had happened to her mother and the cubs? Were they gone like Essie? Serafina couldn't bear the thought that something bad had happened to any of them.

As she stood in the room, she noticed the mirror on the wall.

As soon as she saw it, she froze where she was and her heart began to pound.

"Oh, no, I'm not doin' that . . ." she said firmly.

She didn't want to move toward it. She was too frightened to put herself in front of it and look at it.

What would she see?

Her old self? A whispery haint? A grave-walking ghoul bloodied with the wounds she could see on her torn, blood-stained dress? She was a ghoul. Suddenly she was sure of it. The last thing she wanted to see was the bloody, corpsy sight of her walking death.

Get hold of yourself, you frightened little fool, she scolded herself. *You've got to figure this out! You've got to look!*

She pulled in a long, deep breath.

Then she took a step toward the mirror.

Then another.

Finally, she slowly moved a little bit in front of it and looked at herself.

All she could see in the mirror was a glint of light, a faint blur of motion when she moved, as if she was nothing but air itself.

She had no reflection. She was nobody and nothing.

She remembered back to the time she'd looked into this mirror and noticed her amber eyes starting to change, and her black hair starting to come in, and how proud she'd felt of the beautiful dress she'd been wearing. Now she had no eyes, no hair, nothing.

So much of what she had come to know and love had just slipped away. Was this the work of the sorcerer, or was it simply how time passed?

It felt like it was more than that. It felt as if her world had been shattered into a thousand pieces like a Ming vase on a tiled floor. She kept wondering if she could pick up the pieces and put them back together again.

"Stay bold," she told herself sternly. *Stop this nonsense, feelin' all sorry for yourself. Dream or real, dead or alive, you don't give up, you don't give in to hopelessness. You keep fighting!*

Then, even as she was thinking these thoughts, she saw something very faint in the movement of light and air in the reflection of the mirror. There was something behind her. When she turned to look at what it was, she noticed the tiny particles of dust floating in random motion in the rays of morning light coming through the window.

She stepped toward the floating dust.

She marveled at how she could see the shape of each particle, the way it turned and caught the light as it tumbled through the air. The dust reminded her of the words spoken at funeral rites when a loved one was buried.

"And we commit her body to the ground," the pastor would say. "We all go to the same place. All come from dust and all return to dust. Earth to earth, ashes to ashes, dust to dust."

As she studied the slow swirling motion of the dust in the sunlight, she whispered, "That's what I am now." *Specks of dust floating in the air.*

She lifted her hand and passed it slowly through the rays of light. Her hand caused no shadow, but she could swear that the motes of dust whirled up in little clouds around the movement of her hand.

"I'm here," she said. "Just a little bit . . . I'm still here."

Even if I'm just a minuscule speck of dust or a gust of air, then I still exist. There's still hope.

She looked around at Essie's empty room. The past was behind her. The future unknown. But what now?

She looked out the window toward the mountains. Great banks of dark clouds were rolling across the peaks, vast sheets of rain drinking up the rays of the sun. The water of the French Broad River had risen so high in the last few nights that the ancient river had burst its banks and flooded the lagoon. The lagoon had been drowned in the water of the rains and completely swept away.

The storms are coming, she thought.

And I've got to stop them.

n her way down to the first floor, Serafina descended the long, gentle curve of the Grand Staircase, walking in broad daylight past the guests on the stairs. She jumped up and down in front of them and tried to touch them. She swiped her hands across the long skirts of the ladies' dresses, trying to make the material fly. But it made no difference. She'd spent her whole life hiding, but now she just wanted one person, *any person*, to know she was there.

"Hello, there!" she said loudly to one of the many new lady guests who had arrived for the upcoming summer ball. "Beautiful dress you're wearing today!" she shouted to another. "Your hat is on crooked, sir," she said to one of the gentlemen.

Reaching the main floor, she went into the Winter Garden, where a number of young ladies in beautiful powder-blue and yellow dresses were chatting over English tea. She tried to steal their sugar cubes and knock over their teacups, but she couldn't affect a thing. Then she noticed the faint trace of steam coming off the tea in one of the cups and she had an idea. She bent down and blew gently into the hot vapor, and to her surprise, it actually swirled in a new direction and disappeared into the air. Serafina smiled. She was making progress.

Encouraged, she crossed over to the back corridor and slipped into the Smoking Room with its rich blue damask wallpaper, elegant velvet chairs, and gold-leafed books on the shelves. When she had come here with Braeden on Christmas Eve, they had been dressed in their finest clothes for the first Christmas party she had ever attended. *I just hope it wasn't my last,* she thought glumly.

But she wasn't going to stand around feeling sorry for herself just because she was dead.

She walked over to the room's fireplace, with its finely carved white marble mantel, and was relieved to see that the barn owl was still mounted there.

Her old enemies, the powerful conjurer Uriah and his treacherous daughter-apprentice Rowena, had been shapeshifters, able to change into the white-faced owl at will.

Long ago, Uriah had stolen this land from its rightful owners and formed his dark dominion in the hidden forests of these mountains. He had killed many of the forest animals, as well as

Serafina's panther father. But the arrival of Mr. Vanderbilt and the construction of Biltmore Estate freed the mountain folk and the forest animals from the conjurer's spells and brought new light into the area. Uriah had been obsessed with destroying Biltmore ever since.

Filled with a hateful vengeance, he had created the Black Cloak, which allowed its wearer to steal the souls of its victims. And he had used the Twisted Staff to enslave the animals of the forest and attack Biltmore.

As Uriah was flying in owl form, she had raked him from the sky with her panther claws, sending the bloodied bird tumbling toward the ground. She and her allies had struck down Rowena that same night.

Serafina had hoped that she had destroyed both of them, but the truth was, she didn't truly know. Waysa had told her, *It is the way of his kind that even when he seems to be dead, he is not. His spirit lives on. He hides in a darkness the rest of us cannot see.*

The morning after the battle, Biltmore's groundskeepers had found a dead owl in the forest, and they had it mounted over this fireplace. She remembered that it had looked so lifelike, but now it seemed dead and worn, its feathers graying and tattered, the living spirit gone. It reminded her of the dried, white, desiccated shell of a rattlesnake after it had shed its skin and become anew.

She couldn't help but wonder now if the robed sorcerer she'd seen by the river might have been Uriah in some new form.

Had Uriah been the one who attacked her on the Loggia

the night of the full moon? Was he the sorcerer causing the storms in the forest?

Had he returned to destroy Biltmore once and for all? Or was it some new enemy that she'd never seen before?

Whatever the answer was, she had to stay watchful.

For the rest of the afternoon, she practiced moving particles of dust, shaping tendrils of steam, and causing candles to flicker as she studied the comings and goings of Biltmore. She followed people through their daily lives, watching them from the shadows, a shadow herself, looking for signs of suspicious behavior and clues to where something was amiss.

It wasn't until later that evening that something caught her eye.

The formal dinner in the Banquet Hall started promptly at eight, with many of the guests and staff talking about the heavy rains, the muddy condition of the roads, and the water collecting in the fields where vast acres of crops were being lost to the flooding. Braeden was sitting near his aunt and uncle. Her friend seemed to be in somewhat better spirits than the night before, well enough to at least come to dinner, but there was still a dark and unsmiling gloominess to him.

A mustachioed gentleman at the table tried to speak with him. "It's good to see you, Master Braeden. I was terribly sorry to hear that you've given up your riding. I know you have always enjoyed your time with your horses."

It seemed as if the gentleman was trying to be kind, but Braeden's face hardened at his words.

Serafina wondered if she could get Braeden's attention by swirling the water in his water glass or something. There had to be some way to signal him, to let him know she was there with him. But as soon as she approached him, Braeden became even more upset, muttered that he was tired, and quickly excused himself from the table.

"Good night, Braeden," Mrs. Vanderbilt said, concerned that he was leaving so soon.

"Sleep well," Mr. Vanderbilt said to his nephew, but then touched Braeden's arm, drew him closer in, and spoke to him in a soft and quiet tone. "Remember, the servants will be double-locking all the doors tonight and guards will be posted."

Braeden clenched his jaw and walked away from his uncle without saying a word.

Serafina was taken aback by the rudeness of Braeden's behavior. And she thought that if Mr. Vanderbilt had some inkling of the dangers surrounding Biltmore, then locking the doors and posting guards made perfect sense. But it almost seemed as if Mr. Vanderbilt was telling Braeden that the doors would be double-locked not to keep something out, but to make sure Braeden didn't try to leave the house. And Braeden was none too happy about it.

She followed her friend as he trudged up the stairs to his room, dragging his metal-braced leg behind him. In months past, she had seen him heal a fox, a falcon, and other animals—it was part of his connection to them, part of his love for them—but he couldn't heal humans, not even himself. And it was clear that something had gone terribly wrong with him.

His dog, his horses . . . It was so sad that his grief had kept him from his only friends.

When Braeden arrived at his bedroom door, Gidean was waiting quietly for him outside his room.

"I don't want you following me," Braeden said harshly to Gidean. "Just stay away from me!"

The look on the dog's face was so miserable that Serafina wished she could kneel down beside him and pet him like she used to. "I'm sure he doesn't mean it," she said to Gidean, even though the dog couldn't hear her, and the truth was, she wasn't sure of anything anymore. Maybe Braeden did mean it.

As Serafina followed Braeden into his bedroom, she was surprised by the state of it. The last time she'd seen his room, it had been warm and tidy, but now it was messy and disheveled, with days-old food trays piled on the dresser and dirty clothes all over the floor. The four-poster bed was unmade. The drapes were covered with dust. It looked like he hadn't cleaned his room in months, and hadn't let the servants in, either.

He exhaled a long, tired breath as he collapsed into the leather chair by the small, unlit fireplace. He rubbed his bad leg with his shaking hand. His other leg moved in constant restlessness. And he kept pulling his hand through his hair, then wiping the side of his face. He wasn't just exhausted, but anxious and frustrated.

Serafina remembered visiting him here one night and curling up on the rug in front of the warm fire with Gidean as Braeden slept quietly in his bed. But now he just stared blankly into the dead ashes of the empty black hearth.

Suddenly, Braeden got up. His metal brace thumped the wooden floor as he paced, pressing his trembling fingers to his skull as if there were voices in his head.

More agitated than even before, he changed out of his black dinner jacket and trousers, and put on the rugged clothes he used for hiking. Then he got down onto his hands and knees and pulled a coil of rope out from under his bed.

"What in tarnation are you gonna do with that?" Serafina asked out loud.

As the rest of the house retired for the evening, Braeden opened one of his windows and hurled the rope out into the darkness. It had been raining hard all night, and now the wet spray of it blew into the room.

"Just what's goin' on in that head of yours, Braeden?" she asked him, feeling a terrible tightness in her chest.

She could see that his hands were trembling something awful as he struggled to tie the end of the rope to the bed. The shaking was so bad that he could barely manage it. Then he went over to the window.

"Braeden, whatever you're thinking about doing, don't do it!" she told him.

But he climbed onto the windowsill, his hands and knees slipping on the rain-slick surface, and started to crawl out. He couldn't maneuver his braced leg well enough by its own power, so he lifted it with his hands, then dragged himself over, and began climbing down the rope on the outside of the building.

This was an insanely dangerous thing to do for even an able-bodied person in dry weather, but the sickly, crooked-legged boy was climbing out the window in the middle of a rainstorm. There was a forty-foot drop to the stone terrace below. The fall was going to kill him.

"Be careful, Braeden!" Serafina shouted at him angrily, the storm whipping her hair as she leaned out. All of a sudden, a gust of wind lifted her off her feet, trying to sweep her away with the blowing rain. She felt herself rising upward, pieces of her spirit, her soul, whatever it was, tearing away and disappearing into the gale. All she could do was cling for dear life to the window jamb and try to stay whole.

As Braeden climbed down the outside of the building, she watched helplessly. If he lost his grip, she couldn't save him! He'd fall and die.

Lightning flashed through the sky, then a roar of thunder cracked overhead.

Serafina clung to the window feeling like the universe itself was trying to pull apart what little was left of her, but she finally managed to climb down the side of the building and put her feet on the solid ground. Spirit or ghost or whatever she was, she squatted down and put her hands on the stone tile of the terrace, grateful for the plenum of the earth.

It was becoming clear that the universe was taking her back, that her spirit only had so much more time to roam the earth before it faded into the elements from whence all things came.

When Braeden made it safely to the ground on the Library Terrace beside her, he took a moment to catch his breath and wipe the rain out of his eyes.

"Where are you off to in the middle of the night?" she asked in the rain, still angry with him for endangering himself like that.

As if in reply, he gathered himself and headed into the storm. Tonight there was no party or music, just darkness and rain.

She followed him down the steps and through the garden. He couldn't move quickly with his braced leg. He dragged it behind him, the metal scraping along the stone with each step, but he moved with determination and made pretty good time. It was clear that he knew where he wanted to go.

He followed the winding path of the shrub garden, past the golden-rain tree, then down the steps, through the archway and into the Walled Garden.

She didn't know where he was going, but it felt good to be with him and a part of his adventure into the night, whatever it was. Despite her narrow escape on the windowsill, she was still clinging to the hope that she could figure out what had happened to Braeden since she'd been gone, how she could communicate with him, and somehow get back to him. But she felt a wrenching loneliness, too, a separation from him that tore at her gut. She couldn't speak to him or help him. She couldn't ask him what he was thinking. When she looked at his stark, grim face, it was filled with such desperation that it frightened her.

She followed him down the length of the central arbor and into the rose garden. He ducked into the small stone shed used by the master rosarian, Mr. Fetlan. The shed was filled with rakes, hoes, and other garden tools along with pots, trays, and wired wooden apple crates.

Braeden grabbed a lantern and a shovel and headed back out into the rain again. The boy was soaked to the bone, and she could see him trembling, but he pressed on regardless.

Through the garden he went, then down the path that led toward the pond. After passing the boathouse, it appeared he was going to cross the large redbrick bridge that arched over the eastern spur of the pond, but at the last moment, he diverted to the left and went into the woods.

"This is getting stranger and stranger," she said. "Where are you going now?"

He followed the edge of the pond beneath the overhang of the trees until she heard the sound of rushing water. They had come to the stream that fed into the pond. But the water didn't go straight in. A low brick structure had been built across the stream to block and control its flow. The structure was overgrown with several seasons of bushes, moss, and vines. It took her a moment to remember what it was.

Years before, when Biltmore House was built, her old friend Mr. Olmsted, the estate's landscape architect, had decided that no estate was complete without a tranquil garden pond. He had told her that he had designed a similar pond in Central Park. She'd never been to New York City or anyplace outside the mountains. She couldn't even imagine what flat ground looked like, how strange and disorienting it must be. But she remembered enjoying Mr. Olmsted's stories of the great city's park. There were no natural lakes on the Biltmore property, or anywhere else in these mountains, but years before, an old farmer had dammed the creek to make a mill pond, so Mr. Olmsted expanded it, redesigned it, and made it part of Mr. Vanderbilt's garden.

Serafina remembered that her pa had brought her out to this very spot and showed her the inlet to the pond.

"It's a gentle little creek," her pa had explained, "but every time a storm comes in, it swells up bad and wants to dump muddy water, sticks, and debris into the pond. A farmer and a bunch of cows don't pay no never mind about a muck-filled pond, but it would never do for an elegant gentleman like Mr. Vanderbilt, so Mr. Olmsted had an idea."

As Serafina remembered her pa's words, she couldn't help but think about how happy and filled with life he'd been when he told her these stories.

"Mr. Olmsted had his workers build this brickwork structure across the creek to gather in the water and control how it flowed. You see, the water slips real smooth-like right into that big hole there. If the water's clean, then it runs on toward the pond. But look down in the hole real close, Sera. You see that metal contraption in there? Mr. Olmsted asked me to rig up a steel basket and a sluice gate so that if there's a big storm, and the creek water is all muddy and full of debris, then it won't flow into the pond."

"But I don't understand," Serafina had asked in confusion. "Where's the storm water go? It's gotta go somewhere, doesn't it?"

"Ah, you see! There's the trick of it. When we built this

thing, Mr. Olmsted instructed his work crews to construct a long, winding brick tunnel called a flume under the pond. The tunnel goes from the inlet here, all the way underneath the pond to the far end, nigh on a thousand feet away. So, now, when it rains hard and the creek overflows with muddy storm water, the metal basket fills with sticks and debris, the weight of it tilts the mechanism, the sluice gate opens the entrance to the tunnel, and the whole mess of it pours in. The storm water and debris flows through the tunnel underneath the pond and gushes out at the far end without ever having a chance to muck up the clean water in the pond. From there, the storm water continues on its natural course down the creek, eventually ending up in the big river the way God intended."

As her pa finished his story, Serafina could hear the reverence in his voice. "You see, Sera, you can accept things the way they are. Or you can make them better." And Serafina knew that both her pa and Mr. Olmsted were the kind of the people who made them better.

As Serafina remembered her pa's story, Braeden leaned down into the brick structure and used his lantern to look around inside. The stream was running strong and smooth with a large volume of rainwater pouring down into the main intake hole, but the water was clear of debris, so the metal sluice gate had not yet opened, allowing the water to flow directly into the pond.

Braeden began chucking sticks and branches into the metal basket.

"What in the world are you doing that for?" Serafina asked.

As he filled the basket with the weight of the branches, the sluice gate scraped slowly open. Braeden grabbed his equipment and climbed into the flume tunnel.

"Braeden!" she said in astonishment.

Down in a tunnel that ran beneath the pond was the last place on earth she wanted to go tonight. She'd already been buried once. She definitely didn't want to do it again—especially if it involved getting drowned at the same time.

But as Braeden disappeared, she had no choice. She had no idea where his new recklessness was coming from, but she couldn't let her friend go into that awful place on his own.

Pulling in a frightened breath, she climbed into the tunnel behind him.

Following the light of Braeden's lantern ahead of her, Serafina made her way through the flume. It was a narrow brick passage with a low arched ceiling. An inch of water was running along the floor. At first the tunnel was high enough that they could both walk normally, but the farther they went, the lower and narrower the tunnel became.

She didn't like this place one bit, but what she truly hated was the water dripping down from the ceiling onto the back of her neck, sending tingles down her shivering spine. And she hated the dark runnels of water sliding down the black, slimy, algae-coated walls like spidery tentacles. The heavy, putrid smell of the water hung in the air. She and Braeden were actually walking *under* the water of the pond.

As they went deeper, Serafina felt the cool temperature of the damp air, the clamminess of the walls, and the rising storm water at their feet. She wasn't sure if the sensations she was experiencing were real or shadow, but they felt as sharp as if she herself was part of the water, part of the stone, part of the bits and pieces from which the world was made.

The water in the tunnel was soon flowing around their ankles. Braeden had forced the sluice gate open, so the stream was pouring in. She had no idea why he was going through the flume, but it was even more mystifying why he would do it now, tonight, in the middle of a rainstorm with the water gushing in. What in the world could be so important?

Crack!

Startled by the sound, Serafina hit the floor with a splash, accidentally taking in a gulp of the water.

Crack!

It was steel against brick. Then she heard a prying sound.

She got back up onto her feet and sloshed through the rising water toward Braeden. He had set the lantern on a small ledge to give himself light to work by as he dug into the tunnel floor.

Using the tip of the shovel, he pried up one of the bricks. He pulled it up out of the water, set it aside, then picked up the shovel again and started working on the next one. Working in what was now six inches of rushing water, he was digging out the floor brick by brick!

Braeden's movement was hampered by the metal brace on his leg, but he worked with a steady deliberateness. Soon he had removed a dozen bricks. Then he reached down into the dark water, deep into a hole, and pulled out a dripping metal box.

"You've hidden something here," Serafina said.

With the storm water rising by the second, Braeden seemed to understand the danger he was in. Now that he'd gotten what he'd come for, she expected he'd turn around and go back up toward the opening of the tunnel. But he didn't. Leaving the shovel and lantern behind, he grabbed the box and continued forward into the darkness, down into the narrowest part of the flume.

"Now, where are you going, you crazy boy?" she shouted at him over the sound of the rushing water. "We've got to go back up!"

But he paid her no mind. As they proceeded down the tunnel, the ceiling became so low that she and Braeden could no longer walk upright. They hunched themselves down to fit, then they had to crouch. Finally they had to crawl on their hands and knees, the hinges of Braeden's brace creaking and twisting under the strain of his bending leg. At the same time, the level of the storm water gushing through the tunnel continued to rise. The flood of water pushed hard against her, now inches from her chin, almost to the ceiling, splashing and swirling with great force around her neck and shoulders, making it more and more difficult to breathe.

As she crawled, it felt like the water wasn't just rising around her, but dragging at her, wearing at her, pulling her skin away, tugging at her bones. Soon she'd become nothing more than tiny droplets scattered in the stream. *Just hold on,* she thought, gritting her teeth. *I'm not done yet!*

Braeden crawled faster and faster into the darkness, pushing himself through the water, pressing his mouth up toward the ceiling for air, but still dragging the metal box along with him.

Suddenly, a huge swell with a tumbling raft of branches came gushing down through the flume and crashed into them, filling the entire tunnel with water. She closed her mouth and held her breath, for whatever good that would do, and refused to die. She braced herself against the slimy brick walls so that the water couldn't take her. She had to hold on! But it was no use. The powerful current slammed into her, tore her fingers from the walls, and pulled her somersaulting upside down through the rushing water.

The storm water swept her away, tumbling her down through the narrow chute of the flume. Her arms and legs twisted and crashed with the turbulence of the rushing water. It didn't feel like she was going to drown, but like the last pieces of her soul were going to wash away.

Finally, she shot out of the flume's gushing outlet pipe and splashed into a swollen creek. She came up quickly, gasping for air and struggling to get to her feet. She grabbed frantically at her arms and legs, incredibly relieved that they were still there. She hadn't dissolved into the elements just yet. She'd fought it off one more time.

Braeden lay at the edge of the creek in the torrential rain, exhausted and pulling in great lungfuls of air, but still gripping the metal box as if his very life depended upon it.

Serafina climbed up onto the creek's rocky shore and looked around her in bewilderment, trying to figure out where she was. It took her several seconds to realize that she and Braeden were in the narrow ravine at the base of the pond's dam.

When the water had started coming down the flume in force, Braeden had made the decision that it was better to escape through the outlet rather than trying to fight upstream. That decision had saved his life. And maybe hers too—if the thing she was clinging to was indeed a life.

Serafina couldn't help but smile, relieved that they'd both made it. She gazed up through the pouring rain at the stone face of the dam. The water of the overflowing pond was pouring over the spillway high above her, coming down in a great waterfall into the creek.

As she turned back toward Braeden, a flash of lightning struck the sky with a piercing crack of thunder. Braeden tightened his jaw, wiped his wet hair out of his eyes, and got up onto his feet. Whatever he was doing, it was clear he wasn't done.

He knelt down on the rocks at the edge of the storm-swollen creek and opened the metal box.

Serafina had no idea what was inside it, but the moment he opened it, she could see something extremely black inside.

She stepped back in uncertainty.

Braeden pulled out a long black garment—fine black wool on the outside, and an inner lining of black satin.

A sickening feeling gripped Serafina's stomach and twisted hard.

She could see that the garment had been badly torn. Many parts were nearly shredded, as if by the claws of a wild beast.

A blinding glare of white light glinted on the garment's small silver clasp as a lightning bolt burned up the sky.

Her palms started sweating. Her lips tightened. The rain poured down her face.

As Braeden gathered the garment in his hands, it began to writhe and rattle like a living snake. A smoky cloud began to hiss out from it, as if it was annoyed that it had been closed in the box so long.

Then, with the rain pouring down all around him, and the lightning flashing in the sky behind him, Braeden stood, and with a great sweep of fabric roiling around his shoulders, he pulled on the Black Cloak.

16

Serafina watched in dread.

She could see that the cloak had been badly torn, but it was still the Black Cloak she feared and hated. Its dark, slithering folds hung down from Braeden's shoulders, writhing with power. But in the tears of the cloak was not simply the absence of cloth, but an impenetrable darkness blacker than she had ever seen. *No!* That was wrong. She *had* seen it! It was the same black as the black shapes she'd seen floating in the forest.

Whenever Braeden moved, the cloak's fabric moved with him and the terrible black shapes came wheeling outward into the world around him, tearing through time and space. The cloak threw these torn fragments of roiling, inky black shadow in all directions, blotting out the ground and the leaves of the trees and the stars above.

You've done well, boy . . . the cloak hissed in its raspy voice.

As soon as she heard it, Serafina wanted to pounce on the cloak and kill it. But she had no claws, no fangs, nothing but fear and confusion filling her heart.

I'm not going to hurt you, child . . . the cloak hissed.

Months before, she and Braeden had seen the cloak's evil with their own eyes. It had many powers, but the most sinister was that it allowed the wearer to absorb people, body and soul, deep into the black void of its inner folds. Her mother had been imprisoned in the cloak for twelve years until Serafina cut it to pieces on the angel's sword in the graveyard and freed her back into the world. Destroying the cloak that night had also freed Clara Brahms, Anastasia Rostonova, and the other children who had gone missing.

But the point was that she had slashed the cloak! She had destroyed it! How could it be here again? The last time she remembered seeing any sign of it, there had been nothing left of it but the silver clasp. Detective Grathan had found the clasp in the graveyard and died with it in his hand the night he was killed by the rattlesnakes. Had Braeden somehow retrieved the clasp and reconstituted the black fabric of the cloak? But if so, for what terrible purpose would he bring such an evil thing back into the world? And if it had been remade, why was it so badly torn?

Still wearing the cloak, Braeden stared at the ground, his face clouded with what looked like hatred, violence, and bitter despair all at once, his mind consumed with thoughts he could not bear. "Please forgive me, Serafina," he whispered to himself.

"Forgive you?" she said even though he couldn't hear her. "What did you do?"

She still couldn't believe what she was seeing. Braeden was actually wearing the Black Cloak.

"Tell me what you did, Braeden!" she shouted at him. She didn't understand what was happening. Had he turned evil?

Then, as if in reply, Braeden reached back around his shoulders and gathered the material of the Black Cloak's hood into his fingers.

"Don't you do it!" she shouted at him. "Don't put on the hood!"

But then he slowly pulled the hood up onto his head. His face flashed with terror and revulsion. A storm of torment wrenched through him. As he turned toward her, the hanging pieces of the cloak's shredded fabric went wheeling outward, ripping the air with splintering black shadow, tearing through everything around her.

She knew the black tears were at least as much in her world as they were in his, the connection, the uncrossable bridge between the two planes. She didn't know if he could see her now, or if he even had any idea she was there, but the twisting tears of blackness riving through the air struck her like a physical blow, slicing her with a blaze of searing-hot pain, and knocked her to the rocky ground.

Filled with nothing but blind panic, she belly-crawled frantically over to a tree for cover. But when another black shadow tore through the space around her, the tree made no difference. The blackness cut right through it, bursting a section of the trunk to pieces and bringing the top of the tree crashing down.

Seeing another black shadow coming toward her, she ducked down and tried to scramble away, but she tripped hard and tumbled head over heels. She splashed into the cold depths of the swollen river. And in that moment, she came to understand that sometimes the key to survival wasn't *resisting*, but *giving in*.

"Water," she commanded herself, and she disintegrated instantaneously into millions of droplets of water and flowed away downstream.

In that moment of pain, confusion, and fear when she fled Braeden and fell into the river, Serafina grasped one thing: she was a shape-shifter. Whether in body or spirit, a living whole or a wisp of elements, she was a shape-shifter.

She flowed down the river for a long time, knowing only movement, a constant, sweeping, pulling force that carried her along through the current.

She tried to pull herself back together again into spiritual form, but she couldn't do it. She had shifted into the water, but now the water didn't want to give her back. She could feel her droplets spreading apart, blending with the rest of the water, slipping into eddies, swirling behind rocks, seeping back into the universe.

"Spirit!" she commanded forcefully, using the word to focus her mind, and finally pulled her spirit back together again. She crawled from the river several miles downstream from where she began.

She didn't know exactly what she had done when she splashed into the river, or how she'd done it, except to let herself fade into the water, to will herself into it, to envision herself becoming one with it, but now she clambered up onto the rocky ground and looked around her at the river and the forest. It was still dark and raining. She checked her arms and her legs. She flexed her hands, turned herself around, and moved her head back and forth. She was whole again. Maybe *whole* wasn't the right word. She definitely wasn't *whole*, she knew that, but she was the spirit she had been before.

An idea leapt into her mind. "Body!" she said excitedly.

But nothing happened. She did not change. Some part of her was broken. Her body was gone. Was this what death was, to be pulled back into the elements that made up the world? But if that was true, and she was dead, then why wasn't she already gone? Why hadn't she already disintegrated back into the world? What was her spirit clinging to?

Finally, her mind turned back to Braeden and what she'd seen that night. Picking a direction, she headed into the forest, her only thought to put as much distance between her and the darkness-spewing Black Cloak as she could.

When she was miles away and the rain finally stopped, she slowed down and caught her breath, but she kept moving.

Every few steps, she checked the forest behind her, terrified that Braeden and the Black Cloak would be there.

When dawn came with the dull glow of gray light slowly filling the southern sky, she came into a shaded dell of ferns in a secluded spot she had used before, and there the weight of all that she'd been through finally caught up with her. She collapsed to her knees in exhaustion, grief coiling through her in trembling sobs, then she curled up in a little ball on the forest floor and wept. Her heart ached so bad that it felt like it was going to break apart.

She couldn't believe what had happened. How was it possible that Braeden had the Black Cloak, and why had he put it on? Had he been *using* it to capture people's souls?

Still crying, she tossed and turned in her bed of ferns, her heart filled with anguish. She wasn't sure if Braeden had actually seen her and had been *trying* to attack her with the cloak's searing black shapes. Was it possible that Braeden had truly turned on her?

She ran the back of her hand across her runny nose, wiped her eyes, and sniffled. She was a spirit, but she couldn't separate herself from the memories and sensations of the physical world, the longing and the pain of it. Her chest and legs hurt from running. Her face hurt from crying. But more than anything, the pain was in her heart. Was heartbreak any less painful because it wasn't physically real?

She pressed her eyes shut, curled into a tighter ball, and covered herself with her trembling hands.

After she crawled from the grave, she had rushed back to Biltmore to warn everyone about the evils she'd seen in the forest, to help them fight the coming storms and darkness, but it was hopeless. It was already all over. The darkness had already come. Her enemy had already attacked her and defeated her and pulled Braeden into his evil realm. Or maybe Braeden *was* the evil realm.

What was she going to do now?

She was nothing but a spirit, bodiless, powerless, dead and buried. The storms and the floods were coming to Biltmore. The water was rising. That clawed creature she'd seen in the forest was on its way. The sorcerer had already cast his spells, and she had already lost. She had lost everything. Her world was ending, and there was nothing she could do.

Her only relief was when she fell into an exhausted sleep. She dreamed she was a droplet of water tumbling in the flow of a turbulent river, then drifting into the still waters of a placid lake, then lifting on the heat of the midday sun and sailing on a tumult of moisture-laden clouds, until she was rain, falling back down through the sky again, landing on a leaf, and then dripping down to the earth, and then running along the ground until she slipped into the flow of the river where she began. The water, the sun, the earth and sky . . . It felt as if she could see all the inner workings of the universe.

She knew her time in the living world was coming to an end. She didn't know how many more nights she had left before she faded, or how many times she could shift before she couldn't shift back, but her body and her spirit were being absorbed back into the elements. Soon, she'd become so intermingled with the world, she would cease to be any semblance of what she had been before.

When she woke, the forest was fresh and cool with morning air, but she felt so disoriented that she had to remind herself where she was and how she got there. It took her several seconds to piece together everything that had happened the night before.

And as she lay there on the forest floor trying to understand, she gradually realized that she was not alone. A large animal lay in the grass a few feet away from her. It was a mountain lion, long of body and dark of fur.

Serafina smiled and pulled in a long, deep, pleasurable breath. Seeing the cat lying there filled her heart with joy. It was a catamount she knew well.

18

Not sure if the mountain lion knew she was there, and worried that she might scare him away, she did not move. She watched him for a long time, the gentle rise and fall of the cat's chest, the slow curling of his tail and the small flicking of his huge paws. It was her friend Waysa. And he was dreaming.

As she lay in the ferns beside him, she closed her eyes and tried once again to change into her feline form. But it didn't come. Tears rose in her eyes, and she pressed her eyes shut and gritted her teeth.

She would have loved to have lain in this beautiful shaded place with Waysa in her panther form, to find just a little bit of peace, just a little bit of gentleness at this moment. That was all she wanted right now, to have her thick black fur, and her whiskers, and her claws, and her muscles, and her long tail, and her four padded feet, and her twitching ears. She just wanted to be a cat. She just wanted to be herself.

The breathing of the lion beside her changed. Waysa slowly opened his beautiful brown-and-amber catamount eyes and scanned the forest for friend or foe. As his gaze turned toward her, she lifted herself up and looked at him, hoping beyond hope that he'd somehow see her there, lying in the ferns beside him, but he looked right through her. Waysa could see her no better than the others could.

With Waysa near, she wondered where her mother and the cubs were. A pang of worry rippled deep through her belly. Had the sorcerer killed them like he had killed so many others?

She looked around her and realized that she recognized this tranquil dell of ferns beneath the shade of the trees where she had taken refuge. In all her running and her panic during the night, she hadn't come here by chance. This was a place that she and Waysa had spent time before.

"Waysa, can you hear me?" she asked, her voice quivering with both hope and hopelessness. She missed her friend more than she could bear.

Waysa's ear twitched, but he didn't look at her. He looked in the opposite direction. Then he rose to his four feet.

Serafina heard a faint rustle of leaves, something coming slowly and quietly through the forest toward them.

Waysa crouched down low onto his haunches as the sound approached. She wasn't sure if he was frightened, uncertain, or excited about what was coming.

Then Serafina saw it.

The black head came through the brush first, then the impossibly bright yellow eyes, and the muscled black shoulders, the long black body, and the sweeping black tail. Serafina caught her breath. It was the young black panther she'd seen before.

There can only be one black panther, Serafina thought. *And there she is. It's not me anymore. It's her.*

Serafina felt like she should know who this panther was, but she didn't.

The panther scanned the meadow of ferns and spotted Waysa.

Waysa hunched down his body even further. Serafina wasn't sure if he was getting ready to pounce on her or if he was trying to make himself less threatening—for a cat, sometimes it was both at the same time.

But whatever kind of movement it was, it was enough to spook the young panther. The panther turned away and bounded into the forest the way she came.

Waysa sprang after her. At first Serafina thought he must be defending his territory against her, but then she realized that he wasn't attacking her, he was trying to catch up with her, trying to run with her.

"Good-bye," Serafina said wistfully, as Waysa and the black panther disappeared into the forest together.

Serafina found herself once again alone. Every friend she had made, everything she had gained in her life, was gone now. A deep and overwhelming pain filled her chest. She had to find out what had caused all this. The storm-creech she'd seen in the forest was still out there, and the black shapes were coming, destroying everything in their path. It felt like Biltmore and the people she loved were in more danger now than they had ever been.

But she was powerless. In the physical world, she had no body, no claws, no teeth, no hands, not even a voice. *But what is power?* she wondered. Was it the weapons and tools to act, or the ability to think? Was it talking to someone, or doing something? If you have only a small amount of power, and you're able to do only the tiniest, most insignificant things, does that mean you're *powerless*? Or with that tiny power, do you have all the power in the world?

She dropped down to her hands and knees and pushed at the dirt with her fingers. Nothing happened. Just as before, the world affected her, but she couldn't affect the world. She tried again and again, and then gave up.

The night before, she had shifted into the water of the stream, but she didn't want to *become* the dirt. The grave, the dirt, the dust, that was the last thing she wanted to become. She'd never be able to get back. She wanted to *move* the dirt. To *affect* it. To change *it*, not *her*.

A bumblebee buzzed by her, its dangling legs laden with clusters of yellow pollen. Getting an idea, she followed the bee. She came to a bush blooming with pale red flowers—bees, wasps, and other flying insects hovering around the bush, battling each other for position as they dipped in and sipped the nectar. Tiny yellow grains of pollen floated in the light of the sun. When she raised her hand and moved it slowly through the light, the bees and the pollen seemed to move away from her hand.

Hopeful, she pulled in a lungful of air and blew out at the floating pollen, but nothing happened. She remembered a famous musician, a flute player, who once visited Biltmore. One of the children at dinner asked if she could play his flute. But no matter how hard the girl blew into the instrument, she could not get it to make a flutelike sound. "It takes a lot of practice," the musician said kindly. "You have to do it just right."

And now here Serafina was trying to play the flute of the world. She blew the pollen from different angles and in different ways, slowly but surely figuring out how it worked. If she blew too hard or too soft or at the wrong angle, nothing happened. But if she blew just right, she could get the pollen to float in the way she wanted.

I can't do much, but I can do something, she thought, *and if I can do even the smallest thing, then I am a powerful being.*

As she practiced, trying to figure out what she could do and how she could do it better, she remembered something her pa told her when she was younger.

"Sometimes I reckon the universe we live in is one of God's great machines," her pa had said. "Its gears are nigh on invisible, and its spinning wheels are often silent, but it's a machine all the same-like, with patterns and rules and mechanisms. And if you look real close, you can *understand* it, and for just a spell, in just the smallest way, you may be able to get it to do what you want."

When her pa told her that, he was talking about the mechanical devices he dealt with every day. He definitely wasn't imagining his daughter as a whispery little haint blowing primordial dust, but she reckoned the principle was the same.

By practicing over and over again, she found that she could move dust and pollen floating in the air where she wanted it. She could rustle the edge of a leaf and change the flight path of a bee. And it all made her laugh. The mere act of having an effect on something, *anything*, caused her immeasurable joy. It meant that, at least for a little while longer, she was *real*.

She went over to the bank of the stream and tried to see if she could use her hands to channel the water in a certain way, creating little turbulent eddies near the stream's shore. She found that she couldn't block the water with her fingers or lift it in the cup of her hands. But sometimes, if she focused on the flowing water in just the right way, she could shape its movement.

She slowly realized that one of the most important things was that she had to let go of this idea that she was a human being or a catamount with a physical body in the living world. She had to accept the idea that she was a different kind of thing now, a spirit, just thought, and soul, a tiny wave of energy and elements—dust and wind and water. And when she began to accept this, to let herself slip away with the flow of the world, she began to see the fabric that held everything together, and she could give it a little tug.

Through all this practice, she kept thinking about the terrible evil spreading across the land. Somehow, she had to fight it. But the loneliness of it all was nearly unbearable. She wanted to talk to Waysa and run at his side. She wanted to warn Mr. Vanderbilt about the coming dangers. More than anything, she wanted to ask her pa for advice about what she could do.

But of course, there was no point now. Waysa and Mr. Vanderbilt and her pa and the others couldn't hear her words. There was *no one*, absolutely *no one* in the world, who even knew she was there.

And then she looked in the direction of the dark river she'd seen a few nights before, and she paused.

Or was there?

The sorcerer by the river, Serafina thought.

"I can't see you, but I know you're there," the sorcerer had said. He'd actually *spoken* to her.

But it had frightened her, and she ran away like a startled deer.

If I had only known, Serafina thought.

When she tried to remember the details of that first strange night, she could still feel the fear in her heart. The sorcerer had been walking slowly through the forest by himself in the dead of night, working close to the ground. He had possessed some sort of dark power.

Serafina didn't want to return to where she had seen him by

the river. The thought of it put a twisting knot in the pit of her stomach. But the truth was, she had run out of other paths to take. Her pa had told her once that true courage wasn't because you didn't feel fear. True courage was when you were scared of something, but you did it anyway because it needed to be done. If she was going to get back to the land of the living, she had to stay bold.

She started walking in the direction of the river. As the sun rose toward noon, she thought she still had one more ridge and valley to go. But she heard the sound of rushing water ahead of her and soon came to a deeply flooded area. She realized this was the new shore of the river.

This river in the forest had swollen far past where it had been before, flooding the trees for as far as she could see, the roots and trunks drowning in moving water. The flooding was so deep and wide that she couldn't even make out the main course of the river, let alone the other side of it. The dark brown current rushed by, tearing at the vegetation and carrying it along, swirling in large, twisting whirlpools, and crashing up into whitewater torrents where the water passed through the upper branches of the trees. Her mind was slow to comprehend the unimaginable: the river had filled the valley. The water was tearing away everything in its path, trees and rocks—and now mountains—everything getting swept away.

As she walked along the flooded bank, she realized that the place where she had seen the sorcerer a few nights before was long gone. She could feel the muddy earth she was standing on slipping away beneath her feet, the inexorable pull into the all-consuming current. The thought of it would have frightened her even in the best of times, but in her current state, she was terrified by the thought of getting sucked into a mudslide. She turned tail and headed for high ground.

In the afternoon, she curled up beneath the overhang of a rock to rest. A few hours later, she started awake with a sudden jerk. But when she woke up, she couldn't move her arms or legs. She couldn't raise her body from the ground. She tried to pull air into her lungs, but she felt the solidness of the earth against her, all around her, holding her in and pressing her down. Clenching her teeth, she clawed and snarled, twisted and bent, cracking the brittle stone around her. "Not yet!" she told the earth as she climbed out and brushed herself off.

It's getting worse, she thought, stumbling away from the crevice of stone that had nearly caught her. *I've got to keep moving.*

As she continued her search for the sorcerer and the sun began to set, she came to a steep slope and followed it down into a wet area of bulrushes and cattails. She found her way into a mountain bog where the ground was nothing but thick layers of spongy sphagnum moss and peat, the ancient fiber of a hundred forests that had come before. The bog exuded the dense, vaporous aroma of year upon year of amassed plants and thick black soil. The moss felt damp and strangely buoyant beneath her bare feet as she walked.

Cinnamon fern and swamp laurel with dark pink flowers grew out of the wet, mushy trunks of long-fallen trees. Tiny red cranberries grew all over the leafy ground. And delicate purple and violet dragon-mouthed orchids hung spiraling down.

As she delved deeper into the bog, she stayed alert for any signs of the sorcerer.

In the puddles on the ground, yellow-spotted salamanders scurried this way and that, and small bog turtles with orange necks crawled around. Southern irises, trout lilies, and arrowhead plants were growing everywhere, along with pitchers, sundews, and other carnivorous plants.

Just ahead, she heard a faint, buzzy *peeeent*.

Curious, she moved toward the sound and came to a small meadow in the bog. The sun had set behind the trees just a few minutes before and a soft, dusky orange light filled the western sky.

Peeeent!

She finally saw it: a small, pudgy, well-camouflaged brownish bird with an extremely long bill sat on the ground in the center of the meadow.

It was a timberdoodle.

Hunters who came to visit the estate called the birds woodcocks. Mountain folk called them bogsuckers or brush snipes. She thought it was interesting how different people had different names for the same thing. Mountain lion, puma, panther, painter, cougar, catamount . . . there were many names for her kin. Waysa had taught her that the Cherokee word was *tsv-da-si*.

She wondered what kind of name people had for what she had become. A haint, a haunt, a shade, a phantom, a spirit, a specter, an ethereal being . . .

Suddenly the shy little timberdoodle burst up into the air

in a crazy, spiraling flight, its wings whistling and all a-twitter, flying great sweeping circles up into the twilit sky. When it reached the very top of its spiral, the woodcock hovered for a moment, as if held in the air, then sang out a liquid song. From there it began to fall, tumbling back down toward the earth, folding and fluttering like it had been shot with a gun, but all the while singing through its vainglorious display.

Serafina smiled. She'd never seen the sky dance of the timberdoodle before, but her pa had told her the stories. In this place, in this moment, for just a few minutes during sunset, this normally shy, lonely little bird called out to the world, *I'm here! I'm here!*

He's just looking for a friend, she thought. *I wonder if something like that would work for me . . .* The thought of standing out in the middle of the meadow and leaping in great circles, tilting and twittering, and yelling, *I'm here! I'm here!* brought a cheer to her heart.

Finally, the timberdoodle landed exactly where he'd started.

It was then that Serafina lifted her eyes and saw the silhouette of a person standing and watching from the other side of the meadow.

It was the dark-robed sorcerer she'd seen by the river. Serafina ducked down to conceal herself, not sure if the sorcerer could see her.

When the hooded man finally turned and walked away, Serafina stayed low, gave him a few minutes to put some distance between them, then skirted the meadow and followed him. Serafina moved as quietly as she could through the wet forest bog, but she was determined not to let the sorcerer slip away.

Then the sorcerer stopped and stood very still.

Serafina hunkered down and hid behind the trunk of a large tree.

The sorcerer turned his head and looked in the direction she was hiding.

She thought that after a moment the sorcerer would turn back around and resume walking toward his destination, but he did not.

He lifted his head, then raised his thin, delicate hands and gently pulled his hood down until the dark cloth gathered around his shoulders.

That was when Serafina saw the sorcerer's face for the first time. It was not a man, but a girl! About fourteen years old, she had a pale complexion, dark red lips, and long red hair. The girl's green eyes scanned the forest, looking right where Serafina was hiding. Serafina crouched down even farther, but she couldn't help peeking through the vegetation back at the girl.

Her expression was filled with a grave and somber stillness, as if she had suffered a great loss. She had about her the feeling of someone who was hiding, diminished, but stoically unwilling to relinquish life, like a broken owl who no longer has the heart to fly.

The girl was nearly unrecognizable in manner and form, but Serafina knew exactly who it was.

Fear shot through Serafina. She hunched down low and peered through the bushes. It was *Rowena*! Too close now to flee, Serafina wanted to pounce fast and fight her old enemy. A growling, seething anger rose up inside her for all the terrible things Rowena had done. But the more she watched the wretched girl, the more curious Serafina became.

Rowena had changed. The angles of her face, the movement of her body, and especially her spirit and mannerisms, were all different. Her hair was still red, but it wasn't dressed up into fancy curls like before. It was long and thick around her neck and shoulders. Her face was still pale, but she wasn't wearing any lady's makeup to brighten her lips or shadow her eyes. And she wasn't wearing a stylish dress like she always had.

She wore simple, dark robes, like a hermit who had withdrawn from the world. She did not appear to have a horse or carriage anymore. She walked through the forest alone.

Rowena peered in Serafina's direction for several long seconds, studying the bushes where she was hiding as if she knew she was there. Serafina remained very still, unsure what Rowena could and couldn't sense.

Finally, Rowena pulled the hood back up around her head and continued walking through the misty lowlands of the bog.

Serafina released a long, steady breath, relieved that she'd avoided Rowena's detection. There was a part of Serafina that wanted to turn around and go home, go the other way, let wounded owls lie. But there was another part of her, the bolder, fiercer, more determined part, that was saying, *Don't let her get away.*

Serafina decided to follow her.

Pretty sure that she was invisible to even Rowena, Serafina tracked through the bog behind her, but kept a safe distance, just in case. Sometimes she lost the girl in the gray mountain mist, but then she would catch up again.

Soon they came to a faint path that wound even deeper into the wetlands, through a dark and shadowed grove of old, ragged cedar trees, with leafy ferns all around and moss-covered trunks.

Finally, Serafina watched as Rowena came to a small habitation.

At first it seemed like nothing more than a large clump of tree branches. Thin, twisty twigs had grown downward from the larger limbs of the trees, and the spidery roots had grown upward, creating tight, interwoven walls of sticks with a stick-woven roof overhead. The embers of a small cook fire glowed in front of the shelter's entryway. Various collections of plants lay here and there on logs, as if drying in what little sun might filter down through the trees during the day.

Serafina watched as Rowena tended to a row of carnivorous plants growing near her lair, mumbling strange and unrecognizable words as she pinched small, struggling flies and hornets in her fingers and dropped them into the awaiting mouths of the plants.

A few inches from where Serafina was crouched, and in various other areas of the forest around the shelter, hazes of white spiderwebs stretched between the trees. Feeling a crawling sensation on her spine, she looked more closely into the mass of web and saw thousands of black spiders with crooked legs and red hourglasses on their backs. Sucking in a gasp, she quickly moved away and found a new tree to hide behind. Her pa had taught her that the black widows were the most dangerous spiders around, but she'd never seen them bunched into large nests like this before.

She watched as Rowena worked. Pitcher plants, butterworts, and other carnivorous plants grew all around the shelter, up the walls and the rooftop. Rowena took several small plants out of her satchel, positioned them nearby, and moved her hand over them, mumbling something Serafina didn't understand. When Rowena lifted her hand, the plants had taken root in their new position.

When Rowena was done planting what she had gathered, she went over to the small stream that ran nearby, its water tinted light brown with the tannin of the swamp, where she slowly washed her hands. Serafina couldn't help but notice that it was the only small, gentle stream she'd seen in a long time. She wondered if the storm-creech did not know about this hidden place.

Serafina crept deeper into Rowena's lair, more and more curious about what she was seeing.

Several chickens and gray spotted fowl roamed nearby, along with a tribe of goats with long, shaggy black hair, thick, curving horns, and strange, square pupils in their eyes.

Serafina peered into the shelter of woven sticks. Other than the simple bed and a place for food, it seemed to be filled with glass flasks and orbs containing green, yellow, and milky-white liquids.

As she watched Rowena slowly and calmly gather leaves from some of the plants outside the shelter, Serafina frowned. Rowena had been deceitful and dangerous, but she had been alert and full of life. Now she seemed so grave in spirit. It was as if a great loneliness had grown within her, and now had nearly taken her over, like a thick carpet of moss overtaking a tree that had fallen onto the forest floor.

"I can feel you watching me," Rowena said.

Serafina froze right where she was, her heart pounding.

"I told you to leave me alone," Rowena said harshly. "I'm through with you!"

Serafina moved back a little and crouched down in the bushes.

Rowena pulled back her hood and shouted angrily out into the woods in the other direction, "Just get out of here! I don't want you here!"

It seemed that Rowena couldn't see her after all. But who was she talking to?

Curious to see what would happen, Serafina stepped a little closer.

"No! I told you to go away," Rowena said as if she knew exactly what she was doing. "I can hear you breathing down my neck. I'm not going to do your bidding anymore. I'm through with you, so stop bothering me!"

As Rowena stood up in anger, the air around her compressed and expanded violently, buffeting Serafina back. Frightened, Serafina quickly retreated into the forest.

Serafina knew she should turn and slink away from Rowena's wet, boggy lair. It was obvious that her old enemy had become far more powerful. But in other ways, the girl seemed so diminished.

Serafina thought about abandoning this idea of approaching Rowena and just skulking back to Biltmore and trying to make the best of her situation, but she hated the thought of it. She couldn't talk to them, she couldn't warn them, she couldn't help them in any way. In the nights to come, when the storms finally hit Biltmore and the rivers burst, what was she going to do? And what about Braeden? Had he started sucking up the souls of lost children like the Man in the Black Cloak, greedy for more power and more life, his skin slowly rotting from his body? Was he the root of all this evil or a victim of it? And no matter what he was, could she abandon him? When she thought about Waysa, she remembered him looking straight through her like she didn't even exist anymore. The world was wrecked. It broke her heart to think about enduring another night of this. She pulled in a breath, plucked up her courage, and spoke.

"I haven't been bothering you," she whispered. "I just got here."

Rowena immediately froze, obviously surprised by the sound of her voice.

For several seconds, Rowena did not move or say a word. Her dark red eyebrows furrowed.

"Who are you?" she asked.

21

Serafina couldn't believe it: Rowena had heard her! She was actually talking to her!

"I'm warning you," Rowena said sternly, looking up into the air. "I'll summon you out by force if I have to."

As Rowena lifted her open hand, the trees above Serafina began to shake and rattle with a threatening violence. Serafina could feel the air around her pulsating.

"I know you're there," Rowena said, "so don't just lurk out there. Tell me who you are!"

Serafina was too frightened to answer, fearing that Rowena would destroy her the moment she said her name. She wanted to run while she still had the chance. But Rowena was the only person she'd encountered since she'd crawled from the grave who could hear her.

"Are you living or are you dead?" Rowena demanded.

Serafina froze. She didn't know what to do.

"I asked you a question," Rowena said. "Are you living or are you dead?"

Finally, feeling like she had no other choice, Serafina decided to speak again. "I . . . I don't rightly know," she admitted.

Rowena seemed to understand that answer in ways that Serafina did not.

"But who are you?" Rowena asked again. "Where do you come from?" Her voice was gentler now, almost kind, as if she'd enticed reluctant spirits from the shadows before.

"I . . ." Serafina began, but then stopped, too uncertain to continue.

"Don't be frightened," Rowena said, her voice filled with a compassion that Serafina had never heard from her before. "Just tell me your name. No harm can come from that."

"I'm . . ." Serafina stopped again.

"Yes?"

Serafina ducked down behind a tree. "I'm . . . Serafina," she said finally.

"The cat!" Rowena hissed, her face blanching as she spun around and peered out into the forest. She crouched down and looked all around her like she thought a catamount was going to pounce on her at any moment. And Serafina knew that she probably would have attacked the sorceress if everything had been the way it was before, but in her current form how could she fight Rowena? How could she do *anything*?

"Something's happened to me," Serafina told her.

"But you're still here in this world," Rowena said, her voice filled with uneasiness as she looked warily around her for signs of attack.

"Part of me, at least," Serafina said.

Rowena paused, taking in these words. "But why have you come here?" she asked suspiciously.

"You're the only person I've found who can hear me," Serafina said.

Rowena pressed her lips together and nodded. "I can speak to both sides now."

"You mean the living and the dead . . . Were you the one who woke me from the grave? Were you talking to me?"

Rowena ignored her question.

"Was it you?" Serafina pressed her. "What did you say to me?"

Rowena shook her head. "It doesn't matter now, just the ramblings of a troubled soul, nothing of consequence. I have to be careful when I go to a cemetery, but especially that one." Then Rowena's tone took on a harder edge, like she wanted to change the subject. "Did you come here to my home to kill me, is that it, to seek your revenge?"

Serafina knew it was a fair question. But as she had been talking to Rowena, she felt more and more relieved that she was finally able to interact with someone. Whether she wanted it to or not, her hatred for Rowena was slowly fading behind her into a past that seemed so long ago.

"No," she said to Rowena. "I didn't follow you here to kill you. To be honest, after the battle for the Twisted Staff, I thought you and your father were already dead."

"We're not easy to kill," Rowena said.

"But I don't understand what's happening. Is Braeden on your side now?"

"No," Rowena said.

"But I saw him with the Black Cloak . . ."

"Where did you see him?" Rowena asked quickly, her voice filled with so much interest that it made Serafina reluctant to answer.

"I don't understand," Serafina said. "Where did the Black Cloak come from? I destroyed it on the angel's sword the night we defeated Mr. Thorne."

"We remade it," Rowena said. "The silver clasp is the core of its power, not the fabric."

Serafina frowned in aggravation, regretting she hadn't found the clasp and melted it down when she'd had the chance. Rowena seemed to have so much more knowledge than she did, so much more capability, and yet there was something about her . . . a hopelessness in her, a feeling of resignation, of giving up. And there had been fear in her, too. She'd been frightened of something, telling it to go away. Who or what was she hiding from deep in this forest bog?

"The truth is," Serafina said finally, "I have no wish to harm you, Rowena. With the way I am now . . . I'm just right glad to know that I'm not just a gust of wind."

"A lot has happened since I fought against you," Rowena said, her voice somber and weary. It was clear to Serafina that she, too, had suffered.

"What do you mean?" Serafina asked, moving toward her. "You've corrupted Braeden, haven't you? You've pulled him to your side."

"*No,*" Rowena said again, her voice edged with fierceness. "I haven't."

"But he's not who he was before," Serafina said.

"None of us are," Rowena said.

"He no longer cares about his animals, he's lying to his aunt and uncle, and I told you, I saw him wearing the Black Cloak! You've taken him!"

Suddenly, Rowena turned, looking around her toward an accuser she couldn't see. "You think you know him?" she snarled. "You think you can see what's inside his heart, whether he's good or bad, strong or weak? You don't know anything about any of us, cat. You're such a little fool!"

"But I don't understand!" Serafina screamed at her in reply.

"You think you've lost your friend? Is that it?" Rowena scoffed. "You don't even know what friendship is!"

"And you do?" Serafina snarled.

"I've seen it!" Rowena hissed.

"What are you talking about?" Serafina cried in confusion.

"Sometimes you're blind, cat, with more teeth and claws

than sense," Rowena shouted as she grabbed a flask from her cache. "I will show what I've seen!"

Rowena hurled the glass flask toward the sound of Serafina's voice. It crashed against the trunk of a tree and exploded with a great blast of whirling smoke and a bright, blinding haze. Then Rowena threw another flask and it shattered against the ground, its darkened blue contents rising up in a great swirl. Then she threw another, and the whole world felt as if it were shifting beneath Serafina's feet. Serafina felt cold air all around her, and then the world disappeared.

22

Suddenly, Serafina found herself standing inside Biltmore, the air strangely cold. The French doors to the Loggia were open, the sheer white curtains glowing with the light of the full moon and fluttering in the cold winter breeze.

It's the night I was attacked, Serafina thought.

She stepped slowly out onto the Loggia, the long, beautiful outdoor room with its carved columns and sweeping archways looking out onto the forest and the mountains and the radiance of the stars above.

These aren't just my memories . . . It's like I'm here, living through it all again.

This was her home, her place in the world. She was

Biltmore's Guardian, watching over the people she'd sworn to protect.

She ran her eye along the Loggia's stone railing looking for any sort of creature that might be hiding there. She checked the vaulted ceiling sweeping over her head, looking for shadows that didn't belong. And then she gazed out across the canopy of the forest, her eyes scanning for danger in the distance.

But then she sensed a presence with her on the Loggia. The hairs on the back of her neck rose up as a dark shape emerged from the shadows behind her. She heard a *tick-tick-ticking* sound followed by a long, raspy hiss. She turned just in time to see something coming toward her.

She ducked and leapt aside, then shifted into panther form. Her lungs filled with air and her muscles bulged with power. Her claws sprang out. She roared into an attack even as the hissing folds of the Black Cloak swept over her head and plunged her into darkness.

She twisted her spine around and bit into the attacker's shoulder with her long fangs. Her panther heart hammered in her chest, driving her with dire strength. She clawed viciously at the attacker's side. She couldn't see his face, but she could feel him fighting to capture her in the cloak, pulling it over and around her. An ice-cold darkness soaked into her bones. The awful stench choked her. She fought through the dark rippling void as the Black Cloak engulfed her. She could feel her sharp panther claws slashing through the fabric, shredding it. The sound of the ripping cloth filled her ears. She kept twisting and swiping and striking, swatting wildly with her paws, fighting for her life, like she was drowning in cold black water. The slithering cloak wrapped itself around her, tightening like a coiling snake, even as it wrenched her soul away from her body and sucked her into its dark folds.

She saw inside the cloak a black, swirling, horrible world, but then it all began to change. Her claws had slashed through the cloak's fabric. It could no longer hold what it had captured. The ruptured cloak hurled the inner reaches of its dark void out into the world, and her soul with it.

A boy came running on two strong legs out onto the Loggia and charged toward the attacker. As the attacker turned, the hood fell away and Serafina saw the face. The attacker wasn't Braeden. And it wasn't Uriah. It was Rowena.

Barking a vicious snarl, Gidean leapt upon Rowena, knocked her to the ground and tore into her neck. Braeden, fighting strong, grabbed her and tried to hold her down.

Serafina had already wounded Rowena, but she was still far too strong. The sorceress threw wicked spells, one barrage after another, that gashed Braeden's face, tore at his legs, and threw him against a column.

Gidean lunged for another attack, biting into Rowena's side. She struggled frantically and escaped the dog, then turned to flee. Braeden clutched the shredded Black Cloak and pulled it from her just as she dropped over the railing's edge and disappeared into the dark of night.

Serafina lay wounded in human form on the stone floor of the Loggia, unable to move. Rowena's spells had torn her chest and stomach with gaping wounds. When she tried to take in a breath, a lightning bolt of pain shot through her ribs. She tried to move her bloody arms and legs, but they lay uselessly around her. All she could do was watch the dark red pool of her own blood spread slowly across the floor. She knew she was going to die.

The black fragments, the inner darkness of the Black Cloak that had been riven by her claws, floated all around her in the Loggia and began to drift with the wind.

She tried to tilt her head to see if Braeden had survived the battle, but her neck moved in a painful jerking motion. When she finally managed to look over, she saw a terrifying sight: it wasn't Braeden, but the body of a black panther—*her*—lying wounded on the floor beside her, the panther's flesh torn in the same way hers was, her sides bleeding and her bones shattered.

Both she and the panther were moments from death.

She knew it was the end.

She tried to look for Braeden, but she could not see him.

"Braeden . . ." she gasped, blood gurgling in her throat.

Finally, he came into her view. Her heart leapt when she saw that he was still alive. But his head dripped with long, jagged cuts, and he dragged his leg behind him. She watched as he knelt beside the panther and put his hands on her sides, closing his eyes as he infused the cat with his healing power. He caressed the cat's head and spoke to her in words that Serafina couldn't hear, running his hands down the length of her long, furred body.

When he was done with the panther, Braeden moved quickly over to her.

"Braeden . . ." she tried to say again, but her voice was so weak she knew he couldn't hear her.

As he frantically examined her wounds, she could see how badly she was hurt reflected in the grimace of his face.

"I don't know what to do, Serafina . . ." he said as he ripped his shirt apart and tried to stanch her bleeding with it. He couldn't heal humans the way he could animals.

"I'm sorry," she whispered. "I don't want to go . . . Please say good-bye to my pa . . ."

But with a heavy grunt of pain, he gathered her up into his arms. "Hold on, Serafina . . ." he told her, a fierce determination in his voice.

She wrapped her arms around his neck and tried to hold on to him the best she could, but she could feel her strength waning, her consciousness drifting into a swirling black void.

Braeden carried her outside into the darkness, struggling on his bloodied leg, but unwilling to give up.

"Stay with me, Serafina . . ." he said as he carried her, and she clung to the sound of his voice.

As blood dripped down onto her shoulder and neck, she didn't know whether it was his or hers. They were both shaking, bleeding, and terribly wounded, holding on to each other with their last hope. But Braeden kept moving, carrying her through the darkness.

He took her down into the gardens and set her on the ground outside the master rosarian's shed. Then he shouldered open the door, stormed in, and came out with supplies—old wooden apple crates, a hammer and nails, and other tools. He quickly made a crude stretcher-like box with shallow sides, and dragged her body into it. Then he fastened the end with a rope, called Gidean over, and the two of them began dragging her across the ground toward the trees.

She drifted in and out of consciousness as Braeden and the dog pulled her through the forest, Braeden dragging his bloody leg behind him.

When Braeden finally reached the graveyard, he dragged her to the foot of the statue in the angel's glade and begged for the angel's help. "Take care of her!" he shouted, his voice cracking. "You have to save her!"

As Braeden pulled away from her, Serafina reached out with her last strength and grasped his arm. "Don't leave me here," she whispered hoarsely. "Don't leave me . . ."

"I'm not going to leave you, Serafina," he told her. "I promise you, I will never leave you!"

As she lay dying, with the blood seeping from her body, she looked up at the stars above her head and thought it was the last time she would ever see them. Her body was getting cold now. Her limbs were numb. The pain was receding. She could feel her life slipping away from her, her eyes closing for the last time.

Then she heard the sound of digging. She saw the blurry image of Braeden frantically digging a hole in the ground in the middle of the angel's glade.

The last thing she saw was Braeden dragging the crude coffin that contained her lifeless body into the bottom of the grave he had dug. His only hope was to bury her in the place of eternal spring.

"Take care of her," Braeden begged the angel. "I will find a way to put her back together again!"

And then Serafina saw no more.

The darkness that followed was so black and so long that she did not stir.

Finally, a girl's voice came into the darkness. "You must return now."

When Serafina opened her eyes, she found herself standing in the forest bog by Rowena's lair just where she had been. A warm summer breeze drifted through the trees. The vision was over.

Rowena was standing there alone. Her voice was filled with emotion when she said, "*Now* you know what friendship is."

Serafina, realizing that Rowena, too, had seen what Braeden did on the night of the full moon, looked at her old enemy in amazement. "And so do you . . ."

"And so do I," Rowena said.

Serafina sat down on a log and gazed absently at the things around her. All she could think about, all she could feel, was the vision. She knew now that the Loggia was where she had died. *Died . . .* Was that what happened? She'd been buried, that much was certain. But she wasn't truly dead, was she?

Had Braeden saved her?

She thought about what he must have gone through. He could never let anyone know what truly happened or the horrible thing he'd done. He had dragged the bloody body of his best friend through the forest and buried her. And he hoped that she was still alive when he did it.

In the days that followed, he must have been filled not just with the sadness of losing her but with a terrible guilt. As he lied and covered things up, deceit must have mixed with anguish. His body had been hurt and his heart torn as cruelly as hers.

After months of sorrow and healing, he must have just been finally finding his way back into the world when she crawled from the grave and began to haunt him. She remembered how her presence had upset him. He had seemed so frustrated and hopeless.

Her vision of the night of the full moon was over, and she finally knew what had happened to her.

She thought about her body lying in the grave in the angel's glade all those nights.

She thought about the young black panther she'd seen running wild in the forest.

And then she thought about her whisper of a spirit crawling from the grave and creeping through the gardens back to Biltmore.

Three, she thought. *Three pieces. My human body, my panther body, and my spirit. My trinity was split.*

And as horrible as that was to imagine, and as difficult as it was to accept, everything finally began to make sense in her mind.

She knew from the stories of the mountain folk that there could only be one black panther in the forest at a time.

And it's me, she thought. *It's still me. I'm the black panther running through the forest.*

And I'm the dead girl lying in the grave.

And I'm this lost spirit finding her way through the living world.

On the night of the full moon, she and Braeden had fought an epic battle against Rowena. And they had lost.

She had lost.

The damaged Black Cloak had torn her asunder and flung her pieces out into the world. Time and space, body and spirit, dream and waking, were all a-jumble now.

She was not exactly dead. She was not exactly alive. She was not spirit or body. She was all these things and none, thrown to the winds of chaos, like the black shapes still floating in the forest and destroying everything they touched. They were the torn inner remnants of the Black Cloak.

Still stunned, she looked over at Rowena. "How did you show me this vision? It felt so real. I remember walking onto the Loggia that night and standing at the rail, but once the cloak went over my head, I was torn apart. I couldn't have seen all those things you showed me. Those couldn't have been my memories alone."

"No," Rowena said softly, lowering her head. "Your memories, my memories, the light of the moon, the slip of the stars . . . it's everything that happened that night, the print of our movement on the thread of time."

Serafina began to reply, but she was unable to find the right words, and she was still trembling from the experience of it. "It was startling," she said finally.

"What I did is called scrying," Rowena said. "It provides a vision of past events, a glimpse into the thread."

"And you have seen it before?"

"Yes," Rowena said, and Serafina could see that it had affected Rowena as powerfully as it had affected her.

"You attacked me on the Loggia," Serafina said, trying to connect everything together in her mind. "You tried to kill me with the Black Cloak."

"And I almost succeeded," Rowena said.

"You probably thought you had me as good as dead."

"I did, indeed," Rowena admitted, obviously annoyed. "There was no way you should have been able to survive that."

"I reckon I'm not quite as easy to kill as you figured, either."

"Apparently not," Rowena said with a ghost of a smile.

Serafina frowned in confusion and looked up at her. "But . . . you still showed me the vision . . ."

Rowena turned away, hiding her expression.

"But why?" Serafina asked. "Why did you show me that?"

"Because you were starting to annoy me with all your mewling-weepy-crying about Braeden."

"But I have always been your enemy, and yet you showed this to me . . . You helped me."

Rowena shook her head. "Don't flatter yourself, cat. I'm not trying to be your friend. I just showed you what happened. The truth is the truth. The past is the past. It cannot be changed. But things have changed now."

"What do you mean, things have changed?" Serafina asked, sensing that there was far more on Rowena's mind than she was saying. But Serafina's thoughts kept going back to what happened on the Loggia. "The cloak was torn . . ." she said, trying to grasp what she had learned.

"You've been *splintered* . . ." Rowena said.

Serafina had seen it, experienced it, but when she heard the word *splintered* spoken out loud, her mind recoiled from the sound of it. It seemed too awful to comprehend, that her heart, her soul, had been splintered from her body, and now she was in three pieces.

"How do I fix this?" Serafina asked. "How do I get back?"

Rowena shook her head. "You don't. You're just a spirit now, harmless as a fly, and soon you'll begin to fade, if you haven't already. You can't last in this world, and then you'll be gone. *We all go to the same place; all come from dust, and to dust all return.*"

Serafina looked at her in surprise. It was the passage she'd thought about when she saw the dust in Essie's room.

"So that's why you thought you could show me the vision . . ." Serafina said.

"I'm not stupid, cat," Rowena said. "I know your claws too well."

As Serafina made her way through the forest back toward Biltmore, one thought dwelled on her mind: before she faded away, she had to help Braeden. She didn't know to what extent the Black Cloak had drawn him into its power, but she had to save him, even if she couldn't save herself. She had seen the violent storms in the forest, the claw-handed storm-creech, and the floating black shapes. Something was driving these evils toward Biltmore, something so powerful that even Rowena hid from it. Was it some dark force in the forest? Or someone inside Biltmore itself? Or was it Braeden using the Black Cloak?

When she arrived at the estate, strong winds were blowing through the trees. She felt light on her feet, like if she lifted her arms she would actually float away and become a flurry of drifting air. She was tempted to try it, to keep learning her new skills, but she dared not test the power of the gale, lest she never return.

Crawling through a small shaft in the back of Biltmore's foundation, Serafina found her way back into the house.

Her pa was working on some sort of electrical accoutrements with many copper coils, wires, and bulbs for the summer ball. She wanted to watch him, just *be* with him for a while, but she knew she shouldn't.

As evening came, Mr. and Mrs. Vanderbilt and their many guests gathered in the Banquet Hall for dinner. More newcomers were arriving every day for the ball, and now some sixty people sat around the long oak dining room table, displayed in sparkling fashion with its fine Biltmore-monogrammed porcelain settings and silver candelabras.

She scanned the room. There was an empty chair next to Mr. Vanderbilt, but she didn't see Braeden. She wondered what had become of him after he put on the cloak.

Finally, just before dinner began, Braeden came into the room. He was still limping with the metal brace on his leg, but he appeared fresh and clean, and he was wearing a fine dinner jacket.

She studied him carefully, trying to understand what he was thinking and feeling at that moment, but she couldn't read his face. What had been going on in that head of his? Had the despair of losing her driven him to the Black Cloak?

His dog, Gidean, followed several yards behind him, not at his side. When Braeden took his seat at the table next to his uncle, the dog went over to a distant corner out of Braeden's line of sight and lay down, his head on his paws.

Serafina thought Braeden must have hidden the Black Cloak away somewhere in the house or back in the flume under the pond, but she wasn't sure.

As she watched him talking with the others at the table, it reminded her of watching Mr. Thorne months before in this very room as he lingered among the guests and their children. There was something in the look behind Braeden's eyes that she could not quite fathom, not just the sadness and detachment that she'd seen, but as if he was going through the motions of his life, biding his time, waiting to get to what was important. But that was the question. What was important to him now? Was it using the cloak each night? Is that what he longed for, the dark embrace of its power?

She watched him all through the evening, looking for signs. Was his skin flaking off his hands as it had with Mr. Thorne? Did he watch the children in the room with particular interest? *You have to resist it, Braeden,* she kept thinking.

She looked for signs of good and evil in her friend, of truth and deceit, wondering which side was winning. She could see him doing the things he was expected to do, but was it truly him? Or was he like one of those weird horned beetles that wears the shell of another beetle on its back to hide itself?

But then something happened.

When he thought no one was looking, Braeden slid his hand under the table, and he tapped his fingers lightly on the wooden edge of his chair.

In the corner across the room, Gidean sat up and tilted his head in curiosity.

Braeden tapped again.

Gidean rose to his feet and moved quickly toward Braeden. The dog slipped under the table and put his nose against Braeden's hand to let him know he was there.

Without anyone noticing, Braeden slid the food from his plate and gave it to Gidean beneath the table. The surprised Doberman gobbled the food down in an instant and looked up appreciatively for more.

Serafina smiled. This was new. Something was changing in Braeden. She didn't know if using the cloak had turned him evil or not, or to what degree he could control his use of it, but for the first time in a long time, this was the Braeden she knew, the one who fed his dog from his plate, the one who would fight for his friends no matter what. This wasn't the cloak's doing. This was something else. Somehow, someway, he was still in there, deep down inside, at least a little bit. And this was the Braeden she held on to in her heart.

When the final course was done, Braeden politely excused himself from the table and said good night to everyone. They all wished him a pleasant good night in return.

As Serafina followed him out of the Banquet Hall and around the Winter Garden, she was glad to see Gidean walking with him. But then Braeden took Gidean over to a side door, let him outside, and continued on through the house without him.

"That's strange," Serafina said, and followed Braeden up the Grand Staircase to the second floor.

As Braeden entered his bedroom, she thought he was going to go to sleep, but then he got down on his hands and knees and dragged a heap of outdoor clothes from under the bed. They were dry, so they weren't the clothes he'd worn in the flume, but the shirt, trousers, and boots were stained with dirt. They'd been used before without being washed. He quickly pulled the clothes on and then grabbed the rope out from under his bed.

"Here we go again," she said as he went out the window.

Serafina climbed down the rope to the terrace below and then followed him through the gardens. "Back to the Black Cloak again?" she asked him.

But then Gidean came running toward him out of the darkness. Instead of going toward the pond, Braeden and Gidean followed a path into the forest. It was a path she knew well. And clearly so did Braeden.

He was heading for the graveyard where she was buried.

Serafina followed Braeden through the forest at a distance, uncertain how her presence might affect him. That first night she came to him, he had suffered such anguish. She wasn't keen on driving him afoul again, so she let him get a fair piece in front of her.

She made her way through the darkened cemetery on her own, following the path that she thought Braeden was on. But she could no longer hear him and Gidean walking ahead of her. Either she'd let them get too far up the path or something else had happened. Suddenly, she felt very much alone.

As she crept past the weathered headstones marking the graves, the graveyard's swampy moist air clung to her skin like leeches. A low chorus of crickets, cicadas, and other buzzing insects pulsed around her. Long, wispy trails of mist oozed across the ground at her feet. The twisting roots of the old trees weaved through the damp earth beneath her bare feet, and vines hung down from the trees' crooked, dangling limbs.

She had already read many of the epitaphs chiseled in block letters on these gravestones, and she had no desire to do it again tonight, but as she moved among them, the voices of the dead came alive.

Here lies blood, and let it lie, speechless still, and never cry, one said, but she tried not to look or listen.

Our bed is lovely, dark, and sweet. Come join us now and we shall meet, said the two sisters lying in the ground side by side. It felt as if they were talking to her, inviting her back to where she belonged.

She hurried past the cloven man and through the six-sixty crosses of the buried Confederate soldiers. When she finally made it through the graveyard, she came to the small open area of the angel's glade.

She found Braeden lying stretched out facedown on the dirt mound of her grave. His body was flat to the ground. His left leg was straight, but his right leg was bent beside him, clenched in the metal brace. His arms were up around his head, the fingers of his hands splayed, as if he had been holding the earth. Gidean lay flat on the ground a few feet away, just as still as he.

Serafina's heart filled with fear, for it looked like they were both dead. She couldn't breathe.

But then Braeden's head moved and Serafina exhaled in relief.

Braeden's eyes were closed and his face filled with sadness, but he was alive. He had come to visit her, to sleep there on the ground, stretched out on her grave.

She noticed the dried stains on his trousers and the old dirt on his boots. He'd been here before. Many times. He hadn't been sneaking out of the house every night to use the Black Cloak. He'd been coming here.

She imagined him coming out here night after night, sleeping on her grave when his family thought he was home in his bed.

Had Mr. Vanderbilt come during the night with a search party and looked upon his nephew in dread? Was that why Mr. Vanderbilt had been so concerned about him? Was that why he'd told Braeden that he had double-locked Biltmore's doors?

As Braeden lay on her grave, his shoulders moved with a slow and troubled breathing.

She gazed upon him in sadness, pursing her lips as she felt a thickness catching in her throat.

For a long time, he did not speak or move from the grave. He just lay there in the dirt. It was as if his thoughts had overwhelmed him and he'd collapsed there.

She moved closer to him, her chest rising and falling, slow and steady, with every breath she took, and she knelt down beside him.

She could see that his hands were trembling.

She studied his face, and his closed eyes. When he squeezed his eyes shut even tighter, she watched a tear roll down his cheek, fall, and drop into the dirt. Tiny specks of dust floated into the air around where it fell.

She pulled in a sudden, heaving breath of emotion, and tried to let it out with a measured calm, but her sigh was ragged.

When he finally lifted his face, he looked up at the stone angel. "I gave her to you," he said, his voice shaking. "But what have you done?"

Serafina felt a storm of dizziness passing through her. Tears welled up in her eyes.

As she looked around the gravesite, she noticed that the mound of dirt he was lying on seemed strangely undisturbed. She was surprised that the broken boards of the coffin weren't sticking up out of the ground where she had crawled out.

"What do you want me to do?" Braeden shouted desperately at the angel. "Tell me what to do!"

She wished she could reach out to him, somehow touch him, somehow talk to him. "I'm here, Braeden," she said. "I'm here!"

She put her hand on his. She could not truly feel the living warmth of his hand, and it was clear that he could not feel her, but the closeness of her spirit seemed to rack him with new grief. His face contorted with a dark and terrible sorrow.

Horrified by what she was doing to him, she quickly rose to her feet and stepped back. "I'm sorry," she said, her voice weak.

"I'm not going to leave you, Serafina," he said, getting himself up onto his feet. "I'm not going to abandon you!"

He hadn't heard her words, he was still speaking to her in the grave, but it pulled at her heart. She desperately wanted to show him a sign that she had heard him. No matter what had happened, they were still friends, they were still together. Her death wasn't going to be the end of them. It couldn't be.

She looked around her, determined to find a way to communicate with him.

Dust to dust, she thought. *Of earth they were made, and into earth they return.* That was what was happening to her. She was *returning.* But for the moment, there was still a little trace of her that lingered in the world.

Harmless as a fly, Serafina thought. But even a fly can do things. And now she had an idea.

Wanting to make as big a movement as possible, she stepped onto the mound of the grave and spun around in a circle, shouting and kicking, jumping up and down, trying to make every kind of wild commotion she possibly could.

But nothing happened. The dirt didn't move.

She was useless.

But then she remembered. *Play the flute . . .*

She got down onto her hands and knees, leaned down, pulled some air into her lungs, and blew out a gentle, perfect breath just like she'd practiced.

Suddenly, a tiny flurry of dust swirled up into the moonlight in front of Braeden.

She cheered with a great shout. She'd done it just the way she'd practiced, and at just the right moment!

But Braeden did not see it.

She had accomplished nothing.

More discouraged than ever, she flopped to the ground. The whole thing was hopeless.

But then she noticed that Gidean had sat up and was looking in her direction. His ears were perked and his eyes alert. He wasn't looking at *her*, but at the dust she had stirred.

He was staring straight at it.

He tilted his head quizzically.

"It's me, Gidean!" she shouted.

She blew into the dirt again, and another little cloud of dust curled up.

Gidean rose slowly to his four feet. He tilted his head, trying to understand what he was seeing.

"I'm alive, Gidean!" she shouted.

Finally, Gidean barked in recognition. And then he started digging.

Serafina pulled back in surprise, startled. She wasn't sure what she had been expecting, but she definitely didn't think the silly dog would dig! But she didn't know how to stop him.

Gidean dug furiously with his front paws, throwing a rooster tail of dirt behind him.

Startled, and spitting out the flying dirt hitting his face, Braeden scrambled out of the way.

"What's going on?" he asked in confusion. "What are you doing, boy?"

But Gidean just kept digging straight down into Serafina's grave, throwing dirt like he was a steam-powered digging machine.

"Stop, Gidean. Don't!" Braeden commanded him. He grabbed the dog by the shoulders and tried to hold him back, but the boy was no match for the dog's strength.

"What are you doing?" Braeden demanded, his voice filled with worry and fear. "Don't do this! We can't do this!"

Serafina knew he was scared of what anyone would be scared of digging up a grave, that he'd find her grotesque, putrefied body.

But Gidean didn't stop. He just kept digging.

Braeden stepped back, obviously unsure what to do. He watched as his dog dug a deeper and deeper hole.

Serafina could tell by the horrified look on Braeden's face that he didn't think he was prepared to see what he was about to see. And yet, at the same time, there was something tearing at him, some macabre curiosity, some overwhelming desire for Gidean to keep going. They had to change the dark and terrible world they'd been living in, they had to do *something*, and now Gidean was doing it!

Braeden dropped down to his knees and started digging at Gidean's side. He clawed rapidly at the earth with his bare hands, throwing the dirt behind him.

Serafina didn't know what they were going to find in the grave. Would there be an actual body? But she'd crawled out! She'd been walking through the world. There *couldn't* be a body in the grave! *But was there?* Were they going to find her corpse rotting in the dirt? She could imagine her gray, decaying skin hanging from the broken white bones of her earthly remains.

When Braeden and Gidean finally reached the coffin, Serafina was surprised to see that the lid was unbroken and still in place. Brushing aside the last of the dirt, Braeden pried the coffin's lid away.

Serafina gasped in astonishment at what she saw.

26

Her body was lying in the coffin. She knew she should have expected it, but there was no way to prepare for it. She closed her eyes and shrunk away from the sight of it, bending at her waist and grabbing on to a tree to keep from falling over or collapsing to her knees. She covered her face and eyes with her other hand and struggled to pull in steady breaths of air—but with what lungs, what air? It felt as if her whole world was collapsing in on her. How could this be? How could she be in the grave?

She didn't want to look at the body, but she knew she must.

She slowly turned and looked again, her nose and mouth wrinkling as she expected to see her body's rotten skin peeling back from her bones.

But her body wasn't rotten. Her body was facing upward, with her eyes closed, her hands neatly lying one over the other on her chest, like someone had laid her there with respect and care. As she looked closer, she could see that some dirt had spilled into the grave onto her, but her face and body were not rotted. She was not a grotesque corpse. She appeared to be in some form of suspended animation, as if she lay in eternal spring. Braeden had brought her here to the angel's glade, where decay and seasons and the cycles of the universe had no sway.

Serafina stood over her own grave and stared down into the coffin at her body in disbelief. Braeden and Gidean stood beside her.

Her body was clearly dead in that there was no life in her, no breathing or movement, and yet, her body was not blue or grayish of skin or decayed in any way. It seemed perfectly protected there, as if nothing would ever harm it.

Serafina studied Braeden's expression. He did not seem surprised that her body was in the coffin. He seemed to expect that. He had put it there. But his eyes were wide and his face filled with shock about something else.

"All the wounds are healed," Braeden said in amazement. Her dress was badly torn and stained with old blood, but her body was in perfect condition.

He turned and looked up at the angel.

"You *healed* her," he said, almost apologetically after the accusations he'd slung at her earlier that night. "You've been *protecting* her," he said, as he wiped tears of relief from his eyes.

Serafina gazed all around at the angel's glade, with its beautiful, peaceful willow trees and its lovely green grass. It had always been this way, winter, spring, summer, and fall.

Braeden looked up at the angel again and spoke to her as if she was not only a living, sentient being but a true friend. "But what do I do now? How do I help her?"

He looked at the angel expectantly, but after a long time, his excitement faded, and some of his old sadness returned.

"Don't give up hope," Serafina whispered.

Finally, he laid himself down on the dirt next to her open grave like he himself was dead.

"I'm not going to lose hope, Serafina," he said. "Somehow, I'm going to get you out of here."

She knew he hadn't truly heard her. They had been feeling the same thing at the same time.

Serafina gazed down at Braeden lying beside the grave and she tried to understand it all. Her human body lay in the coffin. Her panther body was out in the forest, a wild animal. Her restless spirit had crawled out of the grave, carrying with it all the trappings and constraints she remembered of the physical world—the steadiness of the earth, the challenges of physical obstructions, the essence of sight and sound and feeling, pain and hunger and sleep. But it had left her body behind, like a cicada crawling out of its dried shell. Her spirit had made it all the way to Biltmore and haunted those within. And now she was back again. Her spirit was here once more.

For a long time, she just tried to understand the difference between thought and action, between dream and waking, between the physical world and the spiritual, between perception and reality.

She tried to figure out what Braeden meant when he said he was going to get her out of here. Out of the grave? Out of her dead body? She didn't understand, but at least she knew now, without any doubt, that even after all this time, after all that had happened, he was still her friend, he was still fighting for her, and he still had hope. He had tremendous hope, brighter than the darkest night.

He was lying on his back now beside the grave and his eyes were open. Gidean crept forward and curled up close beside him, and Braeden put his arm around him. For months, Braeden had been pushing his dog away, ashamed of the boy he had become, but now the rift between them seemed as if it was beginning to heal. Serafina was glad to see them together, but why was it happening here and now? What had changed?

As Braeden stared up through the opening in the trees, she wondered what he was looking at, what he was thinking about in that moment.

She went over to him. She did not go near her dead body lying in the grave. She was scared of what might happen if she did that. But she went to his other side.

As she moved, she noticed a pair of yellow eyes staring from the shadows. The cat's black fur was nearly invisible in the darkness, but Serafina could see the panther's face and the outline of her ears. The panther had crept up close and was lying down now, still and quiet, gazing into the glade toward them.

Serafina slowly made her way over to Braeden and lay down in the dirt next to him.

Lying on her back beside him, she gazed up through the opening of the angel's glade into the nighttime sky. She and Braeden were looking up into the stars just like they had when they used to lie on Biltmore's rooftop together. Those nights seemed so long ago now, like they had been a dream. But it had all been real, and somehow, this was, too.

Lying side by side, they gazed up at the crystalline black ceiling of the midnight sky. It was a beautifully clear night. They could see thousands of points of light splayed above them, clusters of many stars, Saturn and Mars and Jupiter glowing in all their glory, and the bright swath of the Milky Way galaxy splashed across the glistening heavens.

They watched the stars and the planets sliding slowly over their heads, marking time so precisely that it was barely perceptible, like a great, steady celestial clock, keeping the time of their inner lives, showing them that out there in the world everything was always changing, but here in the center of the world, where they were lying side by side, everything would always remain the same.

For the first time, Braeden did not seem upset by her spirit's presence. With her spirit on one side, her human body on the other, and the panther nearby, all was well again. It had been the terrible separation of the three that had caused him such tearing grief. But now, he lay quietly.

As Braeden fell asleep beside her, and she fell asleep beside him, she began to slip away, not into a nightmare like before, but into a lovely dream. She dreamed she was a tendril of moving air, flowing from place to place, without weight or body, only movement, constant movement, from forest to home, from mountain to field, she swept and rolled and turned, like the music of a gentle symphony gliding on the breeze.

For once in a long time, she and Braeden were together, and they were finally at peace.

When Serafina woke, she found herself lying in the angel's glade with Braeden and Gidean standing nearby. She quickly got herself up onto her feet to see what was happening.

"What do you think you're doing?" a male voice asked in a forceful tone.

Serafina looked around the forest.

"I wasn't going to hurt anyone," Braeden replied. "I swear. Nothing happened."

"Something always happens with that thing," Waysa said as he stepped out of the forest. His long dark hair hung down around his shoulders and his brown skin glistened in the morning light. His chest was bare and he wore simple trousers. The pattern of his tribe's ancestral tattoos marked his face and arms.

"What's wrong with you? Why did you put on the cloak?"

"I'm sorry," Braeden said to him, shaking his head. "I . . ."

"What was it?" Waysa demanded. "What happened?"

"My aunt and uncle were having a party in the rose garden with all the guests—"

"Oh, yes, that's a good reason. Lots of excellent victims to choose from," Waysa said sarcastically.

"No!" Braeden said. "I was sitting on the bench up on the Library Terrace away from everybody else. And then a strange feeling came over me."

"What do you mean, a strange feeling?" Waysa said, narrowing his eyes.

"I don't know what it was," Braeden said. "Terrible sadness and pain . . . like I was going through it all over again, like she was actually there and she needed my help, but I couldn't help her. It felt like I could almost reach out and touch her, but I couldn't. I just felt so hopeless, like all this was never going to end. I thought maybe if I put on the cloak I could find her, reach her somehow, and help her . . . I had to do *something.*"

"But not that!" Waysa said. "Never put it on. It's too dangerous. Especially now."

"I won't be doing it again, believe me," Braeden said. "It was awful. I need to find my own way through all this."

Waysa nodded, seeming to understand. "You frightened me, my friend," he said as he walked toward him. The two boys shook hands warmly, with the ease of familiarity, then embraced briefly and separated.

Serafina was happy to see Waysa here, but it surprised her

to see them greet each other so warmly. They had first met during the battle against Uriah and Rowena, but they had not been close. It was a peculiar feeling to have her two friends become friends without her.

She thought it was interesting how different they looked from each other. Waysa was taller than Braeden, and much physically stronger, with muscled arms and legs. He was a boy of action, taut and fierce. Braeden had lighter hair and a younger, softer face. He was a quiet, polite, smartly dressed boy of the house, with his dog at his side.

Waysa turned and looked at her body lying the grave. She could see from the moody look in his eyes that he wasn't in agreement with what Braeden and Gidean had done. "First you put on the cloak, and then you do this . . ."

"I don't understand what comes next, Waysa," Braeden said. "What are we waiting for? What's going to happen?"

But Waysa didn't reply.

"That's all that's left of her," Braeden said despondently, pointing at the body in the grave.

"You know that isn't true," Waysa said, setting his jaw.

"But she's been buried here since the Loggia. How can this go on?"

"This is just her human body," Waysa said. "As long as the angel protects this part of her, then there is hope."

"But hope for what? Where's the rest of her? Where'd she go?"

"I'm right here!" Serafina said.

"I've seen her," Waysa said.

"What?" Serafina said, looking at him in surprise. "You've *seen* me? What are you talking about? You haven't seen me!"

"Sometimes she lingers here, near the grave . . ." Waysa said.

"Yes, I'm here! I'm here now!"

"Does she recognize you?" Braeden asked, keenly interested in what Waysa was saying.

"I don't honestly know," Waysa said sadly. "She seems as wild as the forest itself. The last time I saw her, I tried to follow her, but she attacked me."

Serafina frowned. They weren't talking about her spirit. They were talking about the panther.

Braeden shook his head in sadness. "I've seen her from a distance, but she doesn't come to me . . ."

"Her *tso-i* is split," Waysa said.

"I don't understand what that means," Braeden said.

"Her three, her trinity, has been torn apart," Waysa said, trying to explain it the best he could. "Her *a-da-nv-do* is gone."

"What does that mean?"

"It's her heart, her spirit," Waysa said.

Braeden shook his head as he looked down at her body. "I wish I could have done more for her."

"You did all you could do," Waysa told him.

"But I didn't save her . . ." Braeden said.

"We don't know that yet," Waysa said. "There are still many feet traveling many paths."

Braeden looked up at him. "What do you mean? Is something happening? Have you spoken with Serafina's mother?"

"No, it's not that," Waysa said, shaking his head sadly.

"Her mother was devastated by what happened. After Serafina's death, she lost all hope."

"But where is she?" Braeden asked.

"Everything in these forests reminded her more and more of Serafina: the trees, the rivers, the rocks and sky, even you and me. It was breaking her heart to stay here. She went west with the cubs to the Smoky Mountains to find more of our kind."

"I understand," Braeden said, nodding.

Serafina listened to Waysa's story of her mother with fascination. It made her so sad to think that her mother had gone, but she was relieved to hear that she and the cubs were all right.

Then she thought, *Serafina's death*. That was what Waysa had said. That was what they were calling it. Her *death*.

Braeden looked at Waysa. "But *you* didn't go to the Smoky Mountains with them."

"No."

"But why?"

Waysa lifted his eyes and looked at him, almost angry that he would ask him that question. "The same reason you didn't go to the hospital in New York when your aunt and uncle told you to. The doctors might have been able to fix your leg."

"You're right," Braeden said. "But what did you mean that there are still many feet traveling many paths?"

"Something is coming this way," Waysa said. "I've seen a clawed creature with terrible powers. Dark storms have been ripping through the forest each night. The rivers are swelling, destroying everything in their path. And the black folds are increasing. The people of Biltmore are in grave danger."

"Is it *her*?" Braeden asked, a sudden fierceness in his voice.

"I do not know."

"But you've seen her again, haven't you?"

"No, not since the night she left."

Serafina didn't know who or what they were talking about, but when Waysa said these words his voice was edged with emotion, almost as if he felt guilty about what had happened.

"Not since you helped her, you mean," Braeden said, his voice filled with bitterness. "I still don't understand why you did it."

"When I found her in the forest she was bleeding so badly. She couldn't move or speak. She was going to die, Braeden."

"Yes, I know. You should have finished her off!"

"You don't understand," Waysa said. "She wasn't just suffering from the wounds from the battle on the Loggia. I know what wounds from dog bites and panther claws look like. Something else had gotten her. I found her curled up under a fallen tree, shaking in misery. Something had beaten her savagely, broken her bones, tore into her flesh, even burned her. I've never seen anything like it."

"I don't understand," Braeden said, fear gathering in his eyes. "You mean, like some sort of animal? Or a wicked curse? What do you mean something else had *gotten* her?"

"I don't know what attacked her, but it was the most disturbing thing I have ever seen," Waysa said.

"But she was our enemy, Waysa. Why didn't you destroy her right then when you had the chance?"

Waysa looked down at the ground. He didn't know how to

answer Braeden's question. "You're right that I may have made a terrible mistake," he admitted. "But when I saw her there lying on the ground, suffering so badly, I just kept remembering the night Uriah killed my sister. I could not save my sister from death. No matter how hard I fought, I did not have the strength and speed and fierceness I needed to protect her. But as I was looking at this helpless, wounded girl on the ground, I realized that I could save *this* girl. I have been fighting for a long time now, but that is not what I was before. It's not all I wish to be. My mother and my grandmother taught me that sometimes you win the battle not by fighting, but by helping and healing. Sometimes there is more than one path to follow. It is not always clear which way to go, but I wanted to follow the *du-yu-go-dv-i*, the right path, at least the best I could. When I saw Rowena lying there like that, something stayed my claws. Do you understand?"

For a long time, Braeden did not look at his friend, could not look at him, for he did not want to forgive him, but finally he looked up at him and he nodded. "All right. Tell me what happened next."

"I picked her up and carried her to a safe and hidden place. I bound her wounds and I helped her through the days and nights that followed. I gave her water and food and a place to sleep and heal."

"Then what happened?"

"On the night of the quarter moon, I came back and she was gone. She just disappeared."

"Disappeared?"

"She slipped away. I looked for her for several nights, but she had become nothing but mist in the swamp."

"The creature you spoke of, the storms and the swelling rivers . . ."

"I don't know if she's causing all that," Waysa said. "Or if that creature is the thing that attacked her and caused those terrible wounds."

Serafina couldn't help scanning the forest around them. Waysa had seen the storm-creech. And he knew something was coming.

Braeden looked down again at her body lying in the grave.

"But is this how it's all going to end, Waysa?" Braeden asked. "With Serafina in the ground?"

"We stay bold, my friend, that's what we do," Waysa said. "We fight."

"Even if we've already lost the battle?" Braeden asked in dismay.

"Especially then," Waysa said. "This war isn't over. We stay strong and we stay smart. You still have the cloak, right?"

"I still have it."

"Keep it well hidden. Keep it safe. The cloak is our only hope. And whatever's coming, we'll fight it together."

Braeden nodded his agreement. "And you keep the panther safe."

"I'll do my best," Waysa said solemnly. "Stay bold!"

With this, Waysa leapt into the forest, changed form in midair, and bounded away on four legs.

Braeden watched Waysa go. He and Gidean remained at

the side of the grave alone. He seemed to be thinking about Waysa's words, trying to understand what he should do next.

Then he slowly turned back to the coffin and looked at her body in the grave.

"Come back to me," he said to her.

"Believe me, I'm trying," she said as a pang of sadness moved through her.

Braeden replaced the lid on the coffin and slowly, almost reluctantly, pushed the dirt back into the grave and reburied her.

When the work was done and he was about to leave, he looked up at the angel.

"Take care of her," he told her, and then he turned and headed back toward Biltmore.

Serafina wanted to follow him, but she let him go. There was nothing she could do to help him in that direction. She had to join them in their fight against the coming darkness, and she could see only one path to follow.

28

That night, Serafina made her way through the bog and crept up on Rowena's lair. The sorceress had just returned from one of her hunts with a satchel full of herbs she'd collected. She had also captured a flask full of cicadas and flies, which she dutifully fed to her growing clutch of hungry plants. Her hood was down, her long red hair hanging around her shoulders. Her face was solemn like before, filled with thoughts that Serafina could not fathom.

"I can feel you," Rowena said as she fed a fly to a carnivorous plant. "There's no sense lurking out there."

"What did you mean when you said much has changed?" Serafina said, staying where she was.

"Much is always changing," Rowena said.

"But what specifically were talking about when you said it?"

"I meant that you had no idea what had happened since you took your little catnap in the grave."

"Then tell me," Serafina demanded.

"From the tone of your voice, it sounds like you already know," Rowena said, seeming to realize that Serafina had seen Braeden and Waysa.

"No. Not all of it."

"You've seen all the pieces. You just have to put them together," Rowena replied. "You just don't want to accept it."

Serafina thought about what she was saying. "You mean that I'm dead."

"Of course you are. Or as good as. You're on your way."

"And a dark force is attacking Biltmore . . ."

"You already know that. It always has been. Nothing's changed at all, and yet everything has. The world is circles, and the circles are broken."

"You're not making any sense," Serafina said.

"There can be no sense in the world to someone who doesn't want to understand it. You look at me, but you don't see me. That's what I meant."

"What do you mean I don't see you?"

"You see your enemy."

"You tried to kill me!"

"Yes, I did," she said, almost nonchalantly. "And you me."

"Waysa found you and he saved you."

"Yes, he did," Rowena said quietly, her tone guarded, like she didn't want to talk about it, or her feelings about it, but maybe what Waysa did was the exact point. "There are many paths . . ."

"Are you the cause of all these storms in the forest? Are you going to attack us? Are you trying to destroy Biltmore? What are you doing here?"

"I'm trying to survive."

"But you're speaking in riddles," Serafina said.

"Only to a person who thinks the world is a broken thing that she can put back together again," Rowena said. "Sometimes you can't fix it. Sometimes you have to hunker down and hold on the best you can."

"Or just go ahead and die . . ." Serafina said bitterly.

She wanted to get down to the bottom of what Rowena was hiding, but she began to hear a deep pounding sound all around.

She looked up to see a dark cloud passing over the top of the forest. The stars disappeared. Her legs flushed with a cold surge of sudden fear.

The sound was low in volume at first, but it got louder and louder as it came closer. The earth and trees began to shake, a heavy heartbeat pounding the air. *Boom . . . boom . . . boom . . .*

A swirling wind rose up, and the leaves on the trees began to vibrate. The sticks on the forest floor lifted up and rose slowly into the air, levitating around her. She tried to be brave, but her arms and legs began to tremble, and she couldn't catch her breath. Rowena's goats bleated as they scurried around the lair in terror.

Rowena ran inside and came back out clenching a potion-filled flask. Ducking down in panic, she looked up into the blackened sky and all around her, ready to fight, holding the flask up in her shaking hand like she was going to throw it at the attacker.

"He's found us!" Rowena whispered over to Serafina. "You need to go!"

"But who is it? What's happening?" Serafina asked as she took cover behind a large tree.

"Don't be a fool, cat," Rowena shouted at her. "Get out of here!"

Serafina ran through the forest to escape the storm. The trees twisted and thrashed as branches cracked overhead and came crashing down around her. A gust of wind buffeted her so hard that it knocked her off her feet and threw her tumbling across the ground. She scrambled back up and kept running, but then heard Rowena scream behind her.

Gasping for breath, Serafina turned and looked back.

Serafina could see Rowena cowering by her lair. A great blow of force came crashing through, breaking the limbs of the trees all around. The strength of it pushed Serafina back like a giant wave, lifting her off her feet and dragging her along. She grabbed the swampy earth to stop herself and held firm. Then she began fighting her way back toward Rowena, who was consumed in battle against the unseen attacker.

With the dark, swirling wind and flying branches, Serafina couldn't see everything that was happening, but she saw the figure of Rowena running into her partially destroyed lair, grabbing a potion, and threatening to throw it. "Don't hurt me!" she screamed, her voice shaking in both fear and anger. "I swear I'll fight you!"

Serafina looked all around, searching the trees for a glimpse of the attacker, but she couldn't see him.

Serafina felt her feet getting wet and sticky. She looked down. The mossy ground welled with a dark blood. Insects and worms oozed out of the ground around her.

"Stop it!" Rowena shouted. "Leave me alone!"

A blast of force sent a large, broken tree limb sailing through the air at Rowena. The branch slammed into the girl, knocking her to the ground with a brutal blow. The branches attacked her like tearing fingers, ripping terrible, jagged cuts across her back.

Serafina gasped when she saw not just the fresh bleeding wounds on Rowena's bare back, but the scars of the past all across her back and sides. This wasn't the first time she'd suffered this attacker's wrath. For all her ability to cast spells and change shape, it appeared there were some scars that even a creature of her ilk could not heal.

But Rowena didn't stay down for long. She quickly got back up onto her feet, wiped the blood from her swollen mouth, and looked out into the forest in fierce defiance. Before the next attack came, she scrambled to her cache of potions. She grabbed a flask and hurled it into the forest, filling the bog with a dense mountain mist.

As if in angry reply, a blazing ball of fire came hurtling out of the forest straight at Rowena.

She threw up her arms with an explosive flurry of ice and snow, extinguishing the fireball in a burst of steam.

Through all this, Serafina looked for the attacker, but she couldn't see him.

"Tonight!" a voice blared. "Get the cloak tonight or I'll kill the boy myself!"

"If you kill him, you'll never find the cloak!" Rowena screamed angrily.

But as if to make the final point, another massive fireball came barreling out of the darkness straight at her, this one coming twice as fast as the one before. She leapt out of the way just in time, but the fireball struck the tree behind her and exploded, throwing burning sap in all directions.

Rowena screamed in pain as the searing liquid scalded her bare skin and lit everything around her on fire.

Serafina rushed forward to help her, dodging between the flames. She dropped to her knees beside Rowena as the girl twisted in pain from the burning sap. Knowing that she had to help her, Serafina closed her eyes and let a part of herself fade down into the porous ground, sinking down to where the water lay. Then she focused her mind and swept up her arms and with the force of sheer will began to pull the water up through the spongy moss of the bog, flooding everything around them. The rising water doused the lingering flames and flowed over Rowena's body, sweeping the burning sap away, before receding back into the bog beneath them.

Stunned by what she'd done, Serafina collapsed to the ground in exhaustion next to Rowena.

She and Rowena lay in a heap of scorched, soaking-wet, shredded trunks and branches. The attacker was gone and the fire was out.

The two of them lay there for several seconds, just recovering.

Then Rowena opened her eyes. She slowly crawled out of the wreckage, gathered herself, and struggled to her feet. She seemed barely able to move. Her robes had been torn from her bleeding, dirt-stained body, and she had suffered many bruises and burns. But she was alive.

She gazed desolately around at the destruction, then she took a long breath and seemed to steel herself.

Going into the part of her lair that was still intact, she opened a vial and started rubbing a viscous gray mud onto her burned arms and legs, wincing and gritting her teeth against the pain.

Rowena didn't say anything to Serafina, but the sorceress seemed to understand that Serafina had saved her life, or at least the agony of immeasurable more pain than she had already suffered.

In the next moment, Rowena grabbed her satchel and began to quickly gather some of her crystal flasks and other accoutrements of her dark arts.

Serafina watched in fascination. Rowena did not wallow in fear and misery. She did not cry. She seemed filled with new urgency, a new, angry determination to fight and survive.

Just when Serafina thought she had seen everything strange under the moon, Rowena pressed her hands flat to the top of her head and ran her palms slowly down the length of her hair, changing her hair color from red to black. Then she touched two fingers on each hand to her face just below her eyes. She pressed her fingers onto her cheeks, wiping in a hard, steady motion, changing the contour of her face as she went. Next, she reached down to her feet, pulled off her shoes, and pushed the little toe into each foot until it disappeared. Finally, she touched the center of each of her eyeballs with the pad of her index finger, tinging her eyes with a golden-amber color.

Serafina stared in mystified disbelief. Step by step, Rowena had transformed herself into someone else. Someone who looked disturbingly like *her*!

It was as if Serafina was looking into a mirror, but the girl who was looking back at her was far more beautiful and alluring than she was.

"Wait, Rowena," Serafina said. "I don't understand. What are you doing?"

"You heard him," Rowena said. "I want this over."

"But who was that?" Serafina asked. "Who was attacking you?"

Rowena pulled her torn robes around her and started walking fast through the forest, following the same path Serafina had used to come here.

"Hold on, just stop, where are you going?" Serafina asked desperately. "Please, tell me what you're going to do."

"Stop pestering me, cat, I have a summer ball to go to," Rowena said.

Serafina followed Rowena through the forest, knowing that Braeden was in grave danger. But in the early-morning hours a thick cloud of mist lingered in the mountain valleys and floated along the ridges, drifting slowly, white and eerie, through the trees, obscuring Rowena's path. Serafina wasn't sure if it was a natural fog or one of the sorceress's concealing potions, but one way or another, Serafina finally lost track of her.

As she looked for Rowena's trail, Serafina felt the coolness of the mist on her skin, and sensed that if she stood still a little too long, she'd slip into the vapor, whether she wanted to or not. *Dust to dust, and now mist to mist.*

She had learned to enliven some of the elements in tiny ways, and she had shifted into the water in the stream, but the more she interacted with the elements, the more she sensed herself slipping into them.

It broke her heart to think about leaving the people she loved behind, but she knew there probably wasn't anything she could do about dying now. As Rowena had said, she was already on her way. It felt like she had one more night, maybe two, before she was gone.

Everyone dies, she told herself, trying to stay brave, *but I need to protect the people I love.*

But how? That was the question now.

She'd seen the violent force terrorizing Rowena, bringing in storms, casting fireballs, and burning her as it demanded she retrieve the Black Cloak. Braeden and Waysa were playing a dangerous game by hiding it, but maybe it was the only thing keeping them alive.

All through the afternoon, she searched for Rowena, looking for tracks and other signs, but the sorceress had disappeared.

Finally, she headed back to Biltmore, dreading what was going to happen. It was the night of the summer ball.

She emerged from the forest trees near the statue of Diana, goddess of the hunt, atop the hill that provided the most dramatic view of Biltmore's front facade.

From there, a long stretch of green grass ran down a steep hill to the Esplanade, the flat expanse of manicured grass with its carriageways on each side leading up to the entrance of the house. Biltmore House rose up with its intricately carved limestone walls, its fine statues and strange gargoyles, its steep peaks and slanted rooftops, and the rolling layers of the mountains in the distance. She had once stood here in this spot in a beautiful red-and-black gown, with Braeden and Gidean standing at her side, the three of them gazing down at the house together. But not tonight.

Tonight, she was alone, standing in the moonlight, still wearing the torn, dirty, bloodstained dress that Braeden had buried her in.

Flickering torches lined the grand carriageway that led up to the main door of the mansion, and all the windows of the house were aglow. The slanted, spiraling windows of the Grand Staircase were ablaze with glittering brilliance. But it was the intricate glass panes of the domed Winter Garden—the center of the ball—that shone the brightest of all. It was difficult to imagine, but it seemed as if it would be there that Rowena would try to weave her web around Braeden.

Serafina watched a steady chain of horse-drawn carriages ride through the mansion's gates. The main road to the estate had been muddy and partially flooded, but the bridges were holding, and the carriages had managed to get through. They proceeded in a long line, one after the other, up to the front doors of the house, where two tall, perfectly matched footmen in their formal black-and-white livery uniforms welcomed the arriving guests.

Quiet and watchful, Serafina walked down the hill toward the incoming carriages.

"Oh, it's positively breathtaking!" one fine lady said to her gentleman husband as she opened the carriage window to see the house more clearly.

"Look at it, Mama, it's like a fairy tale!" a young girl in the next carriage said to her mother.

"More like a horror story these days," Serafina grumbled quietly to herself.

Most of the carriages were pulled by two horses, while the wealthiest members of society had carriages that were pulled by four. But then Serafina spotted something she had never seen before.

One of the carriages didn't have any horses at all. It *looked* like a carriage, with four spoked wheels, lacquered wood sides, and four passengers sitting on tufted leather seats, but it appeared to be moving by its own magical power. Serafina's eyes darted around as she looked for the sorceress, thinking that she must have cast some sort of spell, but Rowena was nowhere to be seen.

The carriage with no horses made an odd puttering sound, and the man in the front seat wore a funny hat and goggles. It took Serafina several seconds to realize that it wasn't her enemy's dark magic, but some sort of newfangled machine.

All her life, her pa had been telling her that times were changing, that all over the country men and women were inventing things that were going to change the world. She never knew exactly what he was talking about. But maybe this strange, horseless carriage was the beginning of it. She wished her pa was there to see it and tell her what it was.

Still on the lookout for Rowena, Serafina slipped through the line of carriages, up through the congestion of four-legged hoof stompers, top-hatted coachmen, and glittering ladies.

She skulked up the steps and hid behind the Guardians, the marble lion statues that she had always imagined protected Biltmore from evil spirits. But tonight *she* was the spirit; she was the strange ghost of the night creeping into the house.

As each carriage pulled up to the house, the footman flipped down the carriage's steps and opened the carriage door. The gentleman inside exited first, then offered his hand to help the lady as she alighted in her voluminous gown, carefully navigating the tiny carriage steps in her sparkling shoes. Once she was safely to the ground, she took the gentleman's arm, and they walked through the grand arched doors together into the Vestibule and up the red-carpeted steps into the house.

The light and heat and sound of the ball, with hundreds of guests already inside, poured out of the mansion's broad doorway, and hundreds more were still arriving. As Serafina slipped into the house, it felt as if she were being absorbed into a hot, glowing, gigantic organism.

The only thought on her mind was whether she could find the sorceress in time to stop her from hurting Braeden.

As Serafina entered Biltmore's main hall, it was thick with the aroma of burning candles, fine clean wool, and women's perfumes, all mixed together with the scent of the thousands of roses and lilies that had been strung along the archways and beams of the house. The genteel murmur of the guests' voices mixed with the sounds of rustling satin, pouring wine, and tinkling glasses. There were so many people in the room from wall to wall that the arms of strangers touched each other where they stood, and friends leaned to one another to say a private word, but all the guests seemed happy and respectful, honored to be a part of the grand festivities. Serafina scanned the crowd but did not see Rowena or Braeden.

The gentlemen at the ball wore formal evening attire, dark

tailcoats and trousers, neatly pressed white shirts with wing collars, dark waistcoats, and white bow ties or cravats. Some of the men were lean, others heavy, some with long handlebar mustachios or neatly trimmed beards, others clean-shaven. They all wore white gloves on their hands, and many had watches in their pockets, with long dangling gold or silver chains. A few even had silver-topped canes or formal walking staffs, but none were twisted.

What struck Serafina most was just how pleased the men were to see each other, to be talking and drinking, laughing and carrying on, like a great, gregarious flock of black-and-white jays cawing to each other, with no idea that a young boy of their ranks had buried a body nearby and that the fading, lost spirit of a dead girl walked among them.

The ladies wore long, full, shimmering dancing gowns made from satin, taffeta, and many other fine and luxurious materials, in dark purples, strawberry creams, peach chiffon, lilac, and blue—an endless variety of colors that reminded Serafina of the summer's blooms.

She peered suspiciously at each of the women and girls in the crowd, searching for a girl that looked like her. She had a hunch that the sorceress would be hiding in there someplace among the others, for deceit was her specialty.

Serafina watched the sometimes slow, sometimes flighty interactions between the young ladies and the young gentlemen. Many of the ladies and older girls held embroidered fans, opening or fluttering them to signal interest to a possible suitor, closing or snapping them shut to signal disdain.

As she studied the young ladies and gentlemen maneuvering and interacting with one another, it reminded her of the sandhill cranes that sometimes stopped on their migration to practice their mating dance in the spring fields, hopping and raising their wings, dipping their heads and tossing sticks to one another, spinning and chortling with abandon.

She didn't know exactly why the cranes and the young ladies went through all that or what it all meant, but she sensed that it was a hidden language all its own.

The younger children who weren't yet cranes gathered in small groups together, whispering and watching all the various proceedings in the room. Gaggles of giggling girls pulled each other excitedly through the crowds toward unseen adventures. Clutches of young boys gathered near the food tables.

Among the adults, the room was full of society types and fashion plates, industrialists and politicians, authors and artists, ambassadors and dignitaries of a nature that Serafina did not understand. She missed her old friend, the smiling, storytelling Mr. Olmsted, who had returned to his home far away.

As Serafina made her way into the room, the soft, lovely sound of harps and violins began to fill the hall, and then the deep sound of cellos and other instruments joined in. Row upon row of musicians, each one in black coat and tie, were arranged in the center of the main hall playing the most beautiful, sweeping, romantic music she had ever heard. Mr. Vanderbilt hadn't just arranged for a soloist or a string quartet. He had brought an entire orchestra into his home!

Serafina remembered years before when she was but a little child, sneaking around the house late at night. Mr. Vanderbilt's friend, Thomas Edison, had given him a music-playing phonograph with a crank handle and a large brass horn. She had often watched the master of the house sitting alone in his library listening to his opera music. Mr. Vanderbilt loved *Tannhäuser* so much that he commissioned the famous sculptor Mr. Karl Bitter to depict an epic scene from the opera in the frieze above the Banquet Hall's gigantic triple fireplace.

She remembered that Edison's music machine had produced a scratchy, tinny sound that she hadn't liked, but *this*, this live orchestra, was something else entirely. Mr. Vanderbilt had traveled all over Europe collecting art and furniture for Biltmore, but also attending concerts and operas, and now she understood why. She could finally see and hear what he loved so much.

All the musicians were playing together in such perfect harmony, with all the violins and cellos and other instruments sweeping into gorgeous waves of sound, like nothing she had ever heard before. She overheard a gentleman say to one of the other guests that the music was from a new ballet called *Swan Lake*, which Mr. Vanderbilt had heard in Europe and fallen in love with, so he'd arranged for the orchestra to play it tonight.

The rising music carried through Biltmore's soaring archways to all the grand rooms of the house, to all the elegant ladies in their glimmering dresses and the handsome gentlemen in their evening coats. There were flutes that made the sound of thrushes in the morning, and reedy oboes that sounded like the little grebes that landed in the lagoon in the fall, and majestic French horns like coming kings—instruments of so many kinds that she couldn't name them all.

That was when she finally spotted Braeden. She felt a flush of happiness that her friend was all right. Rowena was nowhere to be seen, and Braeden was safe. Perhaps the night was going to turn out better than she'd feared.

Braeden made his way through the crowd up to his aunt and uncle. He was wearing black tails, a white tie, and white gloves, and he looked every bit the well-to-do young gentleman.

"You look very handsome, young man," Mrs. Vanderbilt said cheerfully.

"Thank you," Braeden said, blushing a little.

"You seem more chipper today," Mr. Vanderbilt remarked.

"I'm feeling a little better," Braeden agreed.

"Well," Mrs. Vanderbilt said. "I know several little ladies who are reserving a spot on their dance cards for you."

Braeden's mood darkened. "I would rather not."

"I know your heart's not in it, Braeden," Mrs. Vanderbilt said gently. "But when the dancing begins, it would be ungentlemanly if you didn't ask some of the girls to dance with you. Many of them have come a long way to be here with us."

"I understand," Braeden said glumly.

"Does your leg feel all right?" Mrs. Vanderbilt asked compassionately. "Do you feel well enough to dance?"

"It's not that. I just . . ." Braeden began, but then faltered.

Serafina could see that he didn't want to lie to his aunt, but he didn't want to tell her what she didn't want to hear, either.

"I know she was a good friend," his aunt said. "But eventually, for your own sake, you're going to have to accept that she's gone."

"I know," Braeden said sadly.

"I'm not gone yet, Braeden!" Serafina cried out despite herself, forgetting her mature and somber acceptance of her death just a few minutes before. "Don't let me go! Hold on to me!" But of course no one could hear her.

In the next moment, the conductor of the orchestra brought the evening's musical prelude to an end, everyone clapped politely, and then he tapped three times on his stand and lifted his white baton.

An excited murmur ran through the crowd. They knew what was coming.

The sound of the orchestra rose up into a lively and sweeping waltz perfect for dancing.

Little bouts of enthused clapping rose up among the guests, everyone happy that the time had finally come. Gentlemen young and old throughout the ball walked over to the ladies of their choice, bowed deeply, took their hands, and asked them to dance.

The palm trees, furniture, and works of art that normally filled the Winter Garden had been cleared away to make room for the dancing. And while many of the mansion's rooms and corridors were lit with candles, the finely carved beams above the dance floor were strung with thousands of tiny electric lights, like fireflies in a magic garden, so that the ladies' dresses glowed and shimmered in the light.

So that's what Pa had been working on, Serafina thought, and at that moment, she caught her breath, for her pa was standing across the room from her in a handsome dark suit, leaning against one of the black marble columns of the Winter Garden.

He was not in the formal, white-tie evening wear of Biltmore's guests, but he was washed and shaved, and he looked more handsome and dignified than she had ever seen him before. He was gazing at the lights that he'd put up for the ball and listening to the pleased reactions of the delighted couples as they walked out onto the dance floor. There was a proud and satisfied look on his face. And all the emotion that she'd been feeling moments before welled up inside her.

She wanted to go over to him and hug him and tell him how proud she was of him and how much she loved him. Her pa had never been to school and knew no magic spells, but tonight he was the wizard of light.

As the elegant couples began filling the dance floor, Serafina noticed a girl standing across the room. She was dressed in a long, beautiful, dark green, iridescent gown. The girl had severely angled cheekbones, long black hair, and large amber eyes. The hackles on the back of Serafina's neck went straight up.

There she is, Serafina thought.

Rowena's face possessed a disturbing resemblance to her own, but it was different from her, too, like a more alluring, better version of herself. It appeared that Rowena wasn't pretending to be her, but an older sister or a cousin. She must have stolen or used some sort of spell to create the dress. And she had fixed her long black hair up into an elaborate arrangement. To Serafina, she looked magnificent and beautiful and evil all at once.

Rowena was almost perfect in her appearance, but when Serafina looked more closely, she saw at the edge of her high collar the trace of the terrible scar on Rowena's pale white skin. Determined to stop the sorceress before she started, Serafina walked straight toward her.

But even as Serafina charged forward, what she heard behind her made her heart sink.

"All right," Braeden said softly to his aunt as he noticed the mysterious but strangely familiar black-haired girl in the green gown. "I'll ask *her* to dance."

"That's excellent, thank you, Braeden," Mrs. Vanderbilt said, barely noticing the girl, but immensely encouraged by her nephew's sudden willingness to do his gentlemanly duty for at least one of the young ladies in the room.

"Do we know that girl?" Mr. Vanderbilt asked, eyeing Rowena with concern.

"I'm sure she's from a good family," Mrs. Vanderbilt said, obviously pleased that Braeden was finally beginning to socialize.

As Braeden moved toward the girl to ask her to dance, Serafina moved toward her as well.

"You shouldn't be here!" Serafina hissed at her.

"Skedaddle, kitty cat, I've got work to do," Rowena whispered beneath her breath, and then lifted her face and smiled a gracious smile as Braeden presented himself to her, bowed, and offered his white-gloved hand.

To those around them who happened to be watching, none of this seemed out of the ordinary. Serafina knew ballroom etiquette enough to know that it was the duty of every young gentleman to ask the young ladies of the ball to dance, and it was in fact rude for a gentleman to allow a young lady to stand for long without a partner. And for her part, if a young lady was properly and respectfully asked, she should not refuse to dance with a gentleman unless her dance card was already full.

"My name is Braeden Vanderbilt," he said in a kind but formal way as he put out his hand to her. "Will you do me the honor of dancing with me?"

"With pleasure, sir," the girl replied in the sweetest, most exquisite Charleston accent that had ever been spoken by a Southern belle, and placed her delicate hand in his.

Serafina watched helplessly as Braeden and Rowena walked slowly and formally out onto the dance floor among the other dancers. It was clear that he didn't recognize who she was, but he seemed strangely drawn to her.

"Not her, Braeden!" Serafina shouted. "Anybody but her!"

Serafina tried to figure out what she could do to stop them. Could she create a blast of air to send all the musicians' sheet music flying from their stands and halt the orchestra? Could she splash the water in the fountain onto all the dancers and send them running?

Rowena leaned toward Braeden and spoke to him in her lovely high-society Southern accent. "I was so positively petrified by the thought that no one would ask me to dance this evening," she said, meeting his eyes with hers. "You are a fine gentleman for rescuing me."

Rowena was acting so sickeningly sweet that it made Serafina want to scream her throat out.

She knew that Rowena was trying to trick him, but she didn't understand her plan. And what was Braeden thinking? Why was he doing this? He had no idea who this girl was! Was he going to dance hand in hand with every creature that slithered in out of the forest in a nice dress and fancy hair? And with the brace on his leg, his dancing was going to be a painful, clumsy affair at best.

But before Serafina knew it, the two of them faced each other in a ceremonial fashion. As was the custom, Braeden put his white-gloved hands behind him and bowed deeply to his dance partner. When it was her turn, his lady did a slow, deep curtsy to him, with one leg out in front of her, her head bowed, and her arms elevated beside her like the wings of a graceful swan. *What on earth!* Serafina thought.

And then the two dance partners came together, holding each other in a formal and decorous fashion. Their dancing started out slow and easy, synchronized with the gentle overture of the orchestra's music and the movement of the other dancers, but when the waltz rose up to its full tempo, they began to move more swiftly, turn and turn and turn and dip, sweeping across the dance floor with astounding grace and beauty.

It made Serafina's heart sink to watch it.

She had no idea Braeden knew how to dance like that. What amazed her even more was that he could move so smoothly and effortlessly with the brace on his leg. He normally dragged it along behind him, barely able to walk, but here he was gliding with the music of the waltz, like his feet were barely touching the floor.

Then Serafina looked down at his feet.

It was difficult to detect, even for her narrowed, suspicious eyes, but when she looked very carefully, she could see an unnatural glint beneath his feet. He wasn't dancing. The sorceress was pulling him along, literally sweeping him off his feet with her power and deceit. But poor Braeden had no idea. He was smiling, euphoric, happy to be dancing, moving with such strength and athleticism on legs that had been weak and pathetic for so long.

Serafina looked around at the other dancers and the people watching to see if any of them could see the sorceress's work.

Mrs. Vanderbilt looked onto the dancing couple with a smile on her face.

Others, too, seemed to be pleased to see the two young dancers enjoying themselves. It was only Mr. Vanderbilt who appeared to be studying his nephew and his dancing partner with a careful eye. There was neither happiness nor rejection in his expression, but a steady evaluation of what he was seeing, as if he sensed that something wasn't quite right.

"It's because she's a sorceress!" Serafina screamed.

"Shush, kitty!" Rowena whispered as she and Braeden danced, knowing that only Serafina would hear her through the sound of the music.

A few moments later, when the music died down and the

dance was over, Braeden and his lady partner stood apart and faced each other once more. Braeden bowed and his lady curtsied, just as they had done before. Then Braeden presented his right arm, his lady took it, and they walked off the floor.

"Did you enjoy the dance?" Braeden asked her.

"Oh, yes, very much so. And you?"

"Yes, my leg is feeling much better than it has in a long time," Braeden said, his voice light and happy.

Serafina followed them up the steps to the promenade that encircled the Winter Garden. The whole area was crowded with mingling guests.

It was customary for the gentleman to escort his dancing partner back to her family or friends, but Braeden did not appear to know where to take her.

"I am here alone," his lady partner said softly.

"She doesn't have any friends," Serafina interjected, "and you definitely don't want to meet her family!"

"I see," Braeden said uncertainly. "Would you like to partake of refreshment in the Banquet Hall?"

"Yes, that would be delightful," she said, and they began walking in that direction.

"Pardon me for asking," Braeden said, "but have you been to the house on a previous occasion? Have I met you before?"

"Yes, I believe we have met," she said mysteriously.

Braeden's expression changed. He leaned toward her and whispered, "Are you a catamount? Are you a friend of Waysa's?"

When the girl did not immediately reply, Braeden asked, "Are you related to Serafina?"

Then he looked down at her feet, knowing that some catamounts had four toes on each foot even when they were in human form. Rowena's feet were covered by her glittering shoes, but at that moment, Serafina began to realize just how carefully Rowena had planned this out. *From head to toe, she's all a trap. She's luring him right in.*

"I came to the ball tonight to speak with you, Braeden," she said, her voice gentle and calm, but filled with just enough urgency to give it an edge.

"With me?" Braeden asked in surprise.

"Perhaps we could go someplace more private," Rowena said.

"Don't fall for her tricks, Braeden!" Serafina shouted at him, wondering if she could swirl her arms and start up a great wind inside the house to send Rowena's hair a-flying and knock her tumbling down the stairs to the basement.

"All right," Braeden said calmly. "Come this way . . ."

Rowena betrayed a crooked smile as she followed Braeden through the Banquet Hall. The room was full of guests, many of them eating and drinking as they enjoyed the lively festivities of the ball.

Serafina looked back through the archway toward the Winter Garden hoping to catch a glimpse of Mr. Vanderbilt watching Braeden and Rowena from a distance, but she couldn't see him.

"What are you doing, Braeden?" Serafina asked. He seemed determined to slip away from the ball and get her alone. It was very unlike him.

Serafina followed the two of them into the Bachelor's Wing and down the dark and empty passage.

"Perhaps we could go in here," Braeden suggested, gesturing toward the Gun Room, with its cabinets full of shotguns, hunting rifles, and other weapons. As was customary for a gentleman, Braeden entered the dark room first to find and turn on the light.

"Rowena, I'm warning you, whatever you're doing, don't do it," Serafina said fiercely. "I mean it. Stop it."

But Rowena ignored her.

"When you were attacked, I helped you!" Serafina reminded her.

"Oh, don't fool yourself," Rowena whispered. "We both know that you're not all cotton balls and kitten paws. You helped me because it was the smart thing to do."

"But what are you doing here?" Serafina demanded. "Leave Braeden alone!"

"My plan should be clear to you now," Rowena said impatiently.

"Pardon me?" Braeden said, looking back at Rowena in confusion.

"I was just saying that Biltmore must be a wonderful place to live," Rowena said more loudly, slipping back into her Southern accent as she stepped into the room with Braeden. Serafina followed her into the room.

"The electric lamp isn't working for some reason, so I lit some of the candles," Braeden explained.

Serafina was surprised when Braeden closed the door. It was highly improper for a young gentleman to lead a girl away from a formal ball into a dark, private room and actually shut the door.

The sights and sounds of the grand ball disappeared. The Gun Room was a small and quiet place, the candlelight flickering on the dark woodwork all around and the glass cases filled with guns. Serafina noticed a table with a display of finely crafted hunting knives. She thought it was odd that one of the knives was missing. Mounted animal heads hung on the hunter-green walls, and there was a small, rustic fireplace in the corner, glowing soft and warm with embers.

"We can talk here," Braeden said.

As Rowena turned to him, it seemed as if she had lured Braeden exactly to where she wanted him. She gazed into his eyes and moved closer to him.

"The truth is," she said in a soft and vulnerable voice, "I need your help."

She spoke the words with the most gentle, sweetest tone, and Serafina thought, *That's it, we're done for! We're lost! She's tricked him, we're all dead for sure!*

Braeden looked at Rowena and said, "I'm not going to help you," as he pressed the point of a wickedly long, sharp hunting knife against the satin brocade of her dress, just where he could push it straight into her side. "I know who you are."

"Oh dear, you have a knife . . ." Rowena said in her sweet Charleston accent, raising her hands, feigning dismay and confusion as she slowly backed up. "I don't understand. What's happening?"

"I know who you are, Rowena," Braeden said, holding the knife out in front of him, his hand trembling and his eyes wide with the fear of facing down a sorceress who could throw a spell at him at any moment.

"Braeden, listen to me," Rowena said in her normal voice.

"You can wear as many masks as you want, Rowena, but you're always a monster underneath."

"I'm not going to hurt you . . ." Rowena said, trying to calm him.

"That's just what the cloak says!" Braeden shouted at her, pressing toward her with the knife in sudden panic, filled with more fear and agitation than Serafina had ever seen in him.

"Don't kill her, Braeden, we need her!" Serafina shouted, but he couldn't hear her.

"Please let me explain," Rowena said, moving away from him as he pushed forward.

"Then spit it out," he said, shaking the knife at her. "What are you doing here? What do you want?"

"Tell him the truth or he's going to stab you!" Serafina shouted frantically.

"I came to tell you that my father is back and he's going to kill you and your family," Rowena said.

Serafina sucked in a breath of surprise. That definitely wasn't the calm and reassuring explanation she was expecting.

But then Rowena's words begin to sink into Serafina's mind. She'd had her suspicions, but now she knew for sure: Uriah had come back. The storm-creech she'd seen in the forest had been him, his talons and scaly skin the remnants of his old owl form. The unhealed wounds across his face had been inflicted by her own panther claws. Uriah was the one bringing the storms, flooding the rivers, and tearing away the trees. He had come to wreak his vengeance on Biltmore.

"This is how you're trying to win my trust?" Braeden said. "By telling me that you and your father are going to kill me?"

"I'm not going to wage my father's war anymore," Rowena said, her voice sharp. "I'm tired of the fighting and the blood, the endless cycle of hate and retribution."

"Another lie," Braeden said.

"I know that I tricked you, I attacked you, I harmed you in so many ways, but I'm through with all that."

As Serafina listened to Rowena's words, everything began to make so much more sense. Uriah had been the one who had inflicted the terrible wounds on Rowena the night Waysa found her and helped her. Uriah had punished Rowena for failing to kill her on the Loggia and for losing the Black Cloak to their enemies. He was the one Rowena was hiding from in the bog, who had been threatening her, attacking her, the one she'd been screaming at the first time Serafina came to her in spirit form. Serafina couldn't even imagine what Rowena had been going through all this time. The girl had become a powerful sorceress in her own right, but it was clear that her father had been twisting her heart and her body for many years. He had a terrible grip on her, and probably always had. Serafina couldn't even imagine her own pa doing that. It was threat, it was hurt, it was a thousand things, but it was not love.

"Then why have you come?" Braeden demanded.

"I need the Black Cloak," Rowena said.

"I don't have it," Braeden spat back.

What surprised Serafina wasn't Rowena's trickery or Braeden's fierceness, but the fact that Rowena hadn't thrown a potion, cast a spell, or tried to outright kill him. So far, she had not only refrained from attacking him, she had told him the truth. This was the weariness, the loneliness, that Serafina had seen in her before. *Much has changed,* Rowena had said. Serafina realized now that she'd been talking about herself.

"You said that you don't want to hurt anyone," Braeden said. "But you want the Black Cloak. That doesn't make sense."

"I'm trying to help you, Braeden," Rowena said, and even to Serafina's suspicious ear it sounded strangely sincere. Rowena seemed to truly care for him.

"Help me?" Braeden snapped at her in disgust. "You killed Serafina!"

Braeden screamed the words with such powerful emotion that it broke Serafina's heart. All the fighting and deception between them, but *this* was the offense that he could not forgive. *You killed Serafina.* The words were so final, so devastating to him. She realized now how deeply his heart had been damaged.

For as long as she had known him, he had always been the trusting one. He had defended his friend Mr. Thorne. He had trusted Lady Rowena when she first came to Biltmore. He had always been the person to open his arms to someone new.

And Serafina knew that she had always been the suspicious one, the one who *didn't* trust people. She had suspected Mr. Vanderbilt was the Man in the Black Cloak because of the type of shoes he wore. She had suspected the footman Mr. Pratt, and the coachman Mr. Crankshod, and the detective Mr. Grathan, and all the others. She was always hunting for the rat.

But now she realized that she had changed, too, maybe just as much as Braeden had, but in the opposite direction. She could feel herself starting to listen to Rowena, wanting to believe what she was saying. She had seen Rowena that first night in the forest walking alone by the river, her spirit so changed. And she had heard the fear in the girl's voice when she shouted out into the darkened forest. And she had seen Rowena fighting off her father's attacks, screaming at him in savage defiance.

Could all of this have been an elaborate trick designed to gain her trust? Serafina knew it could be, but it felt like Rowena was telling the truth.

But more than all that, Serafina knew that it didn't matter how scared she was, how uncertain or suspicious: she needed Rowena. If Rowena didn't succeed tonight, Uriah was going to kill Braeden. That much was certain.

But here was Braeden on the opposite side of it. He *hated* Rowena. Rowena had harmed him, scarred him, and *killed* his friend.

Serafina tried to think. What could she do? How could she talk to Braeden? How could she show him that she was here?

She looked around the softly lit room, the guns in the glass cases, the sizzling embers and gray ashes in the fireplace, the upholstered chairs and the wooden table, and the Persian rug on the floor. She could see Braeden and Rowena's reflection in the cases, but she couldn't see her own. She was just a glint of light in the glass.

Then she looked at the fireplace again.

Ashes to ashes, she thought as an idea sprang into her mind.

"Rowena, listen to me," she said, "we need to get Braeden's attention. Get him over to the fireplace."

Rowena didn't seem to understand and didn't respond.

"Do what I say," Serafina demanded. "He's never going to listen to you alone, not like this. You need my help."

As she watched Rowena pause and think it through, she

realized that even the sorceress had to be careful about whom she trusted.

"Braeden," Rowena said finally. "I need to show you something by the fireplace."

"Good, that's perfect . . ." Serafina encouraged her. "Just get him over there and I'll do the rest."

"No!" Braeden said, pointing the knife at her.

"It's about Serafina," Rowena said.

"What about her?"

"Come over to the fireplace and I'll show you."

"I'm not going to do what you say," Braeden said.

"You've got to convince him," Serafina told her.

"He's not going to do it," Rowena said.

"Who are you talking to?" Braeden asked her.

"Find a way," Serafina said. "Act harmless. Lay on the floor!"

"I'm not stupid," Rowena said. "I'm not doing that!"

"You're not doing what?" Braeden demanded.

"Get on the floor!" Serafina said again. "If I'm going to trust you, you need to trust me."

"Fine!" Rowena snapped resentfully, but then she spoke to Braeden in a softer, gentler tone. "Braeden, I understand that you're frightened of me. I would be, too, if I were you. So let me do this. I will not resist you. Hold your knife to me so that I cannot harm you."

Watching the sorceress carefully, Braeden moved the knife toward her. Rowena slowly lowered herself and lay flat on her back in front of the fireplace. Braeden followed her down, kneeling beside her, and pressed the blade against her throat.

"Your move, cat," Rowena said.

"What are you saying?" Braeden asked.

"Now, ask him to blow into the ashes," Serafina said.

"Braeden," Rowena said, "I need to show you something that I know is important to you. I will not move in any way. I want you to blow into the ashes of the fireplace as hard as you can."

"Who are you talking to?" Braeden asked.

"I'll show you," Rowena said.

Braeden stared at her malevolently, then finally sucked in a deep breath, and blew into the ashes. The ashes and the glowing embers went flying up in a great, swirling cloud into the room.

"That's perfect!" Serafina cheered.

As the embers and ashes floated down, she moved her hands back and forth through the air, guiding the way they fell. Filling her lungs, she blew here and she blew there, bringing new life to the glow of the embers and pushing the ashes up into curling, floating motion, until they all began to fall into tiny lines onto the hardwood floor.

"What's happening?" Braeden asked, his voice trembling with the mystery of what he was seeing.

Serafina guided the ashes and embers down until they fell together into small, scratchy, glowing lines:

ITSME

"What is that?" Braeden asked in fascination. "Does it spell something?"

He leaned toward the glowing ashes and tried to make out

the rough letters in the faint, flickering light of the candles.

"I . . . T . . . S . . . M . . . E . . ." Braeden said as he deciphered the letters one by one. "It says . . . *It's me* . . . But who is it? Who's *me*?"

"Well, you definitely have his attention now," Rowena said as she sat up.

"Who are you talking to?" Braeden asked again.

"The answer to all your questions is the same, Braeden."

"What?" Braeden asked in frustration.

"It's Serafina," Rowena said.

"What do you mean it's Serafina?"

"Serafina is here."

"Here?"

"She's here now, in this room with us."

"You're lying!" Braeden said. "You're a nasty liar!" Angry and disgusted, Braeden blew the ashes away contemptuously, as if to say, *I don't believe a word of this!*

The ashes and the flaring embers swirled up into the air and floated around the room. Over the next few moments they should have gone dark and fallen randomly onto the floor and furniture, but Serafina moved her hands and blew with her lungs and brought them down right back on the floor where they had been before, glowing with new life.

TRUSTHER

Braeden gazed in wonderment at the letters, but then he caught himself.

"Oh, stop it!" he said. "This is just more of your tricks!"

"It's the cat," Rowena said flatly.

"No, it isn't. Serafina's dead. I buried her myself."

"I thought she was, too, but we were both wrong. She's not totally dead. Serafina's spirit is in this very room."

"Just stop this!" Braeden screamed at her, his voice shaking with indignation as the two of them got to their feet and faced each other. "You're always lying!"

"But she's here . . ." Rowena said.

"How do I know that you're not lying to me like you have so many times before? If she's truly here, then prove it to me."

"Rowena," Serafina said. "Tell him to ask you something that only Serafina would know."

When Rowena said these words, Braeden's expression changed. He thought for several seconds, then narrowed his eyes suspiciously at her.

"What were the first words I ever spoke to Serafina?"

Serafina thought back. What were the first words he'd ever said to her? She tried to think. It was the morning after she'd seen the Black Cloak for the first time. She had just crept upstairs into the daylight . . .

"'Are you lost?'" Serafina said. "That's what he said."

"'Are you lost?'" Rowena said.

Braeden's eyes widened in surprise; for a moment he almost believed her. But then he remembered who he was dealing with and became distrustful and angry again.

"It's a trick," he said. "I'll do another. The second time I saw Serafina, I came upon Mr. Crankshod shaking the living daylights out of her. What did we pretend she was?"

Serafina smiled. This one was easy. "A shoeshine girl."

"We pretended I was the shoeshine girl," Rowena said, not just repeating Serafina's words, but taking on the exact sound of her voice, allowing Serafina's spirit to speak through her.

Hearing Serafina's voice, Braeden gazed around the room in shocked amazement.

"Serafina is in this room at this very moment," Rowena said to him softly in her own voice. "She arranged those letters in the ash. She's asking you to trust me."

"But how are you able to do this?" Braeden asked.

"A wise man once said, *That which does not destroy us makes us stronger.*"

"I don't understand," Braeden said.

"After you and the two cats struck me down during the battle for the Twisted Staff, it took time, but I came back, and I was stronger than ever. I'm not just a sorceress now, I'm a *necromancer.*"

"What is that?"

"I can sometimes speak to the spirits of the dead and the in-between."

Braeden stared at her in dread, clearly not sure if he should believe her. "I want to do another test," he said. This time he spoke to the room, like people do when they speak to ghosts at a séance. "Serafina . . . If you're here . . . I once gave you a gift, long and red . . ."

Serafina thought back.

A gift, long and red . . .

What had he given her?

"The red dress!" Serafina said excitedly, and Rowena repeated it in her voice.

"This is amazing . . ." Braeden said, spellbound by the sound of Serafina's voice. "And when was the first time you wore it?"

"I used it to trap the Man in the Black Cloak," Serafina said, and Rowena repeated the words with haunting emotion. "The morning I brought the children back home, I was standing at the forest's edge, with Gidean on one side and my mother in lion form on the other. I saw you up on your horse as you gathered a search party to look for me."

"And you looked so fierce and beautiful standing there at the edge of the forest in your torn dress . . ." Braeden remembered.

Hearing her friend's words, and feeling the ache of his heart in her own, Serafina began to cry.

"Oh, please. You're not beautiful, you're a cat!" Rowena snapped. "He likes cats. That's all it is! Now do get hold of yourself or this whole thing isn't going to work!"

Serafina wiped her eyes and toughened herself, knowing that Rowena was right.

"Look," Serafina said to Rowena sharply. "If I ask Braeden to give you the Black Cloak, what are you going to do with it? What is your plan?"

"You may be fast with your claws, but you sure are slow with the rest of it," Rowena said in a scathing tone. "Have you been following along at all?"

"Braeden, it is truly me," Serafina said, her voice as steady and serious as she could make it, and Rowena repeated the words in the exact same way.

"But where are you, Serafina?" Braeden asked.

"My body is in the grave where you buried me, but my spirit is here with you. I've been with you for these past few nights."

"I thought I could feel you," Braeden said, his voice quivering with recognition.

"You were sitting on the bench on the Library Terrace."

"That's right!" he said, nodding. "That's when it started."

"But I have to tell you, my time is short, a night or two at most, so we have to hurry."

"A night or two before what?" Braeden asked.

Serafina didn't want to answer or even think about his question, so she pressed on the best she could. "Uriah is alive and he wants to kill you. That much is true and certain, but Rowena says she's going to help us."

"But how?" Braeden asked.

"We need the cloak," Serafina said.

"But, Serafina . . ." Braeden begged her. "It's a horrible thing. It's too dangerous! We can't—"

"I know," Serafina said, remembering not just the cloak's sinister powers, but the terrifying fragments of darkness that shot from the folds of the torn fabric.

"What is Rowena going to do with the cloak?" Braeden asked.

Serafina shifted her attention back to Rowena.

"Your move, sorceress," she said. "Before we give you the cloak, tell us what you're going to do with it."

"There are no words to describe what I plan to do, and if I tried to explain it, it would only frighten you," Rowena said.

"Frighten us?" Braeden and Serafina said in alarm at the same time.

"Which of us?" Serafina asked.

"Both," Rowena said. "I cannot explain it in words. I will show you in person. I give you my word that I will not hurt either of you." Here she looked at Braeden. "If you wish, the cloak will never be out of your sight or possession. And I will show you what I'm doing for as long as you wish to watch. But I warn you: you'll not want to watch."

"You're speaking in riddles," Braeden said, staring at her in suspicion and confusion.

"No, I'm speaking as clearly as I can, but the only way for you to understand is to see it."

As she fixed her eyes on Rowena, Serafina tried to think it through. What was the sorceress up to? If she wanted to attack Braeden, she could have already done it. Serafina wished she had some other path she could follow, but she couldn't see it.

"We're going to have to trust her, Braeden," Serafina said, and Rowena repeated the words in Serafina's voice.

"So if we do this," Braeden said, "when are we going to do it?"

"We can't do it here, not right now," Serafina said, and Rowena repeated it. "We've been in this room too long. Your aunt and uncle are going to be wondering where you are and come looking for you. You need to get back to the ball, at least for a little while."

Braeden nodded, knowing she was right. "But when will we be back together again?" he asked, clearly alarmed at the idea of separating from her.

"We'll meet tonight, very soon," Serafina said. "Did you put the cloak back where it was?"

"No," Braeden said. "I moved it to a different spot."

"Good," she said. "To be safe, don't tell Rowena or me where it is. After the ball tonight, when the clock chimes half past one, go collect it and bring it to the place where the three friends once stood beside the stone hunter. Do you know the place I mean?"

"I know it," Braeden said, nodding his head. "Are you sure about this, Serafina?"

"No I am not, but it seems like it's our only path. Be careful."

"And you be careful, too," he said.

With this, Braeden slipped through the concealed door that led into the Smoking Room, and then on through the next concealed door into the Billiard Room. Serafina followed him just long enough to see him walk out into the main corridor and rejoin his aunt and uncle at the ball.

When she returned to Rowena in the Gun Room, she said, "Well, we did it. We convinced him."

"It seems we did," Rowena agreed with satisfaction.

"Now, there's just one more person we need to convince, and he's not going to be so easy."

"Oh, no, we don't need him!"

"He saved your life!"

"He's still a cat! There's no getting around that!" Rowena shot back, feigning annoyance, but her voice betrayed the nervous uncertainty of meeting someone she owed a debt that she knew she could not repay.

"We include him or it's off," Serafina said fiercely.

"You're turning into quite a stubborn little grimalkin," Rowena said.

"Better stubborn than dead," Serafina retorted.

"You're already dead."

"I thought we agreed I wasn't totally dead quite yet."

"My characterization of you being dead was less a comment on your current state than on your future prospects."

"Enough of that," Serafina said in annoyance. "Let's go find him."

A short time later that same night, after Rowena had shifted back to her normal appearance, Serafina guided her to the dell of ferns where she and Waysa sometimes rested. He wasn't there, or in the next place they checked, but they kept looking.

She finally spotted her friend standing in human form gazing at a rocky gully in the forest where a powerful gush of water had rushed through, ripping at the earth and trees, tearing away everything in its path. The flooding was getting worse each night.

Serafina led Rowena to an area of open, rocky ground out of sight from Waysa.

"I don't know how he's going to respond when I approach

him," Rowena said. "He may be angry or violent. He helped me when I was wounded, but he's not going to trust me now."

"You can't approach him. He's a catamount. You have to get him to approach you," Serafina said. "Let him know you're here, from this distance, but don't scare him off."

"How do I do that?" Rowena asked.

Serafina knew that Waysa's reflexes were incredibly strong, that if they approached or surprised him in any way, his first instinct would be to fight or flee. That was how he'd survived so long. She needed to get his attention in a way to get him to think before he reacted.

"Make the sound of a blackbird and then wait," Serafina said.

"But your blackbirds here don't come out at night."

"Exactly. When Waysa and I are in human form in the daytime forest, the blackbird's click is one of the secret calls we use, so if he hears it at night, he'll not know what to make of it."

Rowena nodded, then made the clicking sound of a blackbird.

Within a few seconds, Waysa began moving toward them through the forest. He stopped at the edge of the trees when he saw Rowena standing alone out in the middle of the open area.

"Good. Now stay perfectly still," Serafina whispered to Rowena. "No threatening movements."

Doing exactly what Serafina said, Rowena did not move.

Waysa studied her from a distance, and Rowena studied

him, the two of them gauging whether they could trust the other. It was as if the two of them were looking for the marks of their shared past, the battles they had fought against each other, and the care he had shown her.

"You've come back," he said warily to her from his position in the trees.

"Talk to him, convince him," Serafina said.

Rowena slowly nodded to Waysa. "Yes," she said quietly. "I came to thank you for what you did."

Waysa did not move or speak. He just watched her.

"No one has ever helped me like that before," Rowena said, and then paused.

After a long time, Waysa finally emerged from the trees. He walked slowly toward her until he stood some twenty feet away.

"Why did you save me, Waysa?" Rowena asked gently, her voice soft and uncertain.

Waysa frowned at the question, looked at the ground to collect his thoughts, and then looked back at her. "I do not wish to get lost," he said.

"What do you mean?" she asked him.

"I will destroy the conjurer and make sure those I love are safe, but then I will cleanse myself of blood and fight no more. My heart is on a journey from where it lives. But I must remember my way home."

Rowena stared at Waysa, seeming to understand what he was saying. "I've come here tonight to help you," she said finally. "And to ask for your help once more."

"I've already helped you," Waysa said, as if, despite what

he had just said, there was still a part of him that regretted the foolishness of giving aid to his sworn enemy.

"I know you helped me," Rowena said, "and you have no reason to trust me, but I have a plan to help your friends."

"What are you talking about?" Waysa said, his eyes narrowing.

"Tell him what I told you," Serafina said to Rowena.

"If you need me, winter, spring, or fall, come where what you climbed is floor, and rain is wall," Rowena said. It was the riddle that Waysa had written to Serafina so that she could find him.

"Where did you get those words?" Waysa asked, stepping toward her.

"This is good," Serafina said.

Waysa stared at Rowena, his brown eyes blazing with intensity. He was ready to fight her if he had to, but there was curiosity in his expression as well.

"I want you to tell me. Where did you get those words?" Waysa pressed her again. "And the clicking sound you made . . ."

"I will explain why I've come, and how I know these things," Rowena said. "But first, I want to tell you what I have seen in the past of your people."

"What are you talking about?" Waysa asked again.

"Long ago, many members of your tribe were driven by force away from their homes to the barren lands in the west, but a few stayed behind in these mountains, unwilling to leave their homeland. And you came into this world from them."

"You speak my grandmother's truth," Waysa said, "but how do you know this?"

"When you were taking care of me, I used my powers to look into your heart, to see your past and the past of your people. I know that my father killed your mother, your father, your brothers—"

"And my sister," Waysa said bitterly.

"And your sister," Rowena said, nodding. "I saw it all. I *felt* it all, for it is cut deep into the print of time. And once you see something with your own eyes, once you *feel* something, it becomes part of you. But my father didn't just kill *your* family. He killed many of the catamounts in your tribe. You may be the only one of your clan who survived. But you must remember what your grandmother taught you about injury and rebirth. It is the way of our kind—the catamounts and the owls and the other shifters—that when we are severely injured, we fight through it, we suffer, but we come back stronger than we were before, changed, but more powerful . . . more who we are."

"Yes, I understand . . ." Waysa said, as he moved closer to her. They were just a few feet from each other now.

"You saw the peregrine falcon strike me from the sky," Rowena continued. "I was close to death, but I did not die. You saw what was left of me after my father punished me for losing the Black Cloak to our enemies. Again, I was close to death, but I did not die. With each and every wound, every moment of pain, every night of suffering, I got stronger inside. I *changed.* Injury and rebirth, struggle and ascendance, these are the cycles of our kin. What I've been trying to say is that my powers have changed, Waysa. And my soul has changed as well. I am becoming more of who I am."

Waysa was listening to everything she said. "My grandmother called it *ta-li-ne u-de-nv*, second birth."

"Yes, that's it," Rowena said.

"But you spoke of new powers . . ."

"I can see visions of the past, and I have the power to hear and speak."

"You mean with those who have gone on—"

"—and those who are in between."

"You're talking about Serafina . . ." Waysa whispered in astonishment. "Her *a-da-nv-do* . . . She's lingering . . ."

Rowena nodded very slowly. "Now you're truly beginning to understand."

"Where is she?" Waysa said. Suddenly, there was so much hope in his eyes.

"Do not worry, she is close, here with us," Rowena said softly.

"She's here with us now?" Waysa asked in surprise, looking around them. Unlike Braeden, who had resisted the idea, Waysa didn't seem to doubt that it was possible that spirits existed.

"Serafina and I have spoken with Braeden, and the three of us need your help," Rowena said.

"Tell me what I need to do," Waysa said.

Rowena hesitated.

"Tell him what I said or it's off," Serafina demanded.

"Understand that your instructions come from Serafina, not from me," Rowena said. "She asked that you go to Biltmore tonight and join Braeden. Watch over him. Protect him from my father. But more than anything, protect him from me. If I begin to do anything at all that might harm him or you, then you are to immediately claw my eyes out."

Waysa smiled. "That sounds like the Serafina I know."

"Those are her words," Rowena said.

"I'll do it," Waysa said.

"Good, he's with us," Serafina said in relief.

"Serafina says she's happy to hear that," Rowena said.

"You're speaking to her now?" Waysa looked up excitedly. "Can you tell her something for me?"

"She can already hear you," Rowena said.

Waysa looked around up into the sky where he imagined an *a-da-nv-do* might float.

"No matter what happens, Serafina, you stay fierce, my friend, you stay bold! You hear me?"

As tears welled up in her eyes, Serafina said, "Tell him that I hear him."

But wanting to say more, she moved her hand just so, and a gentle breeze of air blew through Waysa's long dark hair, lifting it for just a moment, then letting it drop down again. *I hear you.*

36

A few hours later, Serafina sat and waited in the darkness on Biltmore's front steps. The summer ball had ended. The Vanderbilts and all the guests who were staying in the house had gone up to their rooms to bed. The others had departed in their carriages. The servants had cleared the tables, and the musicians had packed up their cases and gone home. The house was dark and quiet now. Everything seemed so different from before.

But in her heart, she felt a new sense of contentment. She had finally managed to talk to Braeden and Waysa, and she had seen the smiles on their faces when they came to understand that she was still here. She realized there were many more challenges ahead, and she knew full well that some of them might be insurmountable, at least for her, but at least they were climbing together now. At least they were on the same side, come what may, and as long as that was true, she could keep going wherever she had to go.

Braeden emerged from the house, slipping quietly out the front doors and closing them gently behind him, carrying an old leather knapsack slung over his shoulder. By the size and shape of it, she thought he must have the cloak inside. Braeden stood alone in the darkness on the front terrace, gazing out as if he wasn't sure if he should proceed.

Serafina was relieved that he'd come like they'd agreed, but she felt qualmish in her stomach. It was a grave and dangerous plan to ask him to trust Rowena and give her the Black Cloak. There were a thousand ways it could go wrong. But Serafina knew that she'd run out of time. "Get the cloak tonight or I'll kill the boy myself!" Uriah had blared at Rowena when he attacked her in the bog. Rowena had been holding her father back by telling him that if he killed Braeden he'd never find the hidden cloak, but Rowena's threat had run dry now. Uriah had grown impatient. There was no doubt in Serafina's mind that, one way or another, Uriah was coming for Braeden.

She wished she could talk to Braeden here and now, but without Rowena she couldn't. All she could do was follow him.

Braeden sighed in discouragement when he gazed across the long expanse of the Esplanade and up toward Diana Hill in the distance, where she had asked him to meet her. Serafina knew what he was thinking. Before he'd been injured, he had climbed that hill easily. He'd had fun doing it. But with his bad leg, it was going to be a long way to the top. She wished she had picked an easier spot for him to reach.

Braeden's hands trembled as he tried to fix and adjust the metal brace on his leg. It appeared that one of the metal brackets had broken, making it even more difficult for him to walk.

Pulling in a deep breath, Braeden began his journey. He made his way along the length of the Esplanade, then started the climb up Diana Hill. He breathed heavily and his pace slowed as he trudged, one step at a time, dragging his bad leg behind him.

Then the dark shape of a catamount emerged from the forest.

"Waysa!" Braeden said in surprise. "What are you doing here?" And then he realized. "Serafina asked you to come . . ."

Serafina smiled, glad that Braeden had figured it out so quickly.

Waysa walked in lion form over to Braeden's side, and in a gesture of friendship, hunched down.

"Thank you," Braeden said appreciatively, and climbed onto his back.

Waysa leapt forward with a great bounding leap and ran. Braeden clung to the lion's back as Waysa sprinted straight up the slope of the hill, the cat's powerful legs nothing but a blur.

Now that's the way to travel, Serafina thought, jealous of her friends. She broke into a run in pursuit.

When a breeze stirred, she felt herself getting light on her feet. There was a part of her that thought she might be able to turn into wind the way she had turned into water the night

Braeden put on the cloak, but she was too worried that it would only hasten her fade.

She missed running as a panther, racing Waysa through the forest. But she was happy to see her friends together again, and to be with them, at least in spirit.

With the Black Cloak strapped into Braeden's knapsack as he rode on Waysa's back, and her running along behind, the three of them made their way toward Rowena's lair deep in the forest bog.

A haze of white feathery clouds shrouded the glowing moon as it slowly set and disappeared behind the western mountains. As the darkest shadows of the night fell through the forest trees, Serafina crept with Waysa and Braeden into Rowena's encampment.

The small habitation had been damaged by Uriah's attack a few nights before, and many of the surrounding trees had been destroyed, a grim reminder of why the four of them were there.

The sorceress emerged from the ravaged remnants of her lair wearing the dark hood and robes of her ancient druid kin.

Waysa waited with claws out just a few feet away, as Braeden stepped toward her.

"We've come as you asked," Braeden said. "So what do we do now?"

"You can watch everything I do, but you'll need to give me the cloak . . ." Rowena said.

"What are you going to do with it?" Braeden asked, stepping back from her. "How do we know this is what Serafina wants us to do?"

"Tell him that chicken and no grits is my favorite food," Serafina said, "and that raspberry spoon bread is his."

When Rowena repeated the words, Braeden said, "But tell me what you're going to do with it."

"I am going to try to repair it," Rowena said.

"Repair it?" Braeden asked in confusion. "Are you going to give the cloak to your father?"

"That would be the end of us all," Rowena said.

"Then what? What will happen when you repair it?"

"If all goes well, then it will begin to function the way it was designed."

"Which means what?" Braeden asked. "You're going to start sucking in people's souls and stealing their powers for yourself?"

As Rowena and Braeden talked, a dark and foreboding fear soaked slowly into Serafina. She was beginning to see Rowena's plan.

"When the cloak was torn during the battle on the Loggia, Serafina was splintered out into the world along with the black fragments," Rowena said. "They are the remnants of the cloak's innermost darkness. If I can repair the cloak properly, then it may pull those remnants and Serafina's soul back into its black folds."

"I don't understand, what do you mean *may*?" Braeden asked. "Aren't you sure?"

"No, I'm not," Rowena said. "The cloak is severely damaged."

"And if it doesn't work, what happens to Serafina?"

"If I fail," Rowena said, "I suspect that her spirit will disappear and she'll be lost forever."

"But if you succeed, it's even worse!" Braeden said. "Her soul will be trapped in the cloak."

"Yes," Rowena said.

The frightening image of Clara Brahms's stricken face flashed through Serafina's mind. The girl in the yellow dress had screamed in horror when the cloak absorbed her. Serafina didn't want to do this. She *definitely* didn't want to do this. She hated this plan. She had been running and fighting, biting and clawing, all this time to escape the Black Cloak, to rescue people from it, to protect people from it, to defeat it. There was no way she was going to let herself get sucked into it. She couldn't imagine anything worse than being trapped inside the Black Cloak. She'd rather die. She immediately started trying to figure out how she could communicate with Braeden and Waysa, how she could stop this.

"But if Serafina's spirit gets pulled back into the Black Cloak, then what's going to happen?" Braeden asked, his voice trembling with the same fear that was enveloping Serafina.

"I warned you about this," Rowena said harshly. "I told you this was going to frighten you. You have to trust me."

"But what's going to happen next?" Serafina asked Rowena. "That's what we need to know. Are you going to keep the cloak for yourself? Are you going to steal my strengths and capabilities? Or are you going to give the cloak back to your father? Do you think that will satisfy him and he'll leave you alone? Do you think that will win back his approval? With the cloak, you'll have everything! You'll have all the power and all the choices!"

Rowena suddenly hissed like an owl and turned away, clicking her throat in disgust. "It's impossible to explain it to you," she said again.

"Explain what?" Braeden asked in confusion, not realizing that Rowena was talking to Serafina.

"You keep saying that, Rowena!" Serafina shouted at her. "But you have to explain it, or we're not going to do it! Swear to me that you're not going to hurt Braeden."

"Are you talking to Serafina?" Braeden asked in confusion. "What is she saying?"

"Nothing of consequence," Rowena muttered and began to walk away, the angry flick of her hand casting a blast of force tearing through the forest and snapping branches. Waysa moved rapidly between Rowena and Braeden, ready to lunge at the sorceress.

Bitter-tasting bile rose up in Serafina's throat. This whole thing was beginning to feel like a trick. But then she remembered the night in the graveyard long ago. She had lured the

Man in the Black Cloak into a trap. After the battle, she had tried to tear the cloak's fabric with her hands, but the fabric had been far too strong. Then she tried to pierce it with a dagger. But the cloak could not be harmed by a normal blade. That night in the graveyard, she had pierced the cloak on the sharp point of the angel's steel sword. She had cut the cloak to pieces. That was how she had destroyed it. And when she did, it released its magic in a great cataclysm of heat and smoke and haze, and all the victims that had been captured in the cloak were suddenly set free. She remembered seeing Clara Brahms's body lying in the leaves on the ground. When the girl twitched and began to rise, Serafina had feared that she was a zombie rising from the dead, but she wasn't. She was a little girl, freed from the dark folds of the cloak. And Serafina remembered that she had freed her mother the same way that same night.

"You're going to repair the cloak . . ." Serafina said, "but then you're going to destroy it on the angel's sword . . ."

Rowena stopped and turned, relieved that she finally understood. "I do not know if I can succeed, but I am going to try . . ."

"You're going to try what?" Braeden asked, confused and frightened.

Serafina thought about how she had crawled from the grave and had been living in the spirit world, what she could and couldn't do, who she could and couldn't touch, what paths she could and couldn't take. Dust and water and wind, she wasn't long for this world. She thought about Braeden and Waysa fighting for her with all their hearts, and her pa with his deadened soul going through the motions of his life, and her mother who had lost all hope. She thought about Rowena's father, the coming storms, the raging rivers, his lust for vengeance against the Vanderbilts. He would not rest until Biltmore was destroyed. Then she started thinking about everything she'd seen Rowena do, how they'd first met, all the tricks and betrayals, and all the battles they had fought against each other. Rowena had followed many paths, twisting and intertwining, and there were many ways she could turn.

Through all this, Serafina realized that maybe the most difficult thing wasn't to trust your friend, or even your enemy, but to trust yourself. She had to trust that no matter how dark her future became, she was strong enough, that whatever happened, whether she passed away forever or somehow found her way through to the other side, she had to trust herself, trust her own soul, her own wisdom, her own strength, to pass through the darkness and unknown. She had to trust that she could become who she was meant to be.

Her hands were trembling. Her legs were shaking. Even her voice was unsteady when she spoke. "I have one last request," Serafina said to Rowena. "If I agree to do this, I need you to give me your word that no matter what happens to me, you'll protect Braeden and my pa and Waysa and everyone at Biltmore from your father. Give me your word."

Rowena paused. There was no grimace, no smile, but a face as stone and immobile as the angel's face in the graveyard.

Serafina studied her, trying to figure out what she was

thinking. Was she reluctant to give her word? Or was she actually, in a strange way, satisfied with what Serafina was asking her to do? Had this been what she wanted all along, to join them, to have friends that would fight for her, and that she would fight for in return?

But if Serafina died, Rowena would have to defend all of Biltmore from her father. It was not a fight she could win on her own. She could barely hide herself in the bog to escape him. There was no way she could protect everyone at Biltmore. The friendship Rowena sought came with an almost impossible price, but without that friendship, what chance did Rowena have to survive?

"I need your word, Rowena," Serafina said, but even as she pressed, she realized she didn't know what Rowena's word meant. This could all be a trick. But she could see no other choice. "If you don't help me," Serafina pressed her, "what will happen to you, Rowena?"

"I will survive alone," Rowena said.

"You know that's not true. Is that why you came to talk to me at my grave that night? Maybe you'll survive for a little while against your father. Maybe you can keep hiding from him. But will you truly live? If we trust you to help us, then you have to trust us to help you."

Rowena did not reply at first, but after a long moment, she nodded in agreement. "If you don't make it through, I will do everything in my power to protect them. You have my solemn word."

Serafina studied Rowena. She looked at her face, her eyes, the way she moved when she said the words. How do you know when someone's lying to you, or if they will keep their promise?

"What's going on?" Braeden asked. "What have you given your word to do?"

"We are running out of time, cat," Rowena said, ignoring Braeden.

A cold, black fear like nothing Serafina had ever felt before vibrated through her body. The last thing she wanted to do in the world was to get sucked into the Black Cloak, but she knew she had to do it.

"I'm ready," she said. "I trust you, Rowena. Tell Braeden and Waysa what we're going to do."

Serafina, Braeden, and Waysa watched Rowena work. The sorceress sat down in her lair and took the Black Cloak into her lap. The cloak's dark folds roiled and seethed of their own accord when she moved the fabric with her hands, as if she were holding not a garment but a massive, living snake.

She drew out a long, thin needle of bone and began to sew, slowly stitching the tears of the Black Cloak's torn fabric.

"The outside of the cloak is goat's wool woven with the skin of timber rattlesnakes," Rowena said, "so I've used a fine goat's wool thread for the stitchings. But the lining of the cloak, where its most important power lies, is black satin made from the silk of black widow spiders."

Braeden's face wrinkled in revulsion. "Spiders? The Black

Cloak is made from spider silk? How do you get usable silk from a spider?"

"It is very difficult," Rowena admitted as she worked, "but it is possible if you know the spell."

"A *coercion* spell . . ." Braeden grumbled.

"Yes, obviously, coercion is required," Rowena said, annoyed at the accusation. "Black widow spiders aren't the most willing allies, believe me, and their venom is exceedingly unpleasant. But their silk is much stronger than the silk of many other spiders. Spiders can make six different types of silk: strong silk for dangling, sticky silk for catching prey, flat silk for flying in the wind, and the others, each for their purpose. It takes all of the black widow's silks twined together to create the thread we need. I use a coercion spell to make the spiders do what I need them to do, and a twining spell to spin the thread."

"But isn't a spider's silk white or clear?" Braeden asked, appalled by it all, but beguiled by the gruesome details of the process. It seemed to fascinate him that spiders and other animals were part of the cloak's construction.

"It is the twining process that turns the thread black," Rowena said.

As hour after hour went by with Rowena clutching the twisting cloak, Braeden grew restless. Sometimes, he paced back and forth through the muck outside the lair, dragging his braced leg behind him. Waysa just watched and waited, his claws out, his tail flicking impatiently, as if he were more than ready should battle come.

Serafina watched Rowena carefully, determined to not let the sorceress trick her. She had to stay vigilant, but the truth was, she didn't know how or at what moment Rowena might betray her.

Rowena had gone quiet in her work. Her body began to rock back and forth like she was in some sort of trance, the cloak turning and coiling in her hands. But even as she rocked, she kept mumbling and hissing, casting spell after spell as she stitched the torn fabric, rocking and stitching, a witch knitting a dark and wicked curse, the Black Cloak slithering with power beneath her.

Serafina felt her lungs getting tighter, her breaths getting more difficult. As she watched the sorceress, a dark fear grew within her. She pulled her mesmerized eyes away from Rowena and looked out of the lair's damaged door to Braeden and Waysa, but suddenly they were gone. They had disappeared.

Serafina blinked and rubbed her eyes in confusion, then looked again. Braeden and Waysa were still gone.

As she gazed out at the forest, she realized that the trees seemed to be fading before her eyes, as if darkness darker than darkest night were blotting them out in a terrible black fog. It wasn't just her friends who were missing now, but the entire forest.

Serafina looked down at the ground she was standing on. It was gone, nothing but darkness.

She could not feel it.

She could not see it.

Everything was going!

She pulled in a breath. She could no longer smell the plants of the bog. She could no longer hear the insects.

She turned to Rowena in hot panic. All she could see now was the sorceress, her hooded head down, her face shrouded, the Black Cloak glowing and writhing in her lap as she stitched the last tear closed.

Serafina's world went black.

Serafina could not move.

She could not touch or feel.

All she could see around her was a black, swirling darkness, like she was inside a storm of soot.

All she could hear were the winds of moving fabric.

And all she could smell was ash.

It felt as if the whole world had disappeared and she was all that was left, utterly alone now and forever. Everything she had known, everything she had loved, was gone, incinerated by a prison of incessant darkness.

She tried to be brave. She tried to be bold. But she couldn't do it. She screamed in terror. "Rowena!"

"Do not fight it . . ." came a raspy voice.

Confusion flooded into Serafina's mind. Was it the cloak speaking to her?

Serafina screamed and she fought. She would *not* give up. She would *not* stop fighting. She would tear and tear and tear.

She wanted her mother and Braeden and her pa and everyone she loved. She wanted to see moonlight and sunlight and starlight and every kind of light there was, the light from inside a friend's soul when they smiled and the light from the dawn of a new idea. She wanted it all!

"You have to let everything go . . ." the voice came.

She wanted to hear the rustle of wind in the trees and the sound of music and the murmur of soft voices.

"Just let everything go . . ."

But she wasn't going to give up. She wanted to feel the coolness of the misty night on her skin and the warmth of the morning sun.

"Trust me, cat, just let everything go . . ."

Cat, Serafina thought suddenly. The voice had said *cat.* It wasn't the Black Cloak speaking to her, but Rowena! She was trying to guide her, to show her the way.

The sorceress had been her enemy. They had attacked each other, tricked each other, and slashed each other with wounds. But was she *still* her enemy? Or had Rowena truly switched sides?

And then a different kind of thought came into Serafina's mind.

She knew that despite the many vicious and deceitful

deeds Uriah had forced his daughter to do, Rowena had always wanted Braeden as her friend.

"You don't even know what friendship is!" Rowena had screamed at her in frustration. "I've seen it!"

She's seen it, and she wants it, Serafina thought. *And now I've forced Rowena to promise that if I don't make it, then she'd join with Braeden at Biltmore . . .*

Serafina had thought she had exacted a difficult promise from Rowena, but now she realized that it might have suited Rowena just fine.

All that time playing the role of "Lady Rowena" the sorceress had been pretending to like Braeden, but maybe the trick was that she wasn't pretending.

Was that Rowena's plan now, to get rid of her, and have Braeden's friendship to herself? By persuading Serafina to go into the cloak, had Rowena finally managed to trick her rival out of existence?

Serafina didn't know what was in Rowena's heart, but she saw two paths before her. She could trust Rowena, stop fighting, and let her soul be pulled entirely into the Black Cloak. Or she could try to keep fighting in this storm of oblivion.

She thought about how important it was that Braeden had learned from Rowena's deceit months before that sometimes he shouldn't trust people. And she thought how she herself had learned that sometimes she *should* trust people. Despite all of Rowena's duplicitous shifts and caustic moods, she had helped her talk to Braeden, she had helped her spell the letters in ash in front of the fireplace, and she had revealed the secrets of the Black Cloak. Was it possible that Rowena might have feelings for Braeden, but convincing Serafina to get pulled back into the Black Cloak wasn't necessarily a malicious trick designed to eliminate her? Was it possible that both of those things could be true at the same time?

Serafina realized that she didn't know the answers to the questions. It was a terrifying feeling, but there was no way to know. But she did know that here, in this dark, swirling place, and in the spirit world where she'd been wandering, there was no good path. There was nothing there. Even if she fought back to the place she'd been, *there was nothing there.* No voice. No touch. No love. Her only hope was *forward.* Her only hope was the *unknown.*

Trust me, Rowena had said. *Trust me.*

Serafina knew that she might not return to the land of the living. She might not ever see the world again. In her mind, she began to say good-bye to Braeden and to Waysa. She said good-bye to her pa and to her mother, and the cubs, and Mr. and Mrs. Vanderbilt, and everyone else she knew. One by one, she said good-bye to all of them. Her only hope was that she had somehow helped them.

Finally, she shut her eyes and pulled in a long, deep breath, her chest rising, filling her lungs with the sooty black void. She held her breath for as long as she could, knowing that it would be her last, like a person trapped underwater knows the inhalation that will finally drown her lungs in a watery death.

Then she exhaled, and her mind unfurled as the cloak sucked her soul deep into its void.

And she disappeared into the black folds that she had seen take so many souls before her.

She had no body. She had no wandering spirit. All she had was consciousness, churning through the black prison.

She finally knew what Clara Brahms, Anastasia Rostonova, her mother, and all the other victims of the Black Cloak had experienced.

She had no perception of time or change. Each moment might be a fleeting second—a drop of water as it falls to the floor and splashes into nothingness. Or it might be a whole year of bountiful experience lost—every moment she'd ever spent with the people she loved.

She did not know.

There was no up or down, no action or effect. No hard or soft, no brightness or color, no movement or sensation, no voice or touch, no shape or beauty or love or compassion.

Rowena had trapped her in a black, empty world.

Serafina opened her eyes and saw nothing but black. It was as if she hadn't opened her eyes at all.

She had been deep in the darkened void of a swirling, half-dreaming world when she was awoken to the sound of a muffled voice, but now there was no voice, no sound, no movement of any kind.

Just black.

She closed her eyes and reopened them. But it made no difference. It was still pitch-dark.

But she wasn't floating in the black void of the cloak anymore. She was lying on her back on a long, flat, cold surface.

Where am I? she thought. *How did I get here?*

Then a sound finally came: a thudding in her ears that was more real, more pressing, than anything she had ever heard.

Thump-thump.

For a moment that was all there was.

Thump-thump, thump-thump.

The beat of her heart and the pulse of her blood.

Thump-thump, thump-thump, thump-thump.

As she slowly moved her tongue to moisten her cracked, dry lips, she detected the faint taste of metal in her mouth.

But it wasn't metal.

It was blood—her own blood flowing through her veins into her tongue and her lips.

She tried to clear her throat, but then all at once she took in a sudden, violent, jerking breath and sucked in a great gasp of air, as if it was the very first breath she had ever taken. As her blood flowed, a tingling feeling flooded into her arms and legs and all through her body.

My body . . . she thought, trying to comprehend it. *I'm in my body . . . I'm alive . . . I'm truly alive . . .*

She frantically tried to think back and remember what had happened to her, but it was like trying to grasp the fleeting details of a powerful dream that drifts away the moment you wake.

She pulled air into her nostrils, hoping to draw a clue from what she could smell around her.

Dirt, she thought. *I'm surrounded by damp, rotting dirt.*

Serafina quickly twisted around inside the coffin that surrounded her, pressing her hands against the cold, hard wood.

Her palms were sweating. Her breaths were getting shorter. Her lungs tightened, making it more and more difficult to breathe. A surge of panic poured through her. Her soul had reunited with her body. She was alive! But now she was going to run out of air and die!

She kicked her feet against the end of the coffin. She pounded her fists. She scratched and she scurried, she twisted and she pried, but she could not escape. Just as before, the boards surrounded her on all sides, close and narrow and low.

She hissed with frustration. After all she'd been through, she was going to suffocate in a black coffin buried six feet under the ground! It wasn't right! It wasn't fair! She wanted to scream and cry!

"Quit your mewling, girl, and get on with makin' yourself useful!" she imagined her pa telling her. "Figure out what needs to be done and do it!"

Gritting her teeth, she tore off her dress and wrapped it around her head to protect her nose and mouth. Then she spun around onto her stomach, put her shoulder to the center of the coffin's lid and pushed. She pushed and she kept pushing, over and over again, hammering her shoulder against the center board, *bang, bang, bang.*

When she finally felt the board cracking, she spun around and pulled at the edge of it with her fingers. A massive heap of dirt poured on top of her, crushing her down.

She shoved the dirt into the corners of the coffin until she had packed away as much of it as she could. Then she pushed her head up into the hole and started digging, scraping frantically with her bare hands. The loose earth poured down around her head and shoulders, collapsing onto her faster than she could dig it away.

She felt the pressing, suffocating weight of it all around her, closing in on her, crushing her chest, trapping her legs, but she kept clawing, kicking, squirming her way blindly up through the darkness, desperately trying to breathe.

She dug frantically toward the surface, but she knew she wasn't going to make it. She was too small, too weak, too frail, too dull. Her puny, soft, skin-covered fingers were nothing against the dirt. She was going to die.

"No! No! No!" she growled deep in her throat, until she was making one continuous growl.

She had one moment, and the moment was now. She could stop moving, stop breathing, let the earth win. Or she could envision what she wanted to be and become it.

She growled and she kept growling, the anger building inside her. She felt it coming now. She felt her whole body beginning to change. It was unstoppable now.

She envisioned her mountain lion mother and her black panther father. She was a catamount through and through. She was the *Black One*, the warrior-leader of the forest. It came like a great volcano, exploding from deep within her.

Suddenly, the earth around her expanded with a great heave, giving way to her newly muscled girth. She felt her tail twisting, her four feet clenching and clawing against the dirt. She began digging anew, filled with panther strength and power.

Her claws tore into the earth, ripping it away with lion ferocity. Her powerful legs pushed her upward toward the surface, toward air, toward life.

Her face and whiskers pushed against the dirt, her panther ears pressed back against her head as she shoved herself upward. Her powerful chest filled with a deep, dark, throbbing growl, like the roll of thunder through the ancient mountains where she'd been born into the darkened world.

As she dug, she heard a frenzy of scratching noises, digging down toward her.

Her upstretched claws clacked with the claws of another

catamount. It was Waysa, digging frantically, and Gidean digging at his side!

"You're almost there!" Braeden shouted as he dug toward her.

"Come on, cat, dig!" Rowena urged as she pulled handfuls of dirt away.

Finally, Serafina thrust her panther head up into the air and took in a long, deep, desperately needed breath. She felt the warm night air pouring into her mouth and down her throat and into her lungs. She felt her lungs filling with blessed air, expanding like a great bellows, her chest heaving, pushing easily against the loose dirt still around her. She felt her heart pumping, her bones pushing, and every muscle in her body at her beck and call.

"You made it!" Braeden shouted, as she clambered the rest of the way out. "You made it!"

Standing on four feet now, she threw the dirt from her black coat with a mighty shake. The entire world loomed large. She saw the angel's glade and the forest, and the stars above the trees. Her lungs could finally breathe! She was alive in the world, whole and complete! She was alive! She lifted her yellow panther eyes, and gazed at the smiling faces of her friends all around her.

Serafina shifted into human form and looked around her at the angel's glade, trying to understand what had happened.

"We destroyed it," Braeden told her excitedly.

Serafina looked over at the statue of the angel and saw the molten remnants of the Black Cloak lying in a pile on the ground below the angel's sword. The tight spider weave and binding spells of the cloak's fabric had disintegrated into a hot, smoldering heap as it released the energy within it. The smoky effluent drifted across the angel's glade and the graveyard beyond. They had pierced the cloak on the angel's sword, just as she had done months before when she freed Clara Brahms and the other victims trapped inside the cloak. Even though she knew she should have been expecting it, it took Serafina several seconds to comprehend that destroying the cloak had broken its spell, reunited her three splintered parts, and freed her from its dark imprisonment.

"When we destroyed the cloak, we thought we would find you lying on the ground, like when you freed Clara and the other children," Braeden said. "But we didn't."

"The damaged cloak had torn you apart," Rowena said. "When the spell broke, your freed spirit fled to your human body in the grave."

"And the essence of your panther body was pulled in as well," Waysa said. "It wasn't until I heard you digging that I realized what happened and told the others."

"We all started digging as fast as we could!" Braeden said.

Serafina was amazed. Their plan hadn't worked exactly the way they had expected, but it *did* work.

She looked at Braeden. She could see the exhilaration and relief sparkling in his eyes, a large smile on his face.

"I can't believe it!" he said. "You made it! After all this time, you're truly here! You're alive!" He moved toward her and embraced her, so pleased that he lifted her off her feet and swung her around.

She laughed in joy at his enthusiasm. It felt amazingly good to wrap her arms around him and hug him, to finally embrace him, to truly feel her friend's warm, living body.

As she held on to him, she could feel the rapid beat of his heart against her chest, the movement of air through his lungs as he breathed, and the tremble in his hands as he held her. She could feel everything, and she knew he could feel her. This was the world, she thought, the true and living world, and she was *in* it. In the distance over Braeden's shoulder, a blaze of falling stars streaked across the glistening darkness of the nighttime sky. Down in her soul she felt as infinite as the heavens upon which she gazed, filled with a deep gratitude just to be back with the people she loved.

"Thank you for not giving up on me, Braeden," she said as she held him, unable to control the quiver of appreciation in her voice.

"You're welcome," he said. "I knew that if we could find a way, you'd come back to us."

As she slowly separated from Braeden, she looked at Waysa, who had shifted into human form. Waysa stood before her now, tall and grinning and happy.

"Welcome back," he said, and they embraced. She felt the strength in her friend's arms and the pride in his chest. She felt the warrior in him, the satisfaction of finally winning a battle against their enemy. And she felt the serenity in him, the happiness that they were finally back together. She and Waysa had shared so much together. They had run through the forest, slept behind waterfalls, and swam in mountain pools, but nothing compared to the joy of this moment.

She gazed at Braeden and Waysa and she smiled. Her two friends had waited for her, fought for her, did everything they could to make this night happen, and they had finally succeeded.

Finally, Serafina turned and looked at Rowena. The sorceress in her dark robes, with her hood and her long red hair coiled loosely around her shoulders, stood quietly nearby. She was watching them, her green eyes bright and alive, but flickering with an uncertain wariness.

"I'm not going to embrace you if that's what you're thinking, cat," Rowena said.

Serafina smiled and nodded. "I know," she said. "But thank you, Rowena. Thank you from the bottom of my heart. You saved me."

"I put you there," Rowena said, reminding her. "And now I brought you back."

Serafina wasn't sure if she was saying that she had righted the wrong, or that they were even, or maybe something else, but either way, Serafina said, "I thank you for what you did tonight."

As Serafina spoke with her friends, she couldn't help but take in the world around her. She felt her two feet firmly on the ground, so simple, but so profound, to have weight, to have effect, to not be floating in the air or disintegrating into vapor, but to have substance, to have *presence*, to truly be in a place and in command of her body. She smelled the willow trees around the glade and heard the soft orchestra of buzzing insects. Gone was the feeling of being a droplet of water or a mote of dust. Gone was the feeling of being a gust of wind that might drift away at any moment. She was *alive*, truly alive. She was whole again, solid and firm, body and soul, and had never felt better in her life.

And as she stood there looking around her in amazement, she slowly began to realize there was something else, too, something new. When she tuned her ears just right, she could hear the gentle movement of the breeze in the boughs of the trees far above her. She could sense a drop of dew clinging to a leaf, feel it falling through the vibrating air, and hear it hit the ground and soak into the dusty soil. She could see the breath of the trees with her eyes and the rise of water to the clouds. Everything around her felt closer, finer, more acute.

The rising of the moon, the falling of the stars, ashes to ashes, dust to dust—she knew she'd come close to dying. She had walked *in between*. Her spirit had lingered in the world . . . but now she sensed that the *world* lingered in *her*. She felt the quiet rocks of the earth, the flow of distant rivers, and the drift of the clouds above—she could see and feel the spirit of the world all around her.

As she gazed from one point to the next, trying to understand her new senses and powers, she noticed a faint glint of moonlight on the ground over by the destroyed remnants of the Black Cloak. It was but a small reflection of light at first, but as she walked toward it, the glint became so bright that it was almost blinding to her.

She reached down beside the black pile of the ruined fabric and picked up the cloak's silver clasp. It felt heavy in her hand. In the past, the clasp's design had been a twisting weave of thorny vines. She'd even seen the little faces of children behind the vines. But tonight, the clasp was blank, without any design at all.

Serafina turned and walked back toward Braeden. He smiled at her, still elated with their success.

"You better hide this," she said as she slipped the clasp into his hand.

It still amazed her to think that Braeden had hid the damaged cloak from their enemies all that time, fearing its black, hissing power, but clinging to the hope that one day, somehow, someway, he would be able to bring her back into the world. And tonight was that night. He'd done it!

She moved toward him to embrace him again, but Rowena stepped between them.

"This is a sweet reunion and all, we'll be sure to all have tea together sometime," Rowena said in a biting tone. "But my father is going to sense the destruction of the cloak. He's going to come, and when he does, he'll be bent on a black vengeance like nothing you've ever seen, angry that the cat has escaped, but even angrier that I helped her do it."

Serafina knew Rowena was right. She gazed around at her friends. "Whatever happens, the four of us are in this together now."

As soon as she arrived at Biltmore, Serafina ran down to the workshop. She stopped to catch her breath just outside the door. Then she stepped slowly into the room and gazed upon her pa.

He was near his cot behind the supply racks, the cot he'd slept in for all the years she could remember. He was performing a simple task, straightening the blanket on his bed, but to her it seemed to be the most profound of actions.

Here was the man who had raised her, who had fed her and cared for her all her life, who had taught her all that he could teach her, who had guarded and protected her, and held her close every night.

She was so quiet, so still, standing there behind him, that

for a moment, she almost wasn't sure whether she was spirit or whole.

But then, with hot tears welling up in her eyes, she finally said, "I came home as soon as I could, Pa."

Her pa froze in his movement. He did not turn or say a word.

For several seconds it was as if he had not heard her at all. Or perhaps he did not believe what he had heard.

But then he slowly turned his head to the side, as if waiting for the sound to come again. And then he turned his body and looked at her.

He gazed upon her with awe, like a believing man who has come face-to-face with a winged angel. At first, he was unable to speak, but finally, he smiled, and his face wrinkled, and he wiped tears from his eyes, and he said, "Now you come on over here and see your pa."

She walked forward and collapsed into his arms, not just crying, but bawling.

"I'm sorry, Pa, I'm so sorry, I couldn't get home, I tried and tried, but I couldn't get home," she wailed.

He pulled her against his barrel chest, wrapped his thick arms around her, and held her tight.

She pressed her head against his chest and she held him in her trembling arms. As she let herself fall into him, she pulled in a long, dreaming breath, her chest heaving with the exhilaration of being there with him at this moment. She felt the warmth of his embrace and heard the sigh of his breathing as he held her. It was a miracle. She could *feel* him, truly *feel* him, and he could feel her.

Around her, she smelled the cotton fabric of his shirt, and the grease he'd worked with that day, and the familiar musk of his body, all mixed with the smells of the workshop, the solid oak benches and the half-burned coal in the little stove where they cooked their meals and the gritty stone of the floor and the oiled metal of the hammers, wrenches, and other tools. She was alive. And she was finally, finally, finally back—back in the workshop, back in her pa's arms. She was finally *home*.

In the time that followed, she took a long, warm bath, washed off the grave dirt and the bloodstains, and changed into a simple, clean dress. It felt as if she was living in the lap of luxury.

As they settled in for the night, it seemed like neither of them could quite believe that it was truly real. They kept looking at each other, touching each other, as if constantly wanting to make sure.

Her pa cooked an elaborate supper of chicken and dumplings with his favorite gravy, fried okra, and grits smothered with warm butter and cheese. She was so famished that she ate it all and wanted more. Whether it was drinking a glass full of cool, clear water or eating a meal with her pa, the simplest routines of her life had become the most glorious pleasures.

"You're doin' a good fine job on your supper there," her pa said happily as she scraped down to the bottom of the metal plate.

"It just tastes so good," she said, meaning it true, and it brought a smile to his face.

Over supper, her pa started talking, not with any particular purpose in mind, but just to talk, just to celebrate, like everything was all right again. He spun his usual tales of mending machines and solving the challenges of his day-to-day life. She had always loved his stories in which he was the humble hero fighting against impossible odds with wrench and hammer in hand, and she had never loved the stories more than on this night.

She wanted to tell him that she had seen the beautiful faerie lights he had strung in the garden on the night of the evening party, his shining beacon for her to follow home. And she wanted to tell him how proud she was of him the night she'd seen him smiling, dressed in his suit, in the glow of the glittering summer ball.

Later on, as they washed their dishes, her pa took on a more serious tone.

"I know ya might not be too keen on talkin' about it just yet, Sera," he said, "but what happened to you all this time?"

It was difficult to know how to answer his question in a way that he, or anyone, could understand, but she did the best she could.

She was pretty sure that her pa had an inkling that somehow her mother was a mountain lion, but she didn't think he knew that she too walked on four feet when she wanted to. If he did suspect it, it was something he didn't like to think about, like he didn't like to think about haints and demons and other creatures of the night. To him, she was his daughter, a human being, a twelve-year-old little girl that he cherished more than anything in the world, and he didn't like to think of her in any other way. And she was sure that it would come as quite a shock to him if he ever saw her as a crouched, snarling, clawing, leaping black panther. But she knew he had some idea of the strange and unusual things that happened in the dark of night, for he had warned her of them many times.

"You remember our old enemies . . ." Serafina began.

"The ones who captured the animals in the cages up in the pine forest a few months ago," he said, and she nodded her head.

"They came back, Pa. They attacked me, and I was wounded somethin' awful."

As her pa listened, she could tell by the expression in his eyes that it was difficult for him to hear.

"They caught me in a dark place and I couldn't escape," she said.

As she continued her story, telling him what she could and leaving out what she could not, he listened intently. She had been around him all her life, so she knew it wasn't the kind of story he wanted to hear, but he listened anyway for he knew he must. He knew that what he was hearing was what had happened to her, and she could see in his eyes and his expression that he wanted to understand. He'd been waiting and imagining and praying for her safe return for so long that now he wanted to know everything he could. He wanted to have that bond between them, the bond of *knowing*.

"So it was the young master who finally helped you to escape," he said.

She nodded. "Yes, it was."

"He was a gone miserable lad while you were away," her pa said, recounting a bit of how it was from his side of it all. "The master and I, the two of us as doleful as cold poke, used to talk about it, trying to figure out what we could do for the lad, but I think our talks did more for the pair of us menfolk than they did the poor boy. But in the end, I reckon he figured a way through it all on his own."

"I reckon he did," she said in agreement, but refrained from saying more. Her fondness for Braeden had become immeasurable, but it wasn't something she could easily talk about with her pa.

"And you thanked him kindly for what he did . . ." he said, always wanting to make sure she was doing right by other folk.

She nodded, assuring him that she had thanked Braeden, and that she would again.

"And what about your mother?" her pa asked. He didn't know her personally, but he knew that her mother was important to her. "Have you been able to see her since you returned?"

Serafina's heart clouded in sadness. "No," she said. "She went away and I have no way to reach her."

"Well, I hope she's all right," her pa said, but it was clear that he didn't know what else to say.

Serafina's thoughts lingered. She didn't quite know how to ask the question that had been swirling around in her mind since she'd crawled from the grave, but she thought that if anyone could help her, maybe her pa could.

"Pa, does it feel to you like so much has changed since I've been gone? Everything feels so different . . . but in other ways . . ." Her words dwindled off. She could see right away that she wasn't going to be able to express it the way she wanted to.

But he looked at her and said, "I think I understand what you're gettin' at. The way I see it, everything is always changing and everything is always staying the same."

His words shouldn't have made sense to her, but somehow they almost did.

"You see, everything around us is always changing," he continued, "the machines and the inventions, the people coming and going through our lives, even our own bodies over time— yours is growing up and mine is getting old. The trees in the forest are changing and the courses of the rivers. Even our own minds are changing, growing and learning, finding new paths to follow, shifting and shaping over time."

"But if everything is always changing, what can we hold on to?" she asked.

"That's where the rest of it comes in, Sera," her pa said. "Everything is always changing, but everything is always staying the same, too. The trees are growing and dying, but the forest remains. No matter how the river changes course from year to year, it always keeps flowing. Your body and your mind are changing, but deep down, your soul, your inner spirit, stays the same. I'm the same deep down inside that I was when I was twelve years old, and the spirit you feel inside you tonight will be with you fifty years from now. Yes, you'll be different, the whole world will be different, but the spirit inside you—the thing that makes you you—will still be there."

"But if we're always growing and changing, I don't understand how that can be," she said.

"Look at Mr. Vanderbilt," her pa said. "When he was your age, he was a kind but quiet little boy who loved to read books, study art, and travel to faraway places. Now he's a great man of wealth and power . . ."

". . . but he's a kind and quiet man, who loves to read books, study art, and travel to faraway places," she said, finishing his thoughts.

"That's right," her pa said, smiling. "The twelve-year-old little boy will be the fifty-year-old man. It's been him the whole time, all the way through. His body has changed, and everything around him has changed, but his spirit has always been with him."

Serafina nodded, feeling like she was beginning to understand.

"You asked me what we can hold on to," her pa said. "I'll tell you this: you hold on to the people around you, Sera, to your friends and family, to the people you love, and you hold on to that spirit deep down inside that never leaves you, that spirit that's always flowing, like a river inside you."

Finally, her pa paused. He looked at the floor for a moment, as if thinking about his own words a bit longer, and then looked at her. "Does any of my blither-blather feel like it makes any kind of sense to ya?"

Serafina smiled and nodded. It did indeed. She was pretty sure that her pa couldn't reckon the soul-splitting, haint-walking horror of what she'd been through, but somehow he seemed to have sensed just the right words to say to her.

"There's one more thing, Pa," she said, "that I need your help with tonight."

"Another question?" he asked gently.

"No," she said sheepishly. "I need you to help me make something."

"Make something?" he said in surprise, for in all her life with him in the workshop, she had never expressed any interest to fix something or make something. She was absolutely the least mechanically inclined person who had ever prowled the night.

"You've seen how Braeden wears a brace on his bad leg," she said.

"Yes," he said, a twinge of sadness in his voice.

"One of the metal pieces at the joint broke," she said. "I would like to see if we can come up with some way not just to fix it, but to improve it, maybe something that's less like a bone and more like a tendon."

Her pa looked at her and smiled a broad and happy smile. That was definitely something he could do.

Over the next few hours they worked together shoulder to shoulder in the workshop, long into the night, making little test pieces, and discussing and exploring different ideas, until they constructed a design they liked. She had never worked at her pa's side before, not like this. She had never had a need for man-made constructions. So it was an entirely new experience for her, and it brought her great joy, the act of actually *creating* something with her pa at her side.

Later that night, when they finally went to sleep, she curled up between her sheets, her head on the pillow, and it felt just about as fine as anything she had ever felt. She knew there were dark and terrible dangers out there in the forest. She knew there was still a fight ahead of her, but tonight, she was home with her pa, and for a little while, that's all she wanted. Everything is always changing and everything is always staying the same.

The next morning, Serafina went upstairs straightaway to find Braeden.

All the guests that had come for the ball had fled in their carriages to escape the heavy rains flooding the roads, so the house and grounds felt empty. She passed Mr. McNamee, the estate superintendent, gathering a large group of workers in the stable courtyard to repair the damage caused by the nightly storms.

Out back behind the stables, she spotted Braeden in the distance, walking alone into a pasture toward four black horses. The horses had been his companions for years, but in the months she had been gone, Braeden had fallen into such despair that he had drifted away from his friends. As he approached them for the first time in a long time, the horses stood in the field and stared at him as if he was a stranger.

Braeden folded his leg brace at the knee, and sat in the middle of the field. The horses studied him from a distance for a long time. Finally, they began walking slowly toward him.

The four black horses surrounded Braeden, lowered their heads to his, and gently nuzzled him, as horses in the field who have not seen each other in far too long will do.

Then the lead horse extended his front leg, bowed his head low with a bending neck, and knelt down onto one knee so that Braeden could climb onto his bare back. When the horse rose up again, Braeden was astride him, on four strong legs.

Serafina watched Braeden ride out into the rolling, grassy fields with his horses, up to the top of a great hill where there was a large white oak tree with a huge crown and thick splaying limbs. As the horses grazed at the top of the hill, Braeden stayed among them, once again a trusted member of their herd.

Serafina was about to climb the hill to catch up with them, but then she paused. The golden morning light shone down through the mist rising from the tall grass, and for a moment she felt the coolness of the mist, and the heat of the sun, and the touch of the breeze on her skin. She knew she had returned to the living, but at this moment it felt as if the separation between her and the world around her had slipped away. *We are made of the world, and the world is made of us,* she thought.

Wondering what she could do, she slowly raised her hand

in front of her, shaping her fingers until the mist around her began to move. The mist flowed outward, swirling and turning in a long tendril, propelled by her will. She guided the tendril of mist up the hill, toward Braeden and the horses, then up through the branches of the tree until the tendril of mist met the sun and disappeared. Serafina smiled, sensing that there was much for her to learn.

But she knew she didn't have time to linger. She had won one battle by escaping the cloak, but she knew the real war was yet to come. She continued on up the hill to join Braeden and the horses, but then something happened.

Black crows began flying in, strong and hard, from all directions. Soon, hundreds of crows were flying about the tree at the top of the hill, landing and taking off again, wheeling about the sky, croaking and cawing, as if they were engaged in some sort of raucous, noisy conclave.

When she saw Braeden standing below, looking up at the crows, she thought he was just watching them like she was, but then she realized that he was actually calling them in, trying to speak with them, his voice filled with urgency. As the crows flew in great circles around the top of the tree, he talked to them, sometimes struggling with the phrasing of his words, other times correcting himself, like someone who is gradually finding his way.

Finally, one of the crows flew down and perched on a branch near Braeden, tilted its black shining head, and made clicking-gurgling noises. It appeared that Braeden actually understood what the crow was saying to him, and when Braeden spoke back to the crow in English, the bird seemed to somehow understand him. Many of the other crows came closer and joined in their conversation until there were crows in the lower branches all around him.

As Serafina moved quickly up the hill, she was worried about scaring the crows off, but the birds seemed to have no shortage of boisterous, brazen confidence in themselves, flying all around, buzzing and cawing, flapping their great black wings, as they conversed with the boy.

Braeden seemed unfamiliar with the crows' language at first, as if he didn't understand everything they were saying, but he seemed to become more used to the cadence of it. Serafina had never given much thought to the cawing of crows, but as she watched them now, she began to hear just how many different kinds of sounds they made—long, castigating rattles, impatient clacks, triumphant caws, rowdy jeers and playful chortles, warnings and signals, praise and encouragement, and urgent calls to flight. She realized that the crows had an entire language of their own. And with powers she did not understand, Braeden was learning it.

Finally, he said a few last words to the crows, and they all launched up into the air at once. One flock of the crows flapped forcefully away on strong and steady wings, flying west toward the mountains in the distance. The other crows flew in small flocks in different directions, some toward the house, others the gardens, and still others into the nearby forests.

"Where have you sent them all?" she asked, making her presence known for the first time.

Braeden turned in surprise and smiled at the sight of her. "Serafina . . ." he said, his voice filled with gentle contentment. She was just happy that he could actually see her.

"Did you sleep well?" she asked.

"Better than I have in a long time," he said, nodding vigorously.

"Me too," she said, smiling. "It's good to be home. I was going to come up here and tell you that we have work to do, but I think you've already begun."

"I'm afraid I'm out of practice, so it took me a while to figure out how to speak to them."

She looked toward the flock flying west, their black silhouettes receding into the blue sky beneath a striking, sunlit formation of tumbling white clouds.

"And where is that particular flock going?"

"I asked them to head to the Smoky Mountains."

The sound of that name brought a pang of sadness to her heart.

Looking at Braeden and then the crows again, Serafina wondered what it was all about. "Why so far?" she asked. "What will they find there?"

"They're going to find your mother," he said. "To let her know that you've returned so that she'll come back, and you'll be able to see her again."

Serafina looked at Braeden and felt a deep warmth filling her chest. "That's so kind of you," she said, "to think of that, I mean, to ask them to do that. Thank you. I hope they find her, and the cubs, too. I'd love to see them all again."

"You're very welcome," Braeden said, pleased that she was happy with what he'd done. "Now that you're back, your mother and the cubs belong here with us, in our forests."

Serafina couldn't agree more, and she liked the way he said *our forests*.

As they were talking, she noticed that he was standing in an awkward position, favoring his bad leg. She glanced down and saw that the bracket on the brace was still broken.

"How's your leg?" she asked.

"It's been feeling much better," he said, trying to stay cheerful, but as his trembling fingers began fumbling with the straps and buckles, tightening them the best he could, it was clear that his leg was still sore. "I guess this rickety old brace does need some work," he admitted. "It was brand-new when my uncle got it for me, but after all it's been through, it's definitely suffered some wear and tear. This metal piece here broke off completely, and it's been causing me no end of trouble."

She shyly put out her hand and said, "Maybe this will help."

In her open palm were the two kidney-shaped, multi-holed leather straps that she and her pa had made.

"What are those?" Braeden asked with fascination as he leaned toward her and took a closer look.

"One for each side of your knee," she said, "to replace the metal bracket that broke. My pa and I made them."

"You did?" he asked in amazement, looking up at her. "Thank you!"

"Try them on."

"Yes," he said excitedly. "Let's see how they work . . ."

He took the leather straps out of her hands, his fingers brushing her open palm as he did so, sending a jolt of energy up her arm and down her spine. Then he folded himself to the ground, tore off the broken bracket, and began attaching the new straps.

"I hope they fit," she said.

"They seem like they're going to work very well," he said, standing up and flexing his knee back and forth as if someone had just given him a new, fully functional leg.

Seeing his happiness, Serafina smiled.

She glanced westward across the mountains. The westbound crows had disappeared on their journey.

"Do you think they will succeed?" she asked wistfully. "It's a big forest out there, and she's very good at hiding."

"The crows don't have the eyesight of a hawk, the nose of a vulture, or the speed of a falcon, but they are the smartest birds I know, and they will work together to find her."

"Are the crows always so noisy?" she asked, still a little amused by all the racket they'd been making. It seemed so quiet now up on the hill with only the horses grazing nearby.

"Oh yes," Braeden said. "They love to argue, those crows, and boy, are they quick to take offense. But they're good birds all the same."

"What about all the other crows that flew off in the different directions?"

"Each flock is a small family group that trusts each other, hunts and scavenges together, calling each other when they find something good, and warning each other when danger approaches. Each flock protects their own territory where they've learned to find food, roost at night, and stay safe. I asked all the different flocks in the area to post sentinels all around Biltmore's grounds and keep guard, to warn us if they see anything suspicious. Uriah has been their hated enemy for many years."

Serafina marveled at Braeden's story of the crows, but her gut twisted at the sound of her enemy's name. "And have they seen him?"

"They say he's moving every night, circling Biltmore."

Serafina couldn't help but take a swallow. "I don't like the sound of that one bit."

"Me neither," Braeden agreed. "The crows will be able to give us a short warning, but that's all."

Serafina gazed back at the house and the surrounding gardens, her heart filling with a dark foreboding. Noticing a change in the wind direction, she glanced up at the sky.

In what form would Uriah attack? Would it be a sudden strike like a rattlesnake's bite? Or would the storms and floods come gradually, doing his work for him, sweeping everything away in their destructive path?

"Last night Waysa told me that the rivers are getting worse," Braeden said. "Whole areas of the forest in the mountains above Biltmore are flooded with water and mudslides."

"When Uriah sees his best opportunity, he will attack," Serafina said.

"But what are we going to do?"

"We need to find the others."

"They're down by the spillway of the pond." Seeing her look

of surprise at his quick answer, Braeden said, "Crows have long memories, so they keep a watchful eye on Rowena wherever she goes. They don't trust her any more than they trust her father."

"What about you?" Serafina asked. "Do *you* trust her?"

"Yes, I think she's on our side now," Braeden said. "With the four of us working together, we can defeat him."

Serafina wanted to agree, but wasn't too sure what to make of Braeden's new optimism. A death struggle with a powerful sorcerer loomed ahead, but he seemed happier than he had been in a long time. But he wasn't just returning to his old self. There was something different about him, more focused and determined.

"Let's go," he said, touching her arm, "they're going to be looking for us," and they started down the hill toward the pond, his newly repaired leg brace seeming to provide a new smoothness to his gait.

She felt an unusual sense of satisfaction as she walked at Braeden's side. *This,* she thought, *this is how it should be.* She enjoyed being with him. His leather boot still dragged a little in the grass, and his hands were still trembling, but he seemed stronger and more at ease than he ever had before.

She wanted to keep this sense of peace and belonging for as long as she could, but as she and Braeden reached the bottom of the hill, she felt an unusual stirring in the air. A small flurry of wind swept by her. She might not have noticed such a thing in the past, but her senses were too keen now to ignore it. Suddenly, she caught the scent of a coming storm.

She looked around at the wind blowing in the tops of the

trees. A storm seemed to be moving in with unnatural speed. Even as the light of the sun withdrew from everything around them, a flash of lightning lit up the sky.

"So much for the sunny day," Braeden said. And she knew he wasn't just talking about the weather.

Rolling over the ridge of the closest mountain, a dark bank of clouds loomed like a great wave.

"It's coming this way," she said, eyeing the black front of the storm. "He's attacking now."

By the time they reached the pond, it had begun to rain, like a warm summer shower at first, with the sun still shining bright on the distant eastern horizon, but as the clouds passed directly overhead, the sky grew dark and malevolent, and the heavy rain came pouring down.

"It's been raining like this almost every night," Braeden complained, as they made their way miserably through the deluge.

Serafina was about to reply when her whole body jolted in surprise. A blistering white light blazed in her eyes as a bolt of lightning struck the top of the hill. The oak tree where they'd just been standing exploded into a thousand pieces, sending shards of burning wood hurtling in all directions, whizzing past her head, as the crack of thunder boomed in her chest and rolled across the blackened sky. Braeden's four horses reared up in panic and charged away across the field.

"Serafina!" Braeden said, grabbing her arm and pointing into the distance toward the grassy slope of Diana Hill in front of the house. The hillsides around Biltmore were running with dark rivers of storm water. Rushing currents tore at the earth, and great areas of mud were sliding down toward the house and gardens.

"Gad night a-livin', will you look at that," Serafina gasped. "I hope everyone's holdin' on down there."

As they ran down to the pond, they saw that the small inlet stream had become a turbulent river. The pond was so full that the water had breached the banks and flooded the nearby trees.

Sloshing through inches of water, they made their way toward the stone dam at the outlet of the pond. Normally, the small amount of overflow was nothing more than a trickle, but now a roaring waterfall poured out of the pond and over the spillway, dumping into the ravine below.

"We need to cross before it's too late," Serafina shouted, pointing toward the small wooden footbridge that traversed the top of the waterfall.

As they clambered across the bridge, the driving spray of the rain and the waterfall flew into her face. The blowing wind howled like a horde of ghouls. The wood planking beneath her feet swayed as the pushing current rocked the bridge's supports back and forth. She grabbed the side rail as her eyes darted to the rushing water below her. She felt the bridge suddenly jerk to the side, then tilt violently with the sound of cracking wood.

"Braeden, jump!" she shouted.

Just as she and Braeden leapt to the ground on the other side, the entire bridge split apart and came crashing down, then rolled over the falls in a great heap of broken, twisted boards.

"We made it," Braeden gasped, as Serafina scanned the path ahead for Waysa and Rowena. She spotted them running toward her and Braeden.

"This storm is my father's doing," Rowena yelled through the rain as the last of the bridge's wreckage went over the falls. "It's going to get worse from here."

"Let's get to cover!" Serafina shouted.

As the four of them ran through the rain toward the house, a great mass of mud was sliding into the outer edge of the gardens, tearing through the plants and knocking down the marble Greek statues.

Squinting through the rain, Serafina looked toward the house. A gushing river of water ripped down a side gulley, tearing at Biltmore's foundation.

"There's my uncle!" Braeden shouted.

The wind-torn figures of Mr. Vanderbilt and Superintendent McNamee stood in the middle of the blowing storm, shouting orders to what looked like more than fifty men as they worked frantically to stanch the flow of the water tearing at the house. Serafina watched in horror as a man was pulled into the current and swept away screaming for help.

"What are we going to do?" Braeden shouted, his voice filled with fear and confusion. "We can't battle a thunderstorm!"

Reaching the main house, Serafina led her friends through the side door into the circular room at the base of the Grand Staircase. She and her companions were breathless, sopping wet, and bedraggled from the storm. As she looked around at them, she could see the fear and uncertainty in their faces, and their relief to be in the shelter of the house. She felt it, too. The last thing she wanted to do was go back out there.

And then she realized something.

This was exactly what Uriah wanted, she thought, for them to hunker down and hide. He was pushing them, pressing them back, as he wreaked havoc on the estate.

"We need to attack," Serafina said.

"Now?" Braeden said in surprise. "In the middle of the storm?"

"Exactly," Serafina said. "This is our opportunity. He'll think we'll be hiding, taking cover. The last thing he's going to expect is for us to attack in the middle of the storm."

"Serafina is right," Waysa said.

"I don't think you realize how difficult he is going to be to kill," Rowena said.

"Do you know where he's hiding?" Serafina asked Rowena.

"I suspect he's up on one of the mountain peaks, looking toward Biltmore, directing this storm, but there's no way to tell for certain where he's going to be."

Serafina went over to the door and looked out into the blowing wind and rain. "Braeden, can your crows fly in this?"

"They normally take cover during a storm," he said, gazing

up at the darkened sky, "but they're strong fliers, and they'll jump at the chance to get into a fracas with an enemy they hate as much as Uriah."

"Talk to them and your other friends," she said. "I want to attack Uriah with all our allies at once."

"I'm sure they'll join us," Braeden said. "They've been fighting against Uriah for even longer than we have."

Encouraged, Serafina nodded and then looked at Rowena.

"I will load my satchel with potions and spells," Rowena said. Serafina could see the fear and determination in her eyes. Rowena, more than any of them, knew her father's wrath. She had felt his attacks. She had suffered his blows. She had thrown spells at him only to have them buffeted back. But Serafina could see that Rowena knew the time had come to stand up and fight him.

"You understand that we have to take him by surprise," Rowena warned.

Waysa stepped forward. "I'll attack him first."

Serafina could see the fierceness blazing in Waysa's eyes. She knew her friend wouldn't give up until either he or Uriah was dead. He was honor bound to avenge his family or die trying.

She looked around at her three companions. "Attacking now, in the middle of his attack, is going to be the most dangerous thing we've ever done. But there will be no peace in these mountains for any of us until we destroy him."

"But how are we going to do it?" Rowena asked.

"We'll plan it all out, every detail," Serafina said. "We'll use the crows to find him. Then Waysa and I will lead the attack, charging at him from two different directions at once. Braeden will bring in our animal allies at the same time, and Rowena, you'll attack with every spell you have. We have to hit him so fast and so hard that he never gains his footing."

Serafina looked around at her three companions. They were ready to fight. She waved her hand up at the sky. "Forget about this weather, this rain, this wind. This is nothing to us. We attack now, right through all this. *We* are the storm."

46

As night fell, Serafina and her companions made their way up into the rugged terrain of the mountains. She traveled in panther form with Waysa, the two of them slinking quickly and quietly through the underbrush. Rowena traveled on foot, her dark robes and hood gathered around her against the wind. Braeden rode his horse, with Gidean at his side.

Braeden made a dashing sight, a lionhearted boy in a dark outdoor coat riding atop his black horse, with his black Doberman dog at his side, and his black crows flying above him, and she herself a black panther gliding alongside. She was beginning to notice a trend in his choice of friends.

As they moved up the slope of the mountain, the wind was

still blowing, but they had left the rain and lightning of the storm in the valley behind them. They moved quickly through the highland forest, following the crows that led the way. The crows didn't normally fly at night, but tonight they flew with purpose. They flapped hard through the blowing wind, some of them tumbling in the air, others diving headlong through the buffeting gale, all of them cawing to each other, pressing each other on.

As Serafina and her allies began to reach the top of the mountain, the wind finally died down and the air became deathly still. They entered a forest crowded with large, slanting, jagged rocks. Many of the rocks towered over their heads, jutting up from the ground, cracked and crumbling as if they had been broken by powerful earthen forces. Mottled gray lichen and dark greenish moss covered the rocks, and gnarled trees grew from the cracks, their roots clinging to the stone like the long black, creeping legs of giant spiders.

Making their way slowly up through the denseness of the rocky forest, they came to a bank of fog so thick that they couldn't see ahead. Just as Serafina was wondering how they were going to get through it, she felt a stinging in her eyes and a bad sulfurous taste in her mouth. Suddenly, her nostrils burned. Her throat hurt. A wave of confusion and dizziness came over her. Braeden was suffering as well, coughing badly, his horse throwing its head in agitation as it tried to turn away.

"The fog is poisonous," Rowena said.

Serafina shifted into human form. "Everyone pull back!"

she shouted, coughing and rubbing her stinging eyes as she stumbled down the hill.

"What is going on?" Braeden asked, covering his mouth.

"He's using a spell to protect the top of the mountain," Rowena said in frustration, "but I don't know how to counter it."

Once they retreated down to a safe position, Serafina looked toward the ring of fog that surrounded the peak. "It's a line of defense," she said. "He must be up there."

"But there's no way to get through it," Braeden said.

"Not like this," she agreed. "But I have an idea. Everyone stay here."

As she made her way alone back up the slope of the mountain, she remembered all she had learned. She raised her hand in front of her and pushed it through the air. When she felt the air around her moving, she smiled and tried it again.

She walked slowly up into the poisonous fog, sweeping her hands back and forth, concentrating on the movement and the flow, the wisps of air and vapor, pushing and sliding, until rivers of fog moved to her will through the sky.

She cut a swath through the fog, clearing a narrow path, then called her friends forward to follow close behind her, Braeden on his horse, Gidean at his side, Waysa and Rowena coming up behind.

When they finally reached the other side, the air was clear and the fog behind them. They took cover in a thicket of heath behind a large rock.

"How in the world did you do that?" Braeden whispered to her in astonishment.

"Just something I picked up in my travels," Serafina said, pleased that she was able to hone her powers to useful purpose. But as she looked up toward the mountaintop, she grew more serious.

Like many of the Blue Ridge Mountains, which were some of the oldest mountains in the world, the top of this particular mountain wasn't a sharply pointed peak but a rocky dome, what the mountain folk called a *bald*, worn down by millions of years of wind and rain. Hundreds of the forest's spruce and fir trees lay on the ground like they'd been blown down by the high mountain winds or struck by the vengeance of a sorcerer. The trunks of the fallen trees lay crisscrossed over one another, their limbs broken and twisted, like a hundred titan soldiers lying dead on a hilltop battlefield.

"This is the place," Rowena whispered, as they crouched behind the cracked and weathered rock. "He's close. I can feel him."

Serafina looked back at Braeden on his horse just down the slope from them. "Call in our other friends now. We'll do everything just like we planned."

"There he is!" Rowena whispered, ducking down.

Serafina's arms and legs jolted with sudden strength. The battle was near.

Taking a deep breath, she slowly peeked up over the edge of the rock.

The dark and giant figure of the storm-creech Uriah loomed in the clearing, with the smoky-white haze hanging about him like the fog of the graveyard. He did not appear to be aware of their presence. He wore a long, ragged dark coat so shredded and torn that it looked like the rotting carcass of a dead animal. He stood on two long, bent legs like a gangly man, but he was impossibly tall, grotesquely hunched over, with his long, crooked arms in front of him and his white scaly clawed hands protruding from the ragged sleeves of his coat. The oily strands of his gray hair hung stringy and twisting down the side of his skull. His cracked and leathery face had been slashed by Serafina's four claws months before, and the open wounds still bled and festered after all this time. Uriah paced, lanky and stooping, in the center of the clearing, rocking back and forth as he gazed impatiently toward Biltmore, far in the distant valley, watching over the storm that he had sent to rip it from the earth.

When Serafina had first spotted the clawed creature in the forest, she hadn't been sure what it was, but now she could see that the storm-creech was indeed a man, or at least had been a man before he was consumed by a black and twisting vengeance. *With every injury, we become more of who we are,* Rowena had said. And here was *Uriah,* the sorcerer, the enslaver of wild animals, the murderer of her panther father and many others, the man who had set himself to destroy everything she loved.

By moving in on him the way they had, during the storm and slipping through his ring of poisonous fog, she'd caught him by surprise, and all her allies were ready. *We've got him,* she thought. But just as she turned to signal the attack, a fireball came hurtling over her head, snapping and boiling with terrific force, a long tail of thick black smoke trailing behind it.

It was headed straight for Braeden.

"Watch out, Braeden!" Rowena screamed as she leapt out from behind the rock and threw her arms up into an explosion of ice and frost. It came too late to destroy the fireball, but she managed to deflect it. Instead of hitting Braeden, the fireball struck Braeden's horse, sending it up rearing and striking against the burning flames, killing it almost instantly, collapsing the horse to the ground, and slamming Braeden down with his clothes on fire.

Enraged that Rowena had defended the boy, Uriah struck his arms forward and threw a violent blow across the distance, knocking her through the air with tremendous force and smashing her against a rock. Her lifeless body slid like a bloodied rag doll down to the ground.

Serafina shifted into her panther form and charged into an attack, running straight at Uriah.

Uriah waved his long, gangly arms around him. Suddenly, the branches of the fallen trees began to thrash back and forth, clicking and clacking. The moss hanging down from the limbs of the trees began to smoke. The bark on the trunks began to slowly peel off, as if the trees were burning. The grass turned brown and crackled beneath her running feet.

As Serafina charged toward him, Uriah did not flee or duck.

He threw his hands in one direction and then the other. A mighty wind kicked up, casting out dark, swirling tornadoes that tore up sticks, leaves, and other debris from the ground in front of her. A horrible, loud rushing sound overtook everything else.

Uriah looked straight at her, ready for her attack.

"Are you surprised to see me, Black One?" he roared. "Did you think the swat of a little cat could kill me?" His voice boomed so loudly that it pierced her ears and shook her to the core. "You can't kill me!"

Serafina knew that Uriah wouldn't be standing so fearless if he didn't think he could sustain her attack, and it was foolish to attack him straight on. But it was all part of the trick. She spotted Waysa charging out of the forest at full speed toward Uriah's back. And she knew they had him.

She leapt straight at Uriah's face. Waysa leapt on his back at the same moment. The two catamounts landed upon the man, ripping into him with their tearing claws.

Screaming in outrage, Uriah reached back and grabbed Waysa, pulled him over his shoulder, and threw him off with incredible strength, heaving him so far that Waysa went tumbling across the clearing. Uriah had always been strong, but nothing like this.

Their well-thought-out plan of having Rowena cast her spells, Braeden charge in with their animal allies, and the two catamounts attack from two different directions at once had already gone wrong. Their plans had been wrecked. There was nothing left for Serafina to do but *fight*!

Clinging to Uriah's chest and legs with all four of her clawed paws, Serafina pulled her head back and slammed her long, curved fangs into Uriah's neck. Uriah screamed in pain and grabbed at her, but Waysa came tearing back into the battle and leapt upon his arms with teeth and claws. On the ground, Gidean charged in, chomped onto Uriah's leg, and pulled viciously, snarling and biting, trying to yank Uriah off his feet.

As Uriah struggled to pull Serafina from his chest, she pulled back and bit again, this time, aiming straight for his throat. Her teeth clamped onto his windpipe and cut off his air. Her mother had taught her that big cats kill their prey not just by tearing into them with claws, or breaking their necks, but by blocking their windpipes and asphyxiating them, and that was what she was determined to do now. This time, she couldn't just wound him, she had to kill him. For her peace, for Braeden, for Biltmore, for all that she'd fought for, she had to destroy him. She clenched her teeth and would not let go.

As Serafina fought she glanced back toward Braeden.

He'd been struck down from his horse and hit the ground hard, but he rolled and quickly put out his burning clothes. He immediately scrambled over to his wounded horse lying on the ground. He put his open hands on the horse's body, desperately trying to heal his oldest friend, but his face clouded with anguish as he realized it was too late. His friend was already dead.

Braeden wiped his eyes and ran over to Rowena. It was hard for Serafina to see as she struggled with Uriah, but she made out the silhouette of what looked like some kind of stag with a rack of horns kneeling down, as Braeden dragged the bloody and unconscious Rowena onto its back.

"Take her to safety," he told the animal, as it rose to its feet and drove into the depth of the forest.

A pack of a dozen wolves emerged from the trees, snarling and snapping, as they charged into battle against the sorcerer.

"Attack his arms," Braeden yelled, pointing toward Uriah. "Protect Serafina. Bring him down!"

Uriah thrashed wildly to dislodge her, but Serafina held fast, her panther teeth clamped onto his throat. He grabbed at her with his clacking clawed hands, but Gidean, Waysa, and the wolves attacked him from all directions, biting his arms and legs, preventing him from pulling her away.

If she could just hold on for a few more seconds, they'd kill Uriah once and for all.

Serafina knew this was the ultimate battle. All the allies of the forest had come together at this moment to fight. It was like the battle that her mother and father had fought and lost twelve years before. But this time, she was going to *win*. They were going to finally defeat the most dangerous enemy the forest had ever faced.

Uriah struck Waysa with a heavy blow, knocking him away with his arm. Waysa went tumbling across the ground, but before the catamount even stopped rolling, he spun around and leapt back at Uriah with a vicious snarl, hitting him with such force that it tackled him to the ground with Serafina still attached.

Serafina buried her fangs deeper into Uriah's throat. Through the nerves in the base of her teeth, she could feel the force clamping onto his windpipe, and the slowing of the air to his lungs. He was the storm-creech, the clawed creature, but he still had to breathe. She could feel his struggle diminishing beneath her as she slowly cut off his life.

But suddenly, Serafina felt Uriah's body shaking beneath her, like he'd become possessed by a horrible spirit. His chest expanded with new strength and he began to rise to his feet. He kicked Gidean away from him, sending the dog somersaulting across the ground. Then he grabbed Waysa, tore his claws out of his skin, and hurled the catamount away like an empty sack.

Uriah kicked the wolves off his legs and threw them off his arms. The wolves fell away from him with blazing eyes as he stood to his full height. Then a black, dirty wind began to rip into the wolves around him.

"Now!" Braeden shouted. "Attack him!" A massive bear charged in and slammed into Uriah. Serafina's body swung hard with the force of the blow, her legs and tail dangling now. It took all her strength to hold on as her enemy struck desperately at her side and tore at her head and tried to pull her away.

Yes, pull! she urged him in her mind. *Pull! Yank me away and rip out your own throat!*

And through all this, Serafina held on. No matter what happened, she wasn't going to let go.

But then Uriah burst forth with a deafening explosion that shocked everything around them.

Braeden and the wolves were thrown to the ground. Even the bear went down.

Waysa was hurled through the air, hit a tree, and collapsed, his limp body dangling in the branches, his eyes closed.

Gidean tumbled away, his body dragging through the dirt, biting and twisting, until he finally lay still.

With a terrible new strength, Uriah grabbed Serafina's head and fangs with his hands, and began prying her teeth slowly out of his neck, his fingers dripping with his own blood.

"I told you, you can never kill me!" he spat at her.

She growled and bit harder and tried to stop him from dislodging her teeth, but there was nothing she could do. He tore her off him and slammed her to the ground so hard that it knocked the wind out of her. Then he burst away in an explosion of black air, leaving great flares of orange flame rising all around them.

They had ambushed him with their fiercest allies and all their strength, but he had escaped their attack.

Serafina lay on the ground, stunned. She lifted her head, her eyes looking frantically through the smoke, trying to make sense of the destruction. Was Waysa still alive? Was Braeden still fighting?

The dead and wounded wolves lay strewn across the clearing, their bodies burned and broken.

She glimpsed the bear barreling away through the burning forest, his fur singed by the flames as he ran.

Her heart lurched when she saw Waysa's long lion body hanging in the tree, dangling down from the branches. She still couldn't see if he was alive or dead, but he wasn't moving.

She had to get herself up. Through all the shock and pain of it, through all the strikes and bruises, she had to rise. But as she began to move and breathe again, the blazing-hot air of the burning trees around her scorched her throat and lungs. The forest was on fire.

She gazed through the orange, hazy, firelit clearing. A jolt of fear ripped through her when she spotted Braeden's body lying on the ground, crumpled and still.

Powered by a new surge of energy, she shifted into human form and scrambled toward him, pushing her way through the swirling smoke and embers. When she finally reached him, his eyes were closed. His wounded dog lay beside him. Piles of dead crows and wolves lay all around him.

She dropped to her knees at Braeden's side.

"Braeden, wake up!" she shouted as she grabbed him by his coat and pulled him up.

Finally, he started awake with a violent gasp, and looked around at his fallen friends in horror.

"So many of them are dead!" Braeden said in despair, overwhelmed and disoriented.

"We've got to move, Braeden!" Serafina shouted, trying to shake him out of it as she coughed from the smoke. "We've got to help who we can and get out of here!"

Her chest filled with new hope when Braeden came to his senses and started pulling wolves up onto their feet.

She scanned back through the smoke toward Waysa. Where the fire was burning across the flat ground, it moved slowly, but on the steep slopes around them, the flames tore through the thick vegetation in blinding blazes, sparks and flames swirling upward into the glowing orange sky. She heard the sharp crackling of burning branches all around them, and as the sap within the trees boiled, the tree trunks exploded. Her heart was racing with fear, but there was no time to lose.

She ran over to the tree where Waysa's body was hanging and started climbing. Its trunk was so hot that the sap was popping and steaming, dripping out of it like blood. She knew the tree was going to explode, but she had to keep going.

She climbed frantically out onto the branches. She held Waysa's catamount head in her hands. The concussion of the blast had knocked him unconscious.

"Waysa!" she shouted, pushing hard at his body. "We've got to go!"

She felt a sudden flare of intense heat below her. Flames were spiraling up the trunk of the tree. There was no way to climb down. The sap-filled branches around her began to hiss and boil. Every breath she took from the hot, smoky air felt like she was sucking fire down her throat.

She had no choice. As the flames burned into the creaking, collapsing branches, she wrapped her arms around Waysa's body and jumped.

A sledgehammer of pain thundered through her shoulder and ribs when she hit the ground with a heavy grunt. But she scrambled to her feet. She grabbed Waysa by the shoulders and tried to drag him, pulling and heaving, as the burning tree collapsed around them. She fell to the ground as Waysa finally woke and looked around him in confusion.

"We've got to go!" she shouted at him, and Waysa rose to his feet.

On her way back to Braeden, she pulled Gidean up onto

his unsteady legs. "Come on, boy, let's go, come on!" And the wounded dog sluggishly, obediently, tried to follow her.

"Everyone get up!" she shouted at the surviving wolves as the flames burned around them and the clearing filled with hot choking smoke.

But they had only moments to live before the fire engulfed them. The trees that surrounded them were all aflame and there was no way out.

She wanted to use the wind to blow the flames away, but sensed that it would just make the fire burn faster. She thought about trying to draw water out of the rocky ground, but she knew it wouldn't work. She looked up at the clouds, but she had no idea how to reach up there and make them pour down with rain.

It seemed so hopeless. She looked all around her at the walls of orange fire. The smoke choked her throat. Her eyes stung. The heat burned her skin. They were completely surrounded by flames.

"If we don't find a way out of this, we're going to die here," she shouted to Braeden as she peered through the burning forest looking for a path through.

"No we're not," Braeden said fiercely.

Serafina turned in the direction he was looking. The night sky above them was suddenly full of birds. Hawks and eagles and ospreys.

"Lie down," Braeden said.

"What?" she said in confusion.

"Lie down!" he ordered her. "Waysa, you too. Lie down!"

Waysa came stumbling over to them in human form. As she and Waysa lay down on the ground, Braeden kept shouting at them. "Now spread out your hands and legs. Splay yourself out!"

Serafina had no idea why Braeden wanted her to do these things, but she did as he said. Suddenly, she felt the brush of moving air above her. Many pairs of large, powerful talons gripped her arms and legs, her wrists and her ankles.

"Go!" Braeden shouted to the birds. "Take them!"

Serafina felt her limbs lifting upward, then her body. She couldn't keep the panic from sweeping through her. They were lifting her off the ground. But she didn't want to leave the ground! She liked the ground!

But suddenly, she was in the air, she was floating, she was flying. As she flew upward, she saw the intensity of the forest fire all around them. The mountain was on fire. Braeden's figure standing in the center of the tiny clearing became smaller and smaller as the birds lifted her. Then she was flying across the canopy of the forest like a hawk, above the flames and the smoke.

Waysa was flying beside her, hanging from the talons of the hawks and ospreys like she was.

Within seconds, the blaze of the forest fire fell behind them. The night became dark and cool again as they flew up into the clear moonlit sky over the dark green canopy of the untouched forest.

Serafina craned her neck and looked behind her, searching for Braeden. She could see him in the clearing surrounded by the fire. He was shouting commands as hundreds of hawks and other birds grabbed hold of Gidean and the surviving wolves. The flames were pressing in, the smoke choking him, but he wouldn't leave his friends behind. He was determined to save them all.

"Get out of there, Braeden," Serafina said, but she knew it was useless.

When she looked back a final time, the flames had engulfed the clearing. There was nothing left but fire and great torrents of sparks rising up from the top of the burning mountain.

"Wait," she called to the hawks that were carrying her. "Wait! Go back! Go back for Braeden!"

But they didn't understand her. And they didn't turn.

The birds carried her and Waysa high over the trees and the mountains, which rolled dark and quiet below them. The sorcerer's storm had cleared. Up in the sky, a feathery scattering of white clouds drifted past an impossibly bright moon, with a crush of glittering stars above. Looking down again, she spotted what she knew must be the French Broad River, dark and shimmering, as it wound through the mountains.

As they flew slowly up the valley of the great river, she saw Biltmore House on top of the hill, its gray towers striking up into the sky, the moonlight touching its sides.

But all she could think about was the valiant friend they had left behind.

48

Serafina fell to her knees on the ground in front of Biltmore, her chest heaving with anguish. But she quickly got herself up to her feet again and looked toward the mountain in the distance. She could no longer see the flames. The top of the mountain where they had been fighting had burned black, a thick cloud of smoke pouring from its heights.

Waysa stood beside her, gazing up at the mountain with her, his face filled with dread.

Biltmore's grounds had been badly damaged by the floods, and some of the house's foundation had been torn away, but for now the storm had receded, and the sun was coming up.

"I'm going back up there to find him," Serafina announced and started on foot toward the mountain.

"Wait," Waysa said, grabbing her arm.

Serafina's stomach felt like it was twisting into knots. She hated standing still when she could be moving. "We can't wait here, Waysa. Come on, we've got to help him."

But Waysa turned and looked at something in the distance.

Waves of morning mist were rolling through the trees and across the wide expanse of grass in front of Biltmore, the rising sun casting rays of light between the waves, dappling the front of the house in moving bands of gold.

"The *a-wi-e-qua* have brought him home," Waysa said softly, his voice filled with awe.

Serafina didn't understand what Waysa said until she saw the herd of elk emerging slowly and silently from the mist of the forest.

The elk of the Blue Ridge were large and magnificent forest creatures of old that Serafina knew only from the drawings in Mr. Vanderbilt's books. Seeing the elk here, now, was impossible, for the last of the mountain elk had been killed by hunters more than a hundred years before. Then she remembered the large, stag-like animal that Braeden had called in to carry Rowena to safety the night before.

Was it possible that a few had survived all these years, hidden deep in the mountain coves and the shaded marshes where no one could find them? Had they come out now because Braeden had asked for their help?

The lead elk was an enormous, thousand-pound beast with a massive rack of antlers rising some four feet above his head like the majestic crown of a forest king. Braeden rode on the elk king's back, holding the thick, dark brown mane with one hand and the wounded Rowena draped over the elk's neck with the other. The elk king led the herd in a slow procession across the grass toward her and Waysa.

Serafina felt a swoosh of relief crash through her. She rushed forward and helped her tired, bruised, soot-stained friend down from the elk's back. His clothes were burned and torn, but it appeared that he hadn't suffered any major wounds.

Waysa gently pulled Rowena's limp body from the elk's back and carried her in his arms, her long hair hanging loosely toward the ground.

Braeden turned to the elk king. "Thank you, my friend," he whispered.

As the elk herd turned slowly back into the forest and gradually disappeared into the morning mist, Serafina knew that she would probably never see them again.

She wrapped Braeden in her arms. "I was so worried about you," she said. "What were you doing up there? You almost got yourself killed!"

"I had to save as many of the wolves as I could," he said, shaking his head. "But finally the hawks pulled me out. I still can't believe we lost. I thought we finally had him, but . . . we lost so many of our friends. My horse, and many of the crows and the wolves . . ."

"I'm so sorry," she said. She knew he was hurting.

He shook his head sadly, even as he held her. "I told them

all how dangerous it was going to be, but they wanted to fight anyway. They were very brave."

She hugged him a little tighter before she let him go.

"Our friends fought with great honor, and you led them well," Serafina said. "We fought against our enemy the very best we could."

She and Braeden followed Waysa as he carried Rowena toward the house. Braeden went ahead and opened the front door for him, and then led them upstairs.

Serafina had seen many strange and wondrous things at Biltmore, but this was a sight she had never imagined: a dark-haired Cherokee catamount boy carrying a redheaded young English sorceress up the Grand Staircase of Biltmore Estate at sunrise.

"Let's take her up to the South Tower Room on the third floor," Braeden said, leading the way. "My uncle was worried about my aunt's condition, so he took her into Asheville while the road was still partially clear. We have most of the house to ourselves."

But just as he was saying this, a young dark-haired maid in a black-and-white uniform came bustling down the staircase, clearly not expecting to encounter anyone so early in the morning. Serafina was delighted to see that it was her old friend Essie Walker. Essie seemed so flush and full of life as she bustled down the stairs.

"Oh dear, y'all, pardon me," Essie said in surprise, catching herself up short as she came to an abrupt stop in front of them. Essie caught eyes with Waysa first, and seemed to snag there for a moment, but then she immediately moved her attention to the unconscious girl he was carrying. "Oh my, what's happened to the poor girl? Is she badly hurt?"

But then in the next instant, as Essie's eyes lifted, she noticed the young master Braeden and then Serafina beside him. Essie's eyes widened, like she was seeing a haint. *Not anymore,* Serafina thought.

"Essie, it's me," Serafina said, smiling as she moved toward her old friend.

Essie's face lit up. "Eh law, Miss Serafina, it's you!" she cried. "Where'd you get off to all this time, girl? It's been so long! I'm so glad you're all right! Your poor old pa is going to weep buckets when he sees you!"

Braeden quickly led them all up to the South Tower Room. It was a large, elegant, oval bedroom with an elaborate crown-canopied bed, hand-carved ivory-white molding running along the arc of its curved walls, and a domed ceiling.

As Waysa set Rowena gently down on the bed, Serafina noticed that Essie was staring at him intently. When the catamount boy stepped away from Rowena, Essie's eyes followed him. It was like she had never seen anything like him—neither inside the hallowed walls of Biltmore or out in the wider world—and what she saw now fascinated her.

When Waysa lifted his brown eyes and looked at Essie, she said, "Oh lord, pardon me," and turned aside, her face red. "I'll fetch some warm water and towels right away," she said as she hurried out of the room.

Braeden sat on the edge of the bed beside Rowena, attending

to her the best he could as he tried to examine her wounds. Her head was bleeding and there was a scrape on her shoulder, but there were no gaping cuts or obviously broken bones.

"She's been unconscious since Uriah threw her against the rock, but otherwise, she doesn't seem to be too badly hurt," Braeden said.

When Essie returned with the supplies, Braeden dipped one of the towels in the basin and then wiped Rowena's head and face thoroughly with the wet cloth, trying to clear some of the blood away.

Serafina gazed at Rowena lying unconscious in the bed. Through all the riddles and sharp talk, in the end, Rowena had been true to her word: the sorceress had brought her back into the living world. And Rowena had betrayed her father. But what struck Serafina most was the memory of Rowena leaping into the path of the fireball to save Braeden's life. There seemed to be far more to Rowena than Serafina had realized.

The passing of time and Braeden's attentions with the damp cloth seemed to have an effect on Rowena. She stirred with a groan, and then appeared as if she was slowly coming to. Finally, she opened her eyes and looked around at the four people staring at her.

"What happened?" she asked. "Did the plan work? Is he dead?"

We failed, Serafina thought as she sat in the South Tower Room with the others. *We failed to defeat Uriah.* They had developed a plan, gathered all their allies, and attacked in force, but they had still failed.

Serafina looked around at her three companions.

Rowena, battered and disoriented, rose from her bed and began to pace back and forth, rubbing her face anxiously, worried that her father was still alive.

Waysa went over to one of the room's three sunlit bays, pulled aside the elegant curtains, and opened the window to the outside. He stood looking out across the forested valley of the great river to the misty blue mountains of the southern range. In the distance, toward the rising peak of Mount Pisgah, the dark shapes of storm clouds gathered on the horizon. Serafina thought that he must be keeping a watchful eye for their enemy, but ever since their arrival at Biltmore that morning, Waysa had been restless. As a catamount who had lived all his life with his family in the forest, he wasn't used to being indoors. He didn't trust the smooth, flat ground or the closed-in walls in these unnaturally quiet caves, this place without tree or fern, without the sound of birds or insects, without the feel of the wind in his hair, and he hated not being able to see the sun or moon.

For her part, Serafina was happy to take advantage of the shelter of the room. When Essie brought in a tray of food for them and set it on the fine mahogany table in the sitting area in the center of the room, Serafina gobbled it down with the others.

"Essie, this is my friend," Serafina said. "His name is Waysa."

As Waysa turned and stepped toward her, Essie said, "Howdayado," and curtsied nervously.

"It's very good to meet you, Miss," Waysa said, clearly trying to sound as kind as possible.

"I'm so happy to see you, Essie," Serafina said smiling and hugging her. "I looked for you earlier. Why weren't you in your room on the fourth floor?"

"I've been promoted!" Essie said, filled with pride, but then she quickly remembered everyone else. "I'll tell you all about it, but I'll let y'all talk first."

"Thank you for everything, Essie," Braeden said, as Essie left the room. He, too, seemed relieved to be back in the comfortable routine and relative safety of Biltmore's sunlit rooms.

But they all knew they couldn't truly rest here.

"So, now what are we going to do?" Braeden asked, looking around at the others.

"We have to go back out there," Waysa urged.

When Braeden lowered his head, Serafina knew that he was thinking about his horse and the wolves and his other friends who had died in the battle during the night.

Seeing Braeden's sadness, Waysa said, "I don't wish to fight, but none of us—including our allies in the forest—are safe until we destroy him."

Serafina glanced over at Rowena, who had stopped pacing and was looking at them now, her face clouded with fear and uncertainty. She glanced at the door and then the windows as if she thought her father was going to crash into the room at any moment.

Serafina tried to think about what they should do. She knew that if she stood up right now and called for an immediate attack against Uriah that they would probably join her, and she wanted to do just that, she wanted to fight, but deep down, she knew it would be a mistake.

Finally, she turned to the sorceress.

"What about you, Rowena?" she asked gently. "What do you want to do?"

Rowena shook her head, clenching her jaw, but did not reply.

"Tell me what you're thinking," Serafina urged her.

"It doesn't matter what I'm thinking," Rowena said.

"But I can see you're gnawing on something . . ."

Rowena shook her head again, annoyed that Serafina was pressing her. But then she began to speak.

"I didn't know my father for the first thirteen years of my life," she said. "When I was four or five years old, my mother used to tell me stories about him, that he was traveling in other countries searching for the ancient lore, but I didn't understand what her words truly meant, and she died before I was old enough to ask."

"So you were born with . . ." Serafina began to say.

"I sensed there was something inside me, but I didn't know what it was or how to control it," Rowena said. "All I knew was that I was different from others, that I could do things. When my mother died, the authorities put me into an orphanage, but the adults there couldn't raise me any more than a fly can raise a wasp."

As Rowena spoke, the others listened in silence.

"Years later, my father came to the orphanage and retrieved me. I didn't know him, but I thought that everything I had endured up to that point in my life had been the darkness, the twisting, painful birth of what I was, and that now, with my new father, my life would truly begin."

"Is that when you came to America?" Serafina asked.

"Not at first. First, he trained me how to use the powers within me that had been such a mystery to me all my life. Then he brought me here, back to these mountains where he was born. He'd come to fight his old enemy, and he set me on a path. I followed it gladly. I was appreciative of the chance to help him, hungry for his attention and approval. I wanted to become everything he wanted me to be."

Rowena hesitated, seemingly lost in the shadows of her own

story for a moment, but then she continued, her voice ragged with her determination not to falter. "Trapping animals in cages, killing a man with snakes, hurling a dog from a staircase, throwing a boy from his horse, dragging him over the stones, striking him with wounds, fighting, always fighting, and the blood on the Loggia . . ." Her words dwindled into nothingness and she looked down at the floor. And then, after a long pause, she lifted her eyes to them and said, "What do you do when you realize you are the monster in your own story?"

For a moment, they were all still. And then Serafina answered, "You rewrite the story."

Rowena looked at her sharply, almost malevolently. "The past cannot be changed."

"But the future can," Serafina shot back.

"It doesn't matter now," Rowena said, turning away from her.

Just as Serafina was about to argue that it *does* matter, she realized that Rowena didn't actually believe the words she had just said. It wasn't a trick or a lie, but a shield, and Serafina had heard these words before. *It doesn't matter now,* Rowena had said when they first spoke at her lair, *just the ramblings of a troubled soul, nothing of consequence.*

Serafina looked up at Rowena. "It *was* you. You came to my grave to speak to me about all this . . . The voice I heard . . . You were the one who woke me . . ."

Rowena did not turn, did not look at her. For a moment it seemed as if she was going to walk out the door and never come back.

But then Braeden stepped toward Rowena and touched her

arm. It was like he had cast a spell on her and she could not move. "What do you mean it doesn't matter?" he asked. "Of course it matters. What are you saying, Rowena? You're going to stay with us, aren't you?"

And that caught her. Rowena slowly turned and looked at him.

Serafina could see in Rowena's eyes an awareness of all the suffering she had caused. *A troubled soul, nothing of consequence,* she had said of herself. Somehow Rowena had found a path through it all. But Serafina could see a deep hopelessness in Rowena now, as if the sorceress knew there was no way to make things right, no way to protect Braeden or herself or any of them from her father, that feelings didn't matter, it was all going to end in the same way no matter what she did.

Serafina moved toward her. "You *change,* Rowena," she said firmly. "If you don't like the way you are, you make yourself different. That's what you've done. That's what you've been doing. You've been hiding from your father, finding a new way. I know you're discouraged and scared. We all are. But you *can* rewrite the story. You determine what needs to be done and you do it, whatever it is, no matter how difficult it seems. There's no choice here. You do what's right."

"No," Rowena snarled at her. "That's exactly my point, cat. There *is* a choice. You have a choice between right and wrong at every step you take . . . There's always a choice."

"And you've made your choice, and you're going to keep making it," Serafina said, refusing to back down. "You've chosen to fight with us."

"Yes, I made my choice," Rowena said, her voice strained. "And now we have a war. We surprised my father up there on the mountain. We wounded him. But he'll come back for us now, hunt us, because vengeance, more than anything else, is what drives him. He shifts, he adapts, that's what he does—he's a snake that sheds its skin—but I'm warning you: my father is going to come for us for what we did last night. And he will kill us all. Starting with me."

Waysa stepped toward her. "You are one of us now, Rowena. We'll all fight this together. We're going to stop him before he can hurt you or any of us."

Braeden listened to Waysa, and then looked at Serafina and Rowena. "But we've already fought him and struck him down repeatedly, and he keeps coming back. We threw everything we had at him last night, and lost many good friends, and he still defeated us. How are we going to kill an enemy who can't be killed?"

The room went quiet.

No one had an answer. The young sorceress didn't storm from the room, but she didn't speak, either. She seemed even more distressed by their failure to defeat her father than the rest of them.

When Rowena noticed that Serafina was looking at her, the sorceress turned toward her and said, "Mark my words, he's going to come after us."

50

Rowena's words echoed in Serafina's mind. She was sure she was right. But Serafina had no solution to the problem, no attack or defense, and neither did her companions. None of them knew what to do.

While the others got cleaned up, found some more food in the kitchen, and rested after the long, difficult night, Serafina went downstairs to the workshop to see her pa. She found him cooking up some breakfast in the black iron skillet.

"That was a jenny-wallop of a storm last night," he said, as she walked in. "Me and the rest of the crew were workin' most the night, repairin' what damage we could. Where'd you hunker down?"

"Didn't get much sleep," she said, sitting down at the little table where they ate their meals.

"Everything all right?" he asked, concerned. "You're lookin' a little worse for wear."

"I'm all right," she said.

"But I can see your gears are a-turnin'," he said as he put a plate of food in front of her.

"I just have a question, is all," she said, picking up and chewing on a piece of ham. "Somethin' I need your help with."

"Put me on the scent of it and I'll be off on the bay," he said, using his favorite expression about barking coon dogs to say he was happy to help if she told him what it was about.

"What do you do when you're working on a machine, or some other kind of problem, and you just can't fix it? It just seems impossible," she asked.

Her pa looked at her. She was pretty sure that he could see that it was something important to her.

"When I'm faced with what seems like an unsolvable problem," he said, "I do all that I can do, and when that's not enough, I stop, and I step back. I study it real careful-like, look at it from different angles, try to think about it in ways that I never thought of before, and maybe nobody else has either."

"And does it work?"

"Sometimes. But the main of it is that the most important tool in your toolbox isn't the screwdriver or the wrench. It's your imagination."

Serafina was listening to her pa's words, but he must have seen the quizzical expression on her face.

"Let's try it," he said. "Give me a 'for instance.'"

"Pa?"

"Put me in a fix and let's see how I get out of it."

"All right," she said. "Let's say you want to hammer a nail into a board. You line up the nail, you hold it with your fingers, and you hit the nail on the head with your hammer repeatedly. It goes in a little bit, just enough to stick, but it doesn't go in all the way. You strike the nail with your hammer again and again as hard as you can, and still it doesn't go in. You even get three of your friends to help you, but no matter what you do, no matter how hard you pound, the nail won't go in. So what do you do?"

"I set down the hammer," he said.

She smiled, thinking he was joking, telling her that he'd just give up, but then she realized he wasn't playing. He meant it.

"I set down the hammer," he said again. "I'd take a step back, you see, figure out what I'm truly tryin' to do, and figure out a mend that doesn't involve a hammer. Or maybe even a nail."

Serafina gazed at her pa and tried to reckon his words. She wasn't certain, but she thought she maybe understood.

As they finished their breakfast and washed up the plates, her pa said, "I gonna be fixin' one of the jammed-up coal chutes. It's been leakin' storm water somethin' awful down into the basement every time it rains. I don't know what the rest of the day holds, but I'll be around." Then he looked at her, his eyes steady on her. "What about you?"

"I'll find you," she said, and that was what he needed to hear to know that she'd do her best to keep herself safe, and that he'd see her soon.

Reluctant to separate, the two of them embraced, held each other for several seconds, and then said good-bye.

"I'm glad you're home, Sera," he said softly.

"Me too, Pa," she said in return. "Thanks for the help."

"You stay dry, now," he said.

As she went back upstairs to find Braeden and the others, her mind was filled with thoughts of her pa and what was ahead of her.

She knew Uriah was coming for her and her friends. She knew they had to defeat him. But how? The same question kept rattling around her head: How do you destroy an enemy who can't be destroyed?

She knew she had to stay bold no matter what, but the problem before her seemed impossible. She wasn't strong enough to fight Uriah, and neither were her friends.

But then, deep in the most shadowed recesses of her mind, something began to lurk. The faint movement of an unseen shape. The shaded trace of an idea. It was a dark path, fraught with dangers that could lead to the deaths of her and her friends, and ultimately the destruction of Biltmore.

In many ways, the idea seemed to make no sense at all.

And therein lay its beauty.

Set down the hammer, she thought.

Serafina and Braeden walked together toward the Conservatory, the greenhouse with its tall, arched windows and its slanted glass rooftops shining in the morning sun. Many of the glass panes had been broken by the night's storm, but the brick structure was still standing.

As they entered the thick heat and steaming moisture of the building, the sun filtered down through the palms, ferns, and bromeliads that grew all around them and up over their heads, shading them in a junglelike canopy.

Serafina and Braeden quickly made their way through the plants of the central palm house to join Rowena and Waysa in the orchid room, where they met in the shroud of hundreds of delicate blooms.

They all knew they were there to figure out their next move against Uriah, but Rowena repeated the challenge that they had already faced many times: "How are we going to kill an enemy who can't be killed?"

"I think the trick is that we don't," Serafina said.

They looked at her in confusion.

"We can only hide for so long before he comes for us," Waysa warned.

"I don't think that's what she has in mind," Rowena said as she studied Serafina.

"We can't hunt Uriah down and fight him with tooth and claw," Serafina explained. "We can't beat him in a battle. And even if we do, he won't stay dead."

"But we have no choice," Waysa said.

"I think there may be another way," Serafina said slowly. She looked at Braeden. "In the angel's glade, the night you freed my spirit, I gave you something to keep safe . . ."

"The silver clasp," Braeden said.

"Do you still have it?" Serafina asked.

"I asked a hellbender in the marsh to hide it in the mud where no one could find it."

"Oh dear," Rowena said, shaking her head. "My father's going to be looking for that."

But Serafina smiled. It was perfect. The hellbender was a gigantic, two-foot-long, atrociously ugly brown salamander. The mountain folk called it a grampus, a snot otter, or a mud-devil. If there was anything that could hide the silver clasp, it was the hellbender.

"But what are you thinking about, Serafina?" Waysa asked.

Serafina turned to the sorceress. "It depends on Rowena."

"Do tell," Rowena said.

"If Braeden can retrieve the silver clasp," Serafina asked, "can you use it?"

"Use it to do what?" Braeden asked in alarm.

But Serafina kept her eyes on the sorceress. "Can you do it, Rowena?"

Rowena stared back at her in disbelief. "Well, you little rat catcher . . ." she whispered, her voice filled with the devilish conspiracy of it.

"What?" Braeden asked. "What's going on?"

"You want to remake it . . ." Rowena said.

"Remake what?" Braeden asked, his voice strained with apprehension.

"The Black Cloak," Serafina said.

"I knew it!" Braeden said. "No, Serafina, not that! We just got rid of that infernal thing! We don't want it back again!"

Serafina expected Braeden's reaction, but she fixed her eyes on Rowena. "Can you do it? Can you use the silver clasp to restore the Black Cloak to its full power?"

Rowena held her gaze, as if gauging the depth of her conviction, but she did not speak.

"Serafina, what are you doing?" Waysa said, grabbing her arm. "We don't want to do this."

Serafina looked at him. "Waysa, think about it. The cycle of injury and rebirth, of struggle and rising, it must apply to the cloak as well . . . I destroyed the cloak once and it came back. That means it can come back again."

"The silver clasp is the heart of the cloak's darkness," Rowena said. "The cloth is but its skin."

"But can you do it?" Serafina asked her again, more forcefully this time.

Rowena looked at her. "We would need the wool of black goats, the sheddings of black rat snakes, the entrapping mucilage of pitcher plants, the skin of timber rattlesnakes, and the silk of black widow spiders."

Serafina swallowed. The list got worse as it went. "We should be able to find the goats and maybe the snakes . . ." she said, trying to think it through.

"But we need satin fabric made from the silk of black widow spiders," Rowena said.

"I can't believe you two are even talking about this," Braeden said. "It's way too dangerous to bring the Black Cloak back! What if it falls into the wrong hands?"

"Uriah's hands," Waysa said. "I agree with Braeden. It's far too dangerous."

"And it's also impossible," Rowena said firmly. "I was able to use spider silk thread to sew the areas of the cloak that had been torn, but only my father knows the spells that will force the black widow spiders to weave entirely new fabric."

Serafina's eyes widened in surprise. "Are you saying that the spiders don't just provide the silk for the thread, they actually weave the material?"

Rowena nodded. "The spiders weave the fabric, one spider's thread over the other, like a very tight web. I know the binding spells and the other spells we need, but only my father knows the spells to make the fabric itself."

"Then we're stopped before we've started," Waysa said. "We have no choice but to gather our allies, track Uriah down, and strike with everything we've got."

"We've already hammered that nail and it's not going in," Serafina said, bringing looks of bewilderment from her friends. She turned again to Rowena. "There has to be a way, Rowena."

Rowena shook her head. "There's no way for me to force the spiders to make the cloth we need."

Braeden looked around at his friends in obvious disbelief, incredulous that they would even be thinking about this dire course of action.

"This is a horrible idea," he said.

Serafina knew that he had far too much experience with the Black Cloak to want to bring it back into the world. But as they were talking, she saw Braeden's expression change, and he turned away from them.

"Braeden . . ." Serafina said.

"Is it wrong to use an evil weapon to fight against evil?" he asked, without turning toward them.

Serafina watched him in silence, unsure of where this path was leading him.

"Is this what it has come to?" he asked as he stared at the ground. She thought he was talking about the situation they were in, but then she began to understand.

This was his talent. This was his *love*. Through the bond of friendship, he could commune with animals, speak with them. But just how far could he go? And even if he could, was it the right thing to do? Was it right to create a terrible weapon if it was meant to be used to fight evil? Or was the weapon itself too terrible a thing to bring into the world?

Finally, after a long time, Braeden slowly turned and looked around at the others.

"These black widow spiders you're talking about . . ." he said. "Has anyone actually tried *asking* them to make the silk fabric we need?"

Rowena stared at Braeden and then looked back at Serafina. "If Braeden can persuade the spiders to willingly weave the warp and weft of the black fabric, then it will create a much tighter intertwinement than a coercion spell. That means the Black Cloak will be far more powerful than it was before."

"More powerful?" Braeden said in dismay. "It was bad enough before!"

"We're going to need that power . . ." Serafina said.

"But hold on," Waysa said. "Even if we can remake the Black Cloak, how does that solve our problem? What are we going to do with it?"

ver the next few days and nights, the four companions worked and watched, knowing that Death was coming. A stolen breath, a crushing blow, a ball of fire, Death was surely coming.

All across the grounds, large crews of men worked to protect and repair the storm-damaged roads, bridges, house, and gardens, even when the rain poured down.

Each night, Serafina prowled the grounds with Waysa in feline form, patrolling the estate's boundaries, running together through the forest darkness, their eyes scanning every shadow and their ears prickling to every sound. She knew that their only hope was to be ready.

Serafina loved running through the night. Waysa was fast

and strong, always knowing the way. They often ran side by side, challenging each other to greater speed. Other times they hunkered down near a stream or at the edge of a rocky ledge and just listened to the night forest. When they were in their catamount forms, they were together in body and soul.

But she had learned from hunting rats that she should not follow the same pattern every night, lest her quarry learn to avoid her. So on the third night, as they walked outside for their nightly run, she said, "You follow our normal path tonight. But I'll go a different way, and we'll meet back here."

Waysa was reluctant to separate, but he nodded, understanding the reason. "Remember that we're only patrolling. If you see Uriah, do not approach him on your own. Run like the wind."

"I will," Serafina agreed.

Shifting into her panther form, she went out into the night. She traveled southward at speed, through Biltmore's mud-damaged gardens, past the flooded bass pond, then down along the swollen creek. The area that had once been a small and secluded lagoon where the swans flew was now a large, flooded lake. Whole hills had disappeared. It was frightening how much the landscape had changed and was still changing.

From there she crept through the forest to the flood-breached shore of the mighty French Broad River. She stopped and gazed across the water, looking for any sign of their enemy.

She followed the river northward, wary of mists and shadows and creaks in the night.

Near midnight, she went up into the low, flat ground in

the bend of the great river, into Biltmore's vast farm fields. The fields were flooded. She crossed through acre after acre of ruined corn, potatoes, spinach, and dozens of other crops. She skulked quietly through the darkness past where Biltmore's barns should have been. The rushing water had torn the barns into twisted heaps of broken lumber and washed them away. The farmers had moved the animals to the highest reachable ground, but many were still in danger. The herds of tan Jersey milk cows that Mr. Vanderbilt had imported from England were standing in their pastures in a foot of water. The black Angus cows were huddled together in groups on the mud-wrecked hills that rose like small islands out of the lake that had once been their pasture. The chickens, sheep, and goats were stranded on small strips of rocky ground. But for all the disruption, the animals of the farm were quiet tonight, just a soft rustle of movement in the distance, as if they knew there were more dangers to come.

It made her sad to see Biltmore's once proud and productive farms brought to these conditions. The farms had always been such an important part of life at Biltmore. Mr. Vanderbilt had told her that his vision wasn't just to build a pretty house, but to create a self-sustaining estate that provided its own food for the family, the guests, the staff, and the workers and their families. In a time when the rest of the country was moving into cities, building great factories, and steaming quickly through their lives on black machines, Biltmore was meant to be a community all unto itself, a quiet, pastoral place where people lived close to the earth.

Mr. Vanderbilt had been so successful in his goal that he began donating hundreds of gallons of milk to the hospital, orphanage, and other establishments in Asheville. Biltmore's milk, butter, and cream became famous for its rich taste and high quality. And a new business was born.

Soon, hundreds of horse-drawn wagons emblazoned with "Biltmore Farms" were delivering fresh milk in glass bottles to doorsteps throughout the region. Serafina had sometimes seen the milk wagons trundling down the road in the early mornings.

But now the milk wagons were toppled over and broken to pieces by the storm, and the roads flowed like rivers.

Leaving the farms behind her, she came to where the Swannanoa River met with the French Broad, but instead of one river flowing into another, there was a flooded lake for as far as she could see.

As she traveled eastward, skirting the edge of the lake, she came to Biltmore Village, where years before Mr. Vanderbilt had created a small community for Biltmore's artisans, craftsmen, and other workers. There were many shops and cottages in the village, a school, a train depot, and a beautiful parish church, which Mr. Vanderbilt had named All Souls Church because he wanted folk of all walks of life to join him and his family in worship each Sunday. The village streets were lined with lovely trees, wrought-iron streetlamps, and fine brick sidewalks for its citizens, but tonight, she could see that the village had been ravaged by the recent storms. Most of the cottages had been flooded or outright destroyed. Many of the trees had been toppled to the ground, their great trunks and branches lying across the streets. The once smooth brick sidewalks were wrinkled and broken with strange, snakelike patterns, as if the tree roots beneath had coiled and twisted.

Still in panther form, Serafina prowled through the darkened and abandoned streets of the village. Instead of joyous neighbors out and about enjoying the summer evening, or houses lit up with family warmth, the streets were empty and the houses dark. Slips of whispery ghost fog drifted through the village. Just out of town, she came upon a massive black iron beast half-buried under the wet shifting earth. She stared at the hissing hunk of iron with her panther eyes for several seconds until she finally understood what it was: a train locomotive, knocked on its side, the coals still burning in its belly, half-buried in mud. She could not tell if the train's engineer had managed to escape the iron wreckage or not.

Feeling far more disturbed than she expected by the sight of it all, Serafina turned and started heading southward again, back toward home. She was more sure than ever that somehow she had to stop Uriah. What had started out as a blood feud against Mr. Vanderbilt and his estate years before had become a war not just against her and her companions, but against *everything*. Uriah wanted to destroy it all, and if she didn't fight him, he would soon succeed.

She dove back into the forest again and traveled over the hill and dale of the land back toward the house. Finally, she passed through the house's main gates, coming upon the mansion much like the line of carriages had a few nights before. But tonight was a very different kind of night, still and quiet.

As she looked upon the house, it was dark—not a single lantern, Edison light, or candle was lit. For the first time in her entire life, the house actually looked abandoned.

As she walked toward the house in panther form, she marveled at how quickly its spirit could change, how it could be the brightest, most vibrant and dazzling display of grandiosity one had ever seen, then fall into a dark and moody slumber.

She and her companions had been locking all the doors of the house each night, so she slipped inside using one of her old secret ways through the air shaft in the foundation, then went upstairs.

Waysa had not yet returned. Braeden, her pa, Rowena, and the servants were all asleep. The main floor of the house was empty, dark, and quiet.

For a little while, she took the opportunity to walk the deserted halls of Biltmore in the form of a black panther, her long black body slipping through the shadows, her tail dangling behind her, her bright yellow eyes scanning the darkness. It was a delicious feeling to finally be home in the form she was always meant to be. She remembered creeping through these darkened corridors at night as an eight-year-old girl, wondering why everyone had gone to bed. Back then, her bare feet had made a soft, almost undetectable noise as she walked, but tonight her furred paws were utterly silent on the smooth, shining floors. She had prowled these halls all her life, but never quite like this. It amused her to imagine one of the servants getting up in the middle of the night to use the water closet and coming face-to-face with a black panther.

Shifting back into human form, she continued walking from room to room, watching and listening. She was a twelve-year-old girl and the Guardian of Biltmore.

As she stood in the darkness of the unlit Entrance Hall, the main room in the center of the house, she heard movement down toward the Library.

She walked slowly down the length of the Tapestry Gallery, listening and scanning the shadows ahead, the moonlight falling through the windows casting white slanting rectangles across the floor. The colors in the tapestries that covered the wall and the intricately painted beams on the ceiling seemed to glow in the light.

Then she heard the sound again. Something touching the glass windows. The shuffle of footsteps. Voices. It sounded as if someone outside was trying to get into the Library.

Serafina crouched down, her heart beating heavy in her chest. Her lungs pulled in slow, full breaths, readying her for whatever was about to happen.

She crept forward, using the fine chairs and other furniture in the Tapestry Gallery for cover, but always looking ahead through the archway that led into the darkened Library.

She heard a click and then the movement of a hinge.

Her fingers clung to the top of a settee as she peeked over its edge and watched the French doors. One of the doors swung slowly open into the Library.

Serafina felt the hair on the back of her neck rising.

She spotted a dark hooded figure slipping into the room.

She knew she shouldn't be scared. She was the Guardian of

Biltmore! She had been expecting this! But it didn't matter. She was terrified.

Her heart pounded now. Her chest tightened something fierce, her lungs started pumping, wanting more air, and the muscles in her arms and legs bunched for action.

The dark figure coming into the house pulled back its hood and looked quickly around the room to make sure it was empty. It was Rowena. Her hair lay in a jumble around her shoulders in an unusually unkempt fashion. Her face was smudged with soot and slime. Her eyes scanned the darkness. Serafina could see that it was the sorceress, so she knew she shouldn't be frightened, but she was. Every pore of her body was slowly filling with dread. Rowena looked so different from the last time they had spoken. Everything about her reminded Serafina not of the ally she'd been working with over the last few days, but the dark and mysterious druid girl she'd seen by the river, the young sorceress of the forest, the caster of spider spells, and the speaker to the dead. Serafina knew she should trust her new friend, knew that they had come up with the plan together, but she couldn't stop thinking that everything about the girl she was seeing now oozed a dark and wicked treachery.

Rowena whispered something to someone just outside the door. The sorceress wasn't alone.

Just stay steady, Serafina told herself. *Just stay very still.* But her heart was pounding so hard that it felt like it was going to give her away.

Rowena whispered again, bringing the person with her slowly into the house.

As she watched it, Serafina couldn't believe that it was actually happening. Her hands balled into tight, shaking fists.

She smelled the rotting, earthy stench of the creature first, and then heard the *tick-tick-tick*ing sound of its gnashing teeth. Then she saw the long, dark, ragged coat, and the clawed hands protruding from the tattered sleeves. The mangled, bleeding face came into the room with glowing silver eyes. Serafina's body flooded with cold fear. It was him! It was Uriah, coming right into the house!

"Come this way, Father," Rowena whispered. "They're all asleep . . ."

Serafina watched from behind the settee as Uriah looked slowly around the Library of Biltmore Estate, gazing up and around at all the books and fine furnishings—the secret inner sanctuary of his despised enemy.

Before Uriah had become the bent and hissing creature he was now, he had been the bearded man of the forest, a shrouded hermit whom day folk seldom saw. He had gathered his curses into sap-fueled cauldron fires up in the barren pinelands, but avoided face-to-face battles with his enemies. He never endangered himself. He was like a sniveling rat, a stinking polecat that stays hidden in the darkest depths of the forest. To attack his enemy, he would cast his spells from afar and send his demons into Biltmore to do his bidding. But this night, he had come.

He was entering the very place he most wanted to destroy.

As Rowena led her father quietly into the darkened house, Uriah spoke in his low, gravelly voice. "Have you done everything we talked about?"

"Everything and more, Father," Rowena said in an excited whisper. "It's even better than we hoped."

"Tell me," Uriah rasped.

"You were exactly right. The cat and the boy had the silver clasp all along. But more than that, I now know that the boy can control the spiders."

"What?" Uriah said harshly as he turned angrily toward his daughter in surprise and grabbed her by the throat. "You taught him how to cast the weaving spell?"

"No, no," she gasped, clutching at his scaly hands, tightened around her neck. "Father, listen to me. I swear I didn't! The boy doesn't use spells. He has the power to befriend the creatures of the forest."

"Like he did with the hawks and the wolves . . ." Uriah rasped as he released his daughter's neck.

Still in human form, Serafina watched in amazement as Uriah and Rowena spoke. She knew that Uriah could cast powerful spells and that the Twisted Staff he had created had allowed him to control animals by force at close range, but he seemed to envy Braeden's natural power. He and his daughter had once enslaved many of the forest's creatures, but even he couldn't claim the true and constant alliance of the wolves, the elk, and the other animals.

"Who's inside the house now?" Uriah asked. "Where is the usurper and his woman?"

"The Vanderbilts have gone, Father," she said. "Your storms have pushed them out."

"What about the Black One and the other catamount?"

"They're out patrolling the grounds, but I know the path they take. I waited until they were on the other side of the estate, miles away, before I brought you in."

"So, it is just the boy," Uriah said greedily. "We'll leave his bloody dead body on the floor for the usurpers to find when they return."

"We need to make them suffer, Father," Rowena hissed, "for all that they have done to us."

"And do these others trust you?" Uriah asked.

"They're fools, Father," the young sorceress said. "Even the cat trusts me this time. I pretended like I was conflicted about right and wrong, like I didn't know which path to follow, and then when I told them the secret of the black widow spiders, that clinched it."

"What about the cloak?"

"The boy and I have been working on it day and night," Rowena said. "The boy and his spiders have made the fabric, and I have used the spells you taught me to bind the darkness and suck in souls. But I must tell you, Father, the cloak is far more powerful than anything we've made before."

"More powerful?" he asked, his eyes widening. Serafina could hear the envy seething in his voice. "Where is the cloak now?"

"It's here in the house, Father, but they've locked it away. I can't get to it on my own. I need your help."

Uriah nodded, very pleased. "We'll take the cloak first and then we'll kill the boy."

"This way," Rowena whispered, leading him out of the Library and into the Tapestry Gallery.

As they walked, Uriah put his hand on his daughter's shoulder, a glint of pride contorting his nasty face. He looked as if he was more than pleased with his daughter's talent for treachery, her ruthless and conniving ability to change herself into whatever he needed her to be. Good or evil, dark-haired or fair, human or animal, she was the consummate shifter. His other demons and devices had been flawed, but his apprentice daughter! She was his most perfect creation.

Serafina ducked down into the darkest shadow she could find as Uriah and Rowena walked past her, his earthen stench wafting toward her like the odorous, twisting branches of a diseased and rotting tree.

Suddenly, Uriah stopped in midstride and looked around him.

Serafina froze, her heart pounding.

"What is it, Father?" Rowena whispered.

"Stay quiet," Uriah ordered her, as he listened into the darkness.

Serafina watched from her hiding spot behind the settee as he slowly turned his head and his silver eyes scanned each and every shadow in the long moonlit gallery.

She wanted to flee, right then, just get up and run like the dickens, but she knew she mustn't move or make a sound. She stayed exactly where she was, watching from the shadows of the room.

Uriah tilted his head and sniffed the air, like a predator picking up the scent of its prey.

A pain filled Serafina's chest. Her lungs wanted to breathe, to gasp in rapid gulps of air, but she could not let them, for a hurried breath would kill her now.

Stay very still, she told herself.

She pulled back just a little farther into the darkness, trying to settle her thumping heart and her buzzing legs so that he could not feel her there.

He sniffed the air again.

"She's here . . ." he rasped in a low, hissing whisper.

"Who's here?" Rowena asked.

"The Black One . . ." he said.

"Where?" Rowena asked, looking around them.

"She's here, in this house right now . . ." he whispered. He began moving with a slow and creeping deliberateness among the low tables and soft chairs where she was hiding, his scaly clawed hands raised and crooked like a praying mantis.

"She's in this very room . . ." he rasped.

He began to search behind each piece of furniture, dragging it aside, then going to the next.

He was coming her way.

"THERE!" he screamed, pointing to her.

Serafina broke cover and tried to run.

54

Serafina burst away and sprinted down the length of the gallery, running as fast as she could. Uriah rushed toward her with terrifying speed. The air around her concussed with shaking force. All she could hear behind her was the pushing of the furniture as he shoved it aside and the violent clicking of his gnashing teeth.

As she turned the corner out of the room and dashed across the main hall, she felt a blast of burning air fly past her. The glass on the old grandfather clock cracked, and the wood sides caught on fire.

She ducked down the corridor and darted across the Salon, jumping a chaise lounge as Uriah came barreling around the corner and threw a spell that smashed through the room, toppling everything in its path, and crashed through the far windows with an explosion of glass.

Her chest heaved in rapid breaths as she ran. Her arms pumped. Her legs buzzed with speed. She wanted to change into panther form so bad, but the time had not yet come.

Behind her, she heard the ferocious, attacking growl of Waysa tearing into the room. She glanced back just in time to see the fanged catamount leap upon Uriah's back, biting him and clawing him, pulling at him.

Waysa slowed Uriah down just enough to let Serafina get ahead. But then Uriah slammed Waysa's body into a stone pillar and the catamount collapsed to the floor.

Serafina's heart wrenched when she saw Waysa go down, but she knew he had done what he'd come for, and now the rest was up to her.

She raced away as fast as she could in the moments Waysa had given her. As she scurried through the Breakfast Room, the creature came right behind her, throwing a fireball that lit up the room with blazing orange light and set the leather wallpaper on fire.

There was less than a second between life and death.

Finally, she darted through the door that led into the Banquet Hall.

She'd made it!

She was exactly where she needed to be at exactly the right moment.

As she turned the corner out of sight and ran past the room's three giant fireplaces, she shifted into panther form. She leapt straight up the far wall, clung to the priceless Flemish tapestry with her claws, climbed it with tearing speed, and sprang through the air toward the window, which Braeden had opened for her just moments before.

But the window was far too small for a panther, so she shifted into human form in midair and landed on the windowsill. Unlike normal windows, these small, seldom-noticed windows at the top of the Banquet Hall didn't go *outside*, but to a back corridor of an upper floor high above.

"Here it is," Braeden said, handing her the coiling, hissing Black Cloak, just like they had planned. "Go!"

Grabbing the cloak, she sprinted down the length of the upper corridor, looping back behind where she expected Uriah to be, and came to a second window that looked down into the Banquet Hall. It was similar to the window she'd leapt *into*, but there was a reason she'd chosen this spot in the house.

Rowena had lured Uriah into Biltmore just as they had planned. Waysa had attacked him at just the right moment to slow him down. Braeden had been ready with the cloak right where they had agreed. And now Serafina was positioned directly over the door that Uriah was coming through as he entered the Banquet Hall in search of her.

Seeing Uriah below her, Serafina leapt.

As she fell through the air she stretched out the Black Cloak in her arms, coming down on Uriah like a giant black bat. But as she came down, she realized her timing was off and she was going to miss him. If she'd been in her panther form she could have used the twist of her tail to change the angle of her attack in midair, but she needed to be in her human form to hold the cloak. And now she was going to fall uselessly to the floor behind him. But in the moment of her fall, she used her new powers to shift the air around her with a violent push, and for a split second she wasn't just controlling the movement of the air, she was the air itself. *Ashes to ashes, dust to dust,* she thought. *I am human and panther. I am body and spirit. I am all things in the darkness.*

Her timing was perfect. Just as Uriah came through the doorway, she fell directly upon him and pulled the inner folds of the open cloak over his head and shoulders.

Uriah screamed in rage.

As Serafina landed on his back, he thrashed and struggled, and then heaved himself backward, slamming her into the stone of the fireplace, but she held on to him for dear life. *I am spirit!* she thought, pushing through the crushing pain. *I am power!*

She hung on and she kept hanging on. It was like grabbing a huge, wriggling, biting rat: once you had it, you couldn't let go. You had to grip it, strangle it, do anything you had to do, but you *COULD NOT LET GO!*

She pulled and pulled the cloak, Uriah's head tossing wildly, his arms pushing, his scaly clawed hands clutching blindly around him as he screamed in outrage. He was Uriah, the sorcerer, the master of the forest, the controller of all! He was not going to let this happen!

Suddenly, he began to spin around and around, roaring with a terrible sound as a dirty swirl of darkness poured out of his mouth. He was going to rip himself free. But Serafina pulled in the power of the elements around her, drawing forth a forceful wind from the air, lifting the ashes from the fireplaces up and around them in a great whirling motion.

Their two swirling forces crashed against each other, pushing in opposite directions, each one spinning and twisting against the other until the swirling motion came to a shuddering stop. She held Uriah as still as death with nothing but the force of her will.

Then she heard it.

I'm not going to hurt you, child . . . the cloak said in its hissing, raspy voice.

The folds of the cloak slithered around Uriah like the tentacles of a hungry serpent. The cloak moved of its own accord, wrapping, twisting, accompanied by a disturbing rattling noise, like the hissing threats of a hundred rattlesnakes. Uriah's horrified face looked out at her from within the folds of the enveloping cloak. She realized then that everything had come full circle. It was just as she had once seen Clara Brahms vanish into the Black Cloak. But instead of Clara's innocent bright blue eyes looking desperately out at her for help, Uriah's eyes were consumed with hatred and streaked with all-consuming fear. Then the folds closed over him, the scream went silent, and the man disappeared, body and soul.

Serafina and the cloak fell to the floor. She quickly scurried away from it so that its greedy black folds couldn't get her.

For several seconds, the cloak vibrated violently, and a ghoulish aura glowed in a dark, shimmering haze. A horribly foul smell of rotting guts invaded Serafina's nostrils, forcing her head to jerk back. She wrinkled her nose and tried not to breathe it in.

Suddenly, the cloak clenched into a tight wrenching coil, and an explosion of magical spells burst into the room, sending fireballs and lightning bolts and explosions of ice-cold air in all directions at once. The spears and shields on the walls clattered to the floor. The panther-torn tapestry and its cousins crumpled down. The flags caught fire. The statues tumbled. The entire room filled with a thick, choking smoke.

And then it was finally done.

Serafina jumped up to her feet, still panting, still filled with fear, and she looked around the room. Uriah was gone. She had captured him in the endless void of the Black Cloak. She had finally defeated the man who could not be killed!

She pulled in a long, shaky breath and exhaled, trying not to burst into tears of relief. A pure cool pleasure poured through the cavities of her lungs and the muscles of her legs. She looked around at the devastated, ash-filled, burning room and all she could feel was joy.

"We did it!" Braeden cheered, leaning out the window above her head and pumping his fist triumphantly even as he stamped out one of the burning wall tapestries with a towel.

That was when she came to her senses enough to realize that the room was truly on fire.

She did not run. She did not panic. Her powers had been growing within her, and she felt stronger now than she ever had.

She concentrated her mind, raised her hand into a fist above her, then threw her hand down in a sudden opening motion, and shouted, "Enough!"

The entire room burst with cold air. Every speck of ashen dust hit the floor. Every flame blew out. And the room was still.

"That worked a lot better than my towel!" Braeden shouted happily from the window.

Waysa came limping into the room, bleeding, but with a grin on his face. "I told you to run like the wind, Serafina! I thought for sure he was going to get you there at the last second!"

"Not with you on his back, my friend," Serafina said happily.

Behind Waysa, Rowena was walking into the room as well. Seeing that the sorceress and her other friends were all right, Serafina smiled and then laughed, euphoric with the realization that they had all survived.

But Rowena looked warily at the Black Cloak lying in a heap on the floor of the Banquet Hall right where Serafina had left it.

"It's done now," Serafina said, trying to reassure her.

Rowena slowly lifted her eyes and looked at Serafina. When she spoke, there was no sarcasm in her tone, no aloofness or airs, no whispers or seething voice, just a flat, steady seriousness. "Now we must make certain that this cloak never sees the light of day."

"Or the darkness of night," Serafina said, nodding. "I swear to you, we will hide the cloak well. We'll make sure that your father will never threaten you or anyone at Biltmore again."

Braeden walked into the room through the butler's door that came from the back stairs.

"I wish we could destroy the terrible thing," Braeden said.

"Destroying the cloak will free its prisoner," Serafina said. "We can never destroy it. We must put it somewhere it will never be found, and lock it up forever."

"I know just the place," Braeden said.

And Serafina knew exactly where he had in mind.

When she looked back at Rowena, and saw the sorceress still staring at the Black Cloak in stunned disbelief, Serafina thought she must be thinking about her father.

"It is done," Rowena said, as if trying to convince herself.

"And what will you do now, Rowena?" Serafina asked her gently.

Rowena paused, as if she was thinking about that profound question for the very first time. And then she looked at Serafina and said, "I will *live*."

Serafina smiled a little bit at the corner of her mouth. Rowena was just beginning to realize that she had *survived*. She would go on, free, into a very different world. She would truly live.

"But don't just live," Waysa said, looking at Rowena with kind eyes. "Live *well*. Make all this worth it."

Rowena nodded, appreciating his words. "And you do the same."

Serafina gazed around at her friends, all happy and smiling, looking back at her. They had saved Biltmore. And they had saved each other.

It was hard to take it all in, but they had finally defeated Uriah, the old man of the forest, the conjurer, the bearded man, the sorcerer, the wielder of the Twisted Staff, the creator of the Black Cloak, the enemy who could not be killed.

And through all of this, Serafina thought about her pa working on his machines, and Essie bustling from room to room, and Mr. and Mrs. Vanderbilt and the coming baby, and all the daytime folk at Biltmore. She thought about the wolves, and the crows, and the other animals of the forest, and she thought: *We're finally safe now.*

55

Serafina carefully gathered the Black Cloak up from the floor of the Banquet Hall. The cloak writhed and twisted in her hands.

There are other paths to follow . . . the cloak hissed as it tried to coil up her arms, as if it knew what she was planning to do with it. It wasn't the prisoner within speaking to her, but the cloak itself.

Serafina wanted to drop it, get away from it, but she knew she couldn't. She held the cloak tighter and looked at Braeden. "Get the trowel and mortar."

As Braeden grabbed the equipment, she noticed that the design on the Black Cloak's silver clasp was no longer blank, but entwined with thorny, binding vines twisting around the shadows of a single face.

She and Braeden headed outside with the cloak on their own. They wanted as few people as possible to know where they were going to put it.

They made their way through the darkened gardens and down toward the pond.

With me on your shoulders, you'd have strength beyond imagining . . . you could fly . . . you could live in ways that you never dreamed of . . . the cloak hissed.

She could feel the pull of the cloak on her mind, an aching desire to give in to its hissing pleas. She wanted to put it on, to *wear* it, to *use* it. By sucking in human souls, the cloak provided the wearer the ultimate power, but she knew she must resist it.

"Here it is," Braeden said as they came to the inlet of the pond.

She and Braeden crawled through the metal chute and into the flume.

Together, we could be all-knowing, Serafina . . .

"Don't you dare use my name!" Serafina snarled. She gripped the cloak in her tightly balled fists, refusing to listen.

Braeden carried the lantern, shovel, and tools as they followed the narrow brick tunnel beneath the pond. There was no water running through the tunnel, but it was dripping wet with the sludge of the black algae that coated the walls.

Think about what you've enslaved, the cloak rasped. *It's all in your hands now . . .*

Clenching the cloak tighter, Serafina led the way, delving

deeper and deeper into the tunnel, until they reached its lowest and darkest point.

"This is the spot," Braeden said.

"Hurry," Serafina said.

Just put me on, and all of Uriah's power will be yours, Serafina . . . the cloak whispered.

Serafina tried not to imagine the knowledge and power she'd attain, but she could feel her hands shaking as she held the writhing thing. She wanted so bad to put the cloak on her shoulders.

"Braeden, please hurry!" she cried.

Braeden quickly pried up the bricks with the shovel, then got down on his knees and pulled the bricks away with his hands. There was already a shallow hole where he had stored the Black Cloak before, but Serafina said, "Dig it deeper."

Braeden grabbed the shovel and went to work, digging down into the gravel another two feet.

Together, we shall know a thousand spells . . . the cloak hissed.

"Deeper," Serafina said.

Together, we shall never die . . .

"Deeper!" Serafina told Braeden.

Braeden's hands began to bleed with blisters from the oak handle of the shovel, but he did not argue or complain. He could see Serafina's shaking body, and the anguish tearing through her face, and he kept digging.

"How far?" he asked, but he did not stop.

"Six feet," Serafina said. "Six feet under."

When Braeden had finally finished digging, Serafina

crawled down in and shoved the Black Cloak into the bottom of the hole. She pushed the folds of the material as deep as she could make them go, then pressed them down with the palms of her hands. The cloak hissed and rattled like a snake fighting against her.

"Bury it!" Serafina snapped harshly at Braeden, her voice sounding disturbingly like to the cloak itself.

"Bury it, Braeden, bury it . . ." she hissed, the voice of the cloak coming through her.

His eyes wide with fear, Braeden hurried to push the loose gravel into the hole, handfuls at first, then using the shovel. The dirt began to fill the grave. As Serafina held the cloak down, it felt like she was drowning it. She could feel the sensation of the dirt pressing more and more around her.

"You've got to get out of there, Serafina!" Braeden shouted.

Just put me on . . . the cloak hissed.

"Keep shoveling!" she screamed, holding the cloak down beneath the dirt as it writhed in her hands. *"Bury it!"*

Finally, when the dirt was all around her, and the cloak was buried, she clambered out. Braeden heaved her up to him.

She and Braeden filled in the rest of the dirt, packed it down, and stamped on it with their feet until it was hard.

Then, back down on their hands and knees, they used the trowel to spread a thick layer of mortar over the dirt.

"More," Serafina urged. "As thick as we can make it."

When the mortar was finally down, they pushed the bricks into place. The gray mortar oozed up into the thin spaces between the bricks as they laid them.

Brick by brick, they closed the Black Cloak in.

Brick by brick, they silenced the raspy voice.

And brick by brick they buried their enemy below.

When they were finally done and the mortar had hardened, Serafina stared suspiciously at the brick floor, half expecting to see the insidious black fabric squeezing up through the mortared cracks like little creeping fingers, its voice hissing for her to put it on.

But there was no sound or movement.

They had buried the Black Cloak and Uriah once and for all.

Here the Black Cloak and its prisoner would remain beneath the pond, buried in an unmarked grave and bricked in, seething in the darkness below the darkness.

56

The following day, as Serafina walked through the forested highlands that overlooked Biltmore, she saw a figure moving slowly through the trees. It took her several seconds to realize that it was Rowena coming toward her.

The sorceress was wearing the dark robes and hood of her ancient kindred, and she was carrying a long laurel staff. She wore a twisting bronze-and-silver torc around her neck, and her red hair was tied into a thick braid that fell down into the folds of her hood.

Rowena stopped a few feet in front of Serafina. As the sorceress gazed at her, her green eyes glistened in the sunlight that came down through the forest leaves.

"Have you hidden it?" Rowena asked her.

"We have," Serafina replied, nodding.

"Good," Rowena said, relieved.

The sorceress looked down at the ground for a moment as if collecting her thoughts, then she lifted her eyes and looked at Serafina once more. "Then this is where our paths finally part."

Serafina hesitated, not sure what to say to the girl who had been her enemy and her friend.

"You've decided on what you're going to do . . ." Serafina said.

Rowena nodded. "I am going to follow Waysa's advice. I'm going to live well."

"And where are you going?"

"Once long ago these dark forests and jagged mountains were the hidden domain of a great conjurer, the old man of the forest. As I see it, somewhere out there, there's a vacancy now. And a girl to fill it. In her own way."

Serafina nodded, understanding Rowena's words.

Rowena gazed toward Biltmore visible in the distance and then looked back at Serafina. "You are the protector of that place," she said. "Protect it well, and everyone within."

Serafina nodded, knowing exactly who she meant.

"Live well, sorceress," Serafina said.

"Live well, cat," Rowena said in return.

That night, Serafina slipped out of Biltmore just as the moon was rising in the eastern sky, her four feet trundling easily, silently, along the front terrace, then down the steps, and across the grass toward the trees.

When Waysa spotted her coming, he flicked his tail and ran.

So you want to race . . . Serafina thought, and lunged into a powerful run.

She chased Waysa through the forest, tearing through the ferns, leaping over creeks, dodging between rocks, her heart filling with the joy that only motion can bring.

Waysa doubled back around behind her, crouched at the top of a boulder, and leapt upon her as she ran past. The two catamounts somersaulted in mock battle across the forest floor, then Serafina burst out of it and sprinted away, forcing Waysa to chase after her.

She loved running through the forest with Waysa, her senses alive, and her muscles blazing with power. She loved the speed of it and the rushing wind, the feel of her furred feet flying across the ground, the grace of her tail steering her quick changes in course. When she ran as a black panther, she was everything she had ever dreamed of being.

After the chase, she and Waysa came to the cliff that looked out across the great river. They stopped there at the edge, panting and happy, and gazed out across the moonlit view. The flooding was already receding, the rivers and the forest slowly returning to their natural state.

Serafina's heart skipped a beat when she spotted movement on the high ground in the distance.

She glanced at Waysa. He saw it, too.

The dark figures were far away, and she couldn't quite tell what they were. They were but shadows and a slinking, skulking movement among the rocks of the ridge. Then it became more clear.

The silhouettes of three mountain lions came up over the distant ridge, backlit by the light of the rising moon.

Serafina's heart swelled. One of the lions looked larger than the other two younger, leaner cats.

Filled with excitement, Serafina and Waysa ran toward the ridge to meet them.

The five lions came together, rubbing their heads and their shoulders against each other and purring. Her mother was strong and powerful, and the cubs had grown so much!

Serafina, her mother, and Waysa shifted into human form.

Serafina gazed at her mother's beautiful face with its high, angular cheekbones, her long, lion-colored hair, and her tearful golden-amber eyes looking back at her, and then they moved toward each other and embraced.

"Serafina . . ." her mother purred as she held her.

"Momma . . ." Serafina whispered in return, pressing herself into the warmth of her mother's chest as she wrapped her arms around her.

"When I heard you were alive, I wept with joy and came as fast as I could," her mother said.

Serafina held her mother tight. She could feel the warmth of her mother's love pouring through her body. After all their nights apart, they were finally back together again.

Suddenly, she remembered being a little girl prowling unseen through Biltmore's upstairs rooms looking into the face of every woman she saw, wondering if it was the face of her mother. And she remembered that first night in the forest she saw her mother's eyes and knew who she was. It seemed so long ago now, but the feeling, the love she felt in her heart, was the same.

Months before, when she was first united with her mother, she had learned so much from her, about the lore of the forest and the lives of the catamount. She had learned so much about what it meant to be *Serafina*. But she knew now, even with all that she'd been through since then, that there was still so much more for her to learn. She was just beginning in the world, and she needed her mother to guide her. The spirit and the body, the heart and the soul, the light and the darkness, she wanted to learn it all.

Knowing that it was all ahead of her, Serafina found a great sense of peace.

All through the night, the five cats ran, leaping and diving through the forest, down into valleys and up along the ridges. The night was their domain. Serafina had found her kindred, her family, the primordial creatures to whom she was born.

Deep in the night, they finally returned to the place they began, at the edge of the high ground that looked out across the river to the distant mountains. When Waysa shifted into human form, Serafina did as well.

There was a strange look in her friend's eyes that worried her. She could see there was something on his mind.

Serafina looked at Waysa, but he did not want to look at her.

She stepped toward him and touched his arm.

Finally, he lifted his eyes.

"I need to talk to you, Serafina," he said, a sad tone in his voice.

A sinking feeling poured through her. "Tell me what it is," she said softly, her voice trembling.

"Now that you're safe, and your mother is back, I . . ." Waysa's voice faltered.

"What is it, Waysa?" she asked him again, but she didn't truly want to know the answer. She wanted to pull back time, to go back, back to the way it was before.

"I think it's time for me to go," he said.

Her eyes watered as she looked at him. "No, Waysa . . ."

"When I finally avenged my family, I thought it would restore the balance. I thought it would heal my heart. But when I think of my sister and my brothers . . . my mother and my father . . . there's still . . . an emptiness inside me. My family is dead, I have to accept that, but I want to know if any other Cherokee catamounts survived. Uriah scattered my people. I need to find them. I need to tell them what's happened here, that there's no more need to fear. I need to bring them back together . . ."

Serafina stared at Waysa. She did not want to agree with him. She did not want to let him go. She wanted to yell at him and demand that he stay. She wanted to grab hold of him and *make* him stay.

But she knew she shouldn't. She knew that she should let him go, that it was right for him to go. If his people were still out there, he had to find them, he had to bring them together. That's what he did. He *saved* people, just like he'd saved her.

"I understand," she said softly.

Waysa slowly took her into his arms and held her, and she held him in return, and for a moment she and her friend were of one spirit. She suddenly remembered the wild-haired feral boy fighting for her against the wolfhounds, the pang of loneliness she had felt when she realized he had disappeared into the darkness and she might not ever see him again. She remembered hiding in the cave with the boy who had left her the riddle so that she could find him, how he'd pushed her through the waterfall so that he could teach her to swim, how they'd fought together, run together, how he'd told her that she could be anything she envisioned herself to be.

"You stay bold, Serafina," he said now, his voice shaking with emotion.

"Stay bold, Waysa," she said in return. "Go find your people. And remember, no matter what happens, you have your family here. You have my mother, and my brother and sister, and you have *me*."

He nodded silently as he slowly turned away from her. He shifted into lion form and disappeared into the forest.

Standing with her mother and the cubs at her side, the last she saw of him he was running along the ridge, and then he faded into the silver light of the glowing moon.

58

On a sunny afternoon a few days later, well after Braeden
and Serafina had cleaned up the mess and repaired what damage
they could in the house, the carriages returned from Asheville
with Mr. and Mrs. Vanderbilt and the servants who had been
traveling with them.

The footmen carried the luggage up to their rooms. Mrs.
Vanderbilt's maid and Mr. Vanderbilt's valet began the process
of unpacking. And soon Biltmore was filled with the normal
sounds of the house, the bustling of the servants, the tinkling
of teacups, Mr. Vanderbilt's St. Bernard, Cedric, following him
from room to room. The whole family was home again. The
house resumed its old patterns, with tea at four and dinner at
eight.

Upon hearing the good news that Serafina had returned to Biltmore, Mr. Vanderbilt asked Braeden to have her join the family for dinner.

As was his tradition, Braeden presented Serafina with a dress to wear. She had no idea where he got this one, or how he'd gotten it so quickly. Maybe he'd persuaded one of his feathered friends to deliver it from a distant city by air. She just hoped he hadn't asked the black widow spiders to make it.

Wherever the dress came from, Serafina loved the lustrous deep-blue fabric, which reminded her of a certain mountain stream she knew. It wasn't a full, old-fashioned ball gown like she had seen the ladies wearing at the summer ball, or a light, lacy dress for an evening garden party. Those would have to wait until next year. This dress wasn't for any particular occasion, but a lean and formal dress for wearing to dinner with the family each night. And when she thought about that, it made her smile. That was just about perfect. This was her home now and her life.

She took a lovely warm bath, washed her hair, and then dressed for dinner in the red-and-gold Louis XVI room on the second floor like she had before, with Essie doing her hair. "Aw, Miss," Essie said, as Serafina stood before her for inspection. "The dress goes so well with your black hair. You look right lovely tonight, with the biggest smile that I've ever seen on you."

Serafina and Braeden arrived at dinner together arm in arm. Mr. and Mrs. Vanderbilt smiled and hugged Serafina, overjoyed to see her, and asked her how she'd been. As they sat down to dinner, Serafina was happy to talk with them.

Mr. and Mrs. Vanderbilt seemed to be in warm and pleasant moods, relieved that the storms were over and looking forward to the coming of their child. As there were no guests in the house, it was just the four of them this evening, with Cedric and Gidean lying nearby. Nothing felt out of the ordinary or awkward about any of it. It just felt right. She had to remember where to place her napkin and which fork to use, but her pa had trained her well, and facing a new challenge always did excite her.

Braeden seemed pleased to be sitting at the table with her and his aunt and uncle, content that everything was as it should be. He'd gone out riding in the forest earlier that morning, making sure that everyone was on the mend. She noticed a new brightness in his eyes, and a new confidence in his smile and his manner.

"I was talking to Mr. McNamee this morning about the plans for repairing the gardens," Braeden said. "It all sounds very interesting."

"I'm glad those awful storms have stopped," Mrs. Vanderbilt said.

Mr. Vanderbilt nodded his agreement as he dabbed his mustache with his napkin. "Time to rebuild."

"You're going to rebuild?" Serafina asked, looking at him with interest as she thought about the farms and the village and the other areas that had been damaged.

"Oh, yes, we'll rebuild," Mr. Vanderbilt said. "No matter what happens, we always rebuild."

"I'm going to help," Braeden interjected. "I'll be working on the plans and the reconstruction with Mr. McNamee, learning everything I can. I'm looking forward to it."

"We'll make everything even better than it was before," Mr. Vanderbilt said, nodding. "That's how we keep moving forward. Especially now."

When he said these words, he smiled a little and looked at his wife, who touched her hand to her belly. "We've decided on a name for our little one here," she said happily. "Shall we share it with you two?"

"Oh, yes!" Serafina said excitedly before Braeden could reply.

"Can you keep a secret?" Mrs. Vanderbilt asked, winking at Serafina.

"Believe me," Braeden said. "She can definitely keep a secret. And so can I."

"Well," Mrs. Vanderbilt said happily, "we're going to name our little darling after George's beloved grandfather, Cornelius Vanderbilt. So if it's a baby boy, he'll be Cornelius. But if it's a baby girl, she'll be Cornelia. But no one knows about any of this, so you mustn't tell anyone until it's official."

"That's a wonderful name," Serafina said.

"Yes, we thought so, too," Mrs. Vanderbilt said with satisfaction.

"And what did you two get up to while we were gone?" Mr. Vanderbilt asked Braeden and Serafina.

"Oh, the same old thing," Braeden replied, never wanting to lie to his uncle. For him and Serafina, "the same old thing" meant prowling through the night, fighting sinister demons, and living on the edge of constant death.

"I hope not," Mr. Vanderbilt said, knowing all too well the kind of trouble they were capable of getting into.

It was clear to Serafina by the keen look in Mr. Vanderbilt's eye that he had figured out that something significant had occurred while he was gone. Mr. Vanderbilt knew she had been the one who found the missing children a few months back, and that she'd helped rescue Cedric and Gidean from the cages up in the pine forest. Now that he'd returned from his trip, she was pretty sure that he had noticed the strange scratches on the windowsill above the Banquet Hall and the tears in the room's Flemish tapestry.

"Well, for my part," Mr. Vanderbilt said finally, "I'm just glad that you're back, Serafina. Your home is here with us at Biltmore. And I must say, I feel that Biltmore is a safer place for it."

"Thank you, sir," she said, nodding slowly to him. "I truly appreciate it. I was gone for far too long, but in my heart, it felt like I never left you and Mrs. Vanderbilt and Braeden."

Later that night, Serafina and Braeden walked up the Grand Staircase to the fourth floor and then into the Observatory. From there they climbed the circular wrought-iron staircase to the room's upper level, opened the window, and climbed out onto the roof.

Serafina remained quiet as they walked in the moonlight past the copper dome of the Grand Staircase, among the mansion's tallest towers and slanted slate rooftops, its many reaching chimneys, and its carved stone gargoyles of mythical beasts.

"Do you think we've actually defeated him for good, Serafina?" Braeden asked her. "Is it truly all over?"

"Yes, I think it is," Serafina said, nodding. "But you and I are both the Guardians of Biltmore now, the protectors of this house, its people, and the forest all around, so we must keep a watchful eye and stay ready for whatever danger comes."

"Do you think there's other evil out there?"

"I'm sure there is," she said.

"But what will it be? What form will it take?"

"I don't know," she admitted. "But whatever it is, we'll face it together."

She and Braeden sat on the rooftop to enjoy the warm evening with its graceful breeze rolling through the tops of the trees. She could feel it lifting her long hair and gently touching the skin of her neck. She thought about the wind and earth and water. For a little while, she had caught a glimpse into the movement and flow of the world, and the power of her own soul, and she looked forward to learning more about what she could do.

They gazed across the sweeping lawns, and the gently flowering gardens, and the deep forests that surrounded the house, with the glass of the Conservatory below them glinting in the moonlight and the glow of the house's lights touching everything around. They looked out across the darkened canopy of the trees and the layers of rolling mountains in the distance, with the glistening sweep of the glowing stars and planets rising above.

Suddenly, she remembered a moment from the previous autumn. It seemed so long ago now. She was just a lonely little girl, so small and quiet, standing in the basement at the bottom of the stairs listening to the crowd of fancy folk above, wondering whether she should go up there and tell them that she had seen a girl in a yellow dress get captured by a sinister man in a black cloak.

She remembered that all she wanted to do at that moment was to help.

From that very first moment, with her looking up at that stairway that led from the darkness of the basement to the brightness of the world above, all she wanted to do was to be part of something. That was all she *ever* wanted, not just to see, but to be seen. Not just to hear, but to be heard. Not just to feel, but to be felt by other people, to touch them, affect them in some way, to make their lives different, and to be made different by them. And here, on this night, at this moment, on this rooftop, she knew that time had finally come.

She remembered how it felt when her soul was split from the rest of her, when she was but a lost spirit wandering the living world, but never truly touching it, never truly feeling it or engaging with it.

And she thought back to the conversation she'd had with her pa, that many things changed over time, always becoming something new and always becoming something old. She realized now that the physical things were always changing. Even we ourselves change, learning and growing, getting pulled down and then rebuilding ourselves again.

But for all that, there was a rare and hidden thing, maybe the most important thing, that never changed, and that was the spirit deep inside us, the thing we were when we were a child, and the thing we were when we grow up, the thing we are when we're at home, and the thing we are when we go out into the world—it's always with us—that inner spirit stays with us through it all, no matter how our body changes from year to year or how the world changes around us.

And through all of this, there is one thing we seek. To be connected to the people around us, to touch and be touched, to have a true family and friends of all kinds with which we share the world and its changes. Like our own spirit within us, our family is the hidden, inner core that deep down never changes, the river that is always flowing.

She turned and looked at Braeden. She studied his face, his hair, his eyes, the way he gazed off into the distant forest.

Her heart began to beat strong and steady in her chest.

Her hand began to tremble.

Then she slowly reached over and put her hand on his.

She felt the warmth of it, the living pulse of it, the soft skin and the bones beneath. This was her ally, her friend, the boy she fought her battles with.

Braeden turned and looked at her, somewhat surprised.

Nervous, she felt like she needed to give him a little bit of an explanation of why she had touched him in this way.

Thinking back on everything they had been through, she said, "I just wanted to make sure that I was truly here."

Braeden smiled, understanding.

"You are," he said. "We both are."

Author's Note

Thank you for reading this third book in the Serafina series. I hope you enjoyed it. This concludes the story of the conjurer Uriah and the Black Cloak, but it is not the last you'll hear from me, or from Serafina and Braeden.

Disney Hyperion will be publishing my next book, which is called *Willa of the Wood*. This next story takes place in Serafina's world in the Blue Ridge Mountains, but is focused on a new character named Willa, a twelve-year-old forest girl with special powers that I think you're going to like. In the future, Willa's story will blend and intermingle with Serafina and Braeden's story. I hope you'll join us for these future books.

If you enjoyed *Serafina and the Splintered Heart*, I encourage you to let people know about it, post reviews and comments online, and share your impressions with others. Thank you for helping to spread the word. But please avoid revealing how the story starts with Serafina in spirit form, the appearance of Rowena and the Black Cloak, and other details. Enjoying this book depends on the reader knowing no more than Serafina does at any particular moment, so it's important to avoid spoilers.

I would like to touch on a few elements of this story. The Cherokee are an important part of our community here in Western North Carolina today. I would like to thank the Eastern Band of the Cherokee Indians (EBCI), the Museum of the Cherokee Indian, Western North Carolina University, and members of the Cherokee tribe for their assistance with the depiction of Waysa, the Cherokee people, and the Kituhwa dialect of the Cherokee language that is spoken here in the mountains of Western North Carolina.

When you read this story, you may have thought that the idea of making fabric from spider silk sounds a bit far-fetched, but in reality, spider silk is an exciting new area of textile research. This includes using natural spider silk, creating synthetic spider silk, and gene-splicing spider silk DNA into other animals to achieve enhanced qualities. One of the most impressive uses of natural spider silk is a golden-colored cape made from silk harvested sustainably from thousands of golden orb spiders. Creepy but true.

As I've mentioned in my previous author notes, Biltmore Estate is a real place, which you can visit and explore. I've worked hard to be historically accurate with my depiction of the house and grounds. I would like to thank Biltmore Estate and the descendants of George and Edith Vanderbilt for their continued support and encouragement of my writing efforts, and for all they are doing to preserve and protect an important part of our American history.

I write at home, nearly every day, and work in close connection with my family. I would like to thank my daughters, Camille, Genevieve, and Elizabeth, for helping me to create this story and improve many of its details. And I would like to thank my wife, Jennifer, for working closely with me to refine the writing. My family is an integral part of my writing process.

And once again, I would like to extend my thanks to my agent, my beta readers and consulting editors, and everyone on the Serafina Team in Asheville and around the country who have helped make the Serafina series what it is.

I would also like to give my sincere gratitude to Laura Schreiber and Emily Meehan, my editors at Disney Hyperion, and the rest of the wonderful Disney Hyperion team. I am so honored to be part of your efforts to bring high-quality, imaginative books to readers of all ages.

Finally, I would like to thank *you*, the reader. In an era of easy distraction, I am so thankful for your willingness to journey with me into the heart and imagination of Serafina's world. Thank you for reading my stories, and for all your support and encouragement.

Stay Bold,

—Robert Beatty
Asheville, North Carolina